Taking Time

Pam Farley

Ukiyoto Publishing

For my beautiful, brave friend, Beck

Contents

Chapter One

The prison officer to the left of Ravi kept sniffing as they walked along the grey passageway. The bloke stopped just short of the door to the main corridor and blew his nose. Ravi held his breath while the man blew snot into the bunch of tissues in his chubby hand. They moved again, and Ravi was now distracted by the officer on his right. The man's shoe was squeaking. Every time his nearest foot touched the floor, it sounded like someone was torturing a mouse. If his situation wasn't so dire, Ravi might have been amused. But Ravi's left leg was trembling so severely beneath him it buckled, and he fell to his knee. His bowels felt liquified, and he clenched his anus as the officers hauled him upright. Up ahead was the last corner, and beyond that, his awful fate. Ravi could barely stand as shivers wracked his body. There was nowhere to run and no escape from his sentence.

The wrought-iron gate ahead slid to fully open with a clang, and Ravi was taken into the custody of two new corrections officers. They didn't look friendly. But then, since he was caught trying to steal a car, and subsequently injured the owner to flee the scene, Ravi hadn't seen an affable expression at all. Even his mother had been glum since hearing of his stupid actions, which was out of character for the perennial optimist. During any stressful situation in his life, she had always kept his spirits buoyed, but this time, his mother appeared floored. Especially when the sentence was read out.

Ten years was a long time. A big chunk of Ravi's life.

His girlfriend hadn't even shown up, which he guessed was hardly surprising since she'd been planning to break up with him. He had known for weeks that she was seeing Andreas from the local gym. Ravi hadn't wanted to believe it, but her absence confirmed it. Piper, it seemed, had been won over by that testosterone-pumped freak. Well, good luck to her. If she wanted someone young and fit, that wouldn't be Ravi after his punishment. He would be hitting middle age.

Was he just unlucky to have been a recipient of the harsh new felonious penalties? Previously, and with good behaviour, he may only have served a couple of years for his offences. But sentences had been doubled when the new Criminal Ageing System had passed legislation the previous year. The effect of the treatment was immediate and convicted felons were aged according to the length of their sentence. Ravi had heard of prisoners balding within seconds. He'd heard of some losing their libido and others still suffering rapidly from age-related diseases, crippling arthritis, cancers and cardiac problems to name a few.

Ravi halted for a moment. His two attendants didn't speak, but the larger of the two gave him a forceful push between his shoulder blades. But a few steps on, Ravi stalled again. This time he broke into tears, head bent and dripping onto the floor.

'Come on mate. It'll be over soon,' the shorter bloke said.

'I don't want to get old!' Ravi wailed.

The two officers looked at each other, clearly not impressed.

The greyer of the two said, 'Listen, kid. You got ten years. You will still be younger than me when it's over, so stop fucking moaning. If you'd got twenty, you might have something to whine about. Now get going!'

The other man pushed him harder this time, causing Ravi to stagger. He bit at the inside of his bottom lip, fighting the fear and the tears, but the closer they got to the treatment room, the more terrified he became. It took both men to muscle him through the doorway and deliver him to the waiting therapist.

The woman glanced down at her clipboard. She read out his name, and Ravi nodded. Next, he signed a form on the line indicated. Once finished, she read a page-long diatribe about the drug he would receive. Ravi had no idea what telomere attrition, cellular senescence or mitochondrial dysfunction were, but apparently, he was to receive a metered injection that would create changes, effectively ageing his cells by ten years. Instead, Ravi fixed his stare at the mole on the side of the therapist's left nostril. It took another few minutes for the corrections officers to restrain him on the surgical table and for the treatment to begin.

The steel beneath him was ice cold, making it impossible to stop shivering. If Ravi's arm was not held in a vice-like grip, the cannula would have missed its mark, but it didn't, and Ravi cried out as the stylet bit through his skin. He'd always been terrified of needles.

As the therapist injected the milky looking substance, Ravi held his breath, waiting for the pain and burning, but he felt nothing.

Following the administration of the drug and the observation time it took to ensure he had no adverse side effects; Ravi was free to leave. He collected the belongings taken from him when he arrived at the prison and went to the bathroom.

The person that stared back from the smudged mirror had a receding hairline, shot with grey, and deep crow's feet that were not present before. There was a roll of fat around his midriff and the beginnings of a double chin. Ravi's lips trembled as he examined his face. He looked like his father. He'd gone from a young man to a middle-aged slob in less than a day.

What was this madness? How could they treat him so cruelly? If he'd spent ten years in jail, then fair enough. He would have ten years of memories, even if they weren't happy. He would have gradually noticed the changes in himself and come to terms with them. But this! This was sick. So what if the states saved millions on correctional facilities and the federal government could boast? Who cared if the country's prisons were practically empty? What about his sanity? What about his right to age as an average person should?

He screamed at his reflection, railed at the aged image, and finally punched the face that looked so much like his neglectful old man. The mirror shattered, but it did little to calm Ravi. He bashed the remaining shards until both his fists were bleeding. His throat was raw from shouting. When the anger finally diminished he was spent, and withered to the sticky, piss-covered floor. Black thoughts shuffled through his mind, and now his misery was as all-consuming as his rage. There was nothing to look forward to in life. He picked up a mirror section, tilting it from left to right, examining his face. The puffy bags under his eyes made him look sad.

'I am fucking sad,' he said to his reflection. His image mouthed back the exact words. 'No,' he whispered. 'No, no, no!' He raised the piece of glass with his chubby old man's hand. Reflected light glinted off it, and for a moment, he thought about throwing it, smashing it into tiny slivers, but the hairs he saw on the back of his hands toppled his depression over the edge.

He grimaced and plucked at them wildly, swearing, dribbling. But he couldn't remove that repugnant fuzz that resembled pubes. This was the final straw. Ravi had detested those hairy hands on his father, but he loathed them even more on himself. He would never be that person. For once, he would be in control and have the final say.

'No,' he muttered one last time. He raised the shard to his neck and slashed his jugular vein. There was nothing unpleasant about the feeling of hot blood running down the inside of his shirt; in fact, he enjoyed it. Ravi gave a few self-satisfied grunts before everything went dark.

*

Ravi woke to the bright overhead lights of the ambulance as it careened its way through the city streets. Two more corners and the sensation of travelling backwards became too much. He spewed over the side of the stretcher, earning a look of disgust from the paramedic attending him.

'Sorry,' he managed before heaving again.

This time the woman had a bag ready. She helped him hold it steady while he retched, then wiped his mouth clean with a white face washer. Ravi's neck was throbbing, and he could hardly move his head. A thick bandage held him rigid. When he tried to touch it, the ambo grasped his hand. She pointed to the cannula inserted into his arm and the line that led to the fluid bag hanging on the vehicle's side wall.

'Please, keep still. You've lost a lot of blood. They can give you a blood transfusion at the hospital but don't move for now.

Ravi stared at his hand, not at the IV line but at those pubic-looking hairs. Then he recalled his image in the mirror, so devastating then, now only mildly disappointing. His anger was gone, and so was his misery. Was he fitting into his new self? Was he reacting the way a man nearing his forties might? Is that how the treatment worked?

'Can you answer some questions for me?' the woman asked.

'Sure.'

So, Ravi did his best to answer her enquiries about allergies, medications and his medical history. Then she asked if he had thoughts of self-harm.

'I don't think so,' Ravi answered honestly. 'I was overcome with ageing so fast. It hit me hard, losing my youth.' He shrugged. 'I don't know how to describe it, but it was overwhelming. First so angry and then so sad, but now - I feel a bit numb.'

The woman nodded; her expression sympathetic.

'I lost ten years,' he explained.

Again, she nodded. 'We are seeing this response more and more these days.'

'Really? I'd heard some things, but I imagined they were exaggerated.

'No. It's a concept which is hard for the brain to comprehend.' She looked him in the eye and covered his hand with her own. She looked friendlier now. 'You worry about getting better and staying positive. You still have a lot of life to live. Live it well.'

He would have asked more questions, but the ambulance began to slow, the siren and motor suddenly silenced, and the back doors flung open. In a matter of minutes, he was being wheeled into the emergency department.

*

Ravi was released into his mother's care the following day. He still felt weak, but without private hospital cover, it was either leave or suffer in the overcrowded wards, which he worried were rife with infectious diseases.

He showered without help and dressed in donated clothing which would have looked more at home on an American rapper. As he returned from the small bathroom to his bed, his mother, Emily, appeared in the doorway. She looked shocked.

'Oh dear!' she said.

Ravi understood her reaction. Instead of having twenty-two years between them, it had been whittled down to twelve. And although he didn't find her attractive, he could appreciate her good looks for the first time. Emily was petite and muscled, and her face, while not beautiful, was blessed with large hazel eyes giving her a wholesome appearance.

'You – look just like your dad used to.' She gazed at the ground.

Ravi nodded. It went without saying that since he hit the booze, his father now looked more like an eighty-year-old Gulag survivor.

'I'm sorry, mum.'

She hugged him tightly and then shook him by the shoulders. 'Don't be silly. You've had a terrible shock. That treatment is evil. As much as prisons are horrid, so is that unnatural punishment. The government should never have introduced it.'

'Well,' Ravi said. 'I have to learn to live with it.' His legs were beginning to tremble. 'I need to sit down, mum.'

'Okay, but I'm taking you home.'

Emily helped him to his bed and then rang the nurse's call bell. Within twenty minutes, his mum had organised a wheelchair and rolled him down to the bus stop at the front of the hospital. She pointed to a space on the end of a bench.

'Just stay here while I return this.' She manoeuvred the wheelchair. 'I'll be right back.'

Ravi found the air, redolent of cigarette smoke and car fumes, cloying. He cleared his throat and tugged at his collar. He gazed around at the people who strode past, some appearing to have a purpose, some without, but no one was smiling. The misery he'd felt in the prison bathroom overwhelmed him once more.

He'd always loved the city. The hustle and bustle, something new going on around every corner. The nightclubs, the crazy streets after midnight. The lights. The colours. But today, everything was grey and dreary.

A bus pulled up with a squeal of brakes and the bash of automatically opening doors. More miserable-looking people alighted and made their way past in a rush. Ravi's hands were shaking.

'Are you okay, son?' Emily asked.

Ravi began to nod but then shook his head. 'I want to go to grandma's house.'

'To the country?' Emily looked confused. 'You hate the county.'

He swallowed, tasting the fumes and building nausea. 'Not anymore. I need to be somewhere else. Somewhere quiet that doesn't stink.'

To his surprise, she broke into a grin. It caused him to scan around at all the surrounding faces, scowls and frowns, and then back to hers. It was like the sun peeking through clouds.

'It's a good idea, isn't it?' he asked.

Emily kissed him on the cheek and stepped to the curb, throwing out her arm to hail an approaching cab. 'Come on, Ravi,' she said.

Chapter Two

While most of the coastal towns in South Australia were popular with visitors, some places were too distant from the city or not on the way to somewhere desirable. Sometimes the hordes of caravaners would stop for a look, but most gave the town of Henderson, on the Eyre Peninsula, a wide berth. Limited funds in the town meant little was spent on infrastructure. As the population further dwindled, so did the council coffers. The town was bland, but the beaches were pristine.

It took half a day to drive to Henderson from Adelaide, and although Ravi offered to take the wheel when Emily began yawning, she insisted on continuing. Ravi's grandma, Edith, was his maternal grandmother. She had lived in Henderson all her life, initially as a sheep farmer with her husband and now as a widowed retiree. Ravi's mother had tried to convince Edith to move to the city to be closer to medical facilities as she aged, but Edith would have none of it. So instead, she was determined to see out her life in her hometown.

Ravi wasn't sure if any of his paternal relatives were still alive or, if they were, where they lived. His father had left Chennai, in southeast India, almost thirty years before. Randeep Singh had changed his name to Randy and embraced the Australian way of life. For a time, it had worked for him. Within five years, he was living with Emily and produced two children, Samantha and Ravi, but just a few years later, Randy changed. He became bitter that he had given up his culture and heritage to live in a country that still treated him as an alien, angry that he was the victim of passive racism. As a result, he was repeatedly overlooked for promotion at the insurance company where he toiled.

When his relationship with Emily broke down, he began drinking. Ravi hated to see him that way. His father had become a sullen man, full of regrets. Although Ravi rarely saw him anymore, when he did, there was always a communication obstacle, either real or perceived, that prevented the two from being anything more than strangers. It was an interaction that it seemed neither of them relished, so it was preferable to keep apart.

Ravi gazed out the window at the distant flashes of coastline. Another half an hour and they would arrive at their destination. Then, as the road tracked westward, the sun warmed his cheek, and he closed his eyes.

As a teenager, Ravi had thought about changing his name. His surname was Sanders, the same as his mother and sister, but his first name was a sore point. He was named after his dad's younger brother, who died as a baby. It was a name that encouraged teasing at school and beyond. It was a name that, when mentioned, seemed to confirm to people that he was "not from around here." He guessed it answered the question of his year-round tan and dark hair. But he had his mum's eyes, hazel and piercing. Now he wondered how much of his father's weaknesses he carried.

'Almost there.'

Emily's words woke Ravi from his doze. He struggled to sit up straight in the seat, and he pulled up the collar of his skivvy to conceal the bandage.

'Don't worry about it. Your grandma knows what happened. She won't ask questions, but if you want to talk to her, she is a good listener.'

'You told her?'

'Of course. Grandma knew you'd been charged and about the punishment. I had to tell her.'

'I guess she's locked up the silverware,' Ravi said miserably.

'Ravi, you tried to steal that car.'

'I know. I was an idiot. But Piper was being threatened. She said it was a simple job and completely legal – not theft. And besides, if she didn't pay her debts, she would get hurt.'

Emily raised an eyebrow and asked, 'Really? So, after you got caught and were arrested, how come she was unharmed? I mean, her debts would still have been unpaid, wouldn't they?'

Ravi shrugged and then frowned, the heat of embarrassment creeping up his neck. He'd been such an idiot.

'I think Piper could always look after herself,' Emily continued. 'I think she was dishonest and knew she could rely on you to get things for her. She had a good job but let it go because you said you would support her. Where was her ambition? What woman these days wants to depend on someone else? She spent all her time and money working on her looks. It's not normal.'

'Let it go mum!' And then, in a gentler tone, Ravi said. 'I don't deny that I've been a fool and probably been fooled, but that's my fault. Not hers. Right now, I need time to get my head around who I am.'

'Good. I'm glad to hear that. Oh look, your grandma's been waiting for us.'

Edith Sanders waved from the front gate as the car pulled closer. Before Ravi and Emily could exit the car, she was standing by his door.

'Grandma!'

'Oh, Ravi!' She hugged him and smiled, not showing any surprise at his physical changes. 'Come on in. I've just boiled the kettle.'

The two women embraced briefly before being greeted by Hank, Edith's Staffordshire terrier. The dog was a twenty-kilo cube of muscle that bounded like a spring.

'Hank the tank!' Ravi called. At first the dog hesitated, but then came closer and sniffed Ravi's hand. Hank raced away, running two laps around the yard. He went so fast that he almost toppled, then changed direction and repeated his crazy run. Finally, he stopped just as suddenly as he started.

Hank's mouth was open, nearly ear to ear, foaming saliva, a long pink tongue lolling to one side as he panted. He flopped onto his back across Ravi's feet, looking up.

'Oh yuck! He just pissed with excitement!' Ravi said in horror.

His runners were wet. But Hank's tail kept wagging, and the yellow fountain kept flowing.

'Well, at least he's glad to see you,' Edith said, laughing as Ravi discarded his shoes.

As soon as Ravi entered the hallway, he felt a tug of nostalgia. When he was young and the family came here for holidays, this place seemed like paradise. Long days of playing on the beach, backyard picnics and night-time barbeques. But as he and his sister grew older, coming here seemed like a chore. The internet was slow when it worked at all. There was nowhere to go and nothing to do. Ravi spent all his time wishing he was somewhere else. He loved his grandma but detested the boredom associated with this town. Today it was different. It felt like coming home.

While his mother and grandmother fussed around with mugs, coffee and packets of biscuits, Ravi wondered how long he would stay here. The infamously crap internet service hadn't improved, but he found it hard to care. And the idea of mundane didn't faze him either. Part of him wondered if he had turned into an old man because the thought of strolling along the beach didn't irk him as it once would have. He was surprised by just how satisfying coffee and biscuits sounded. Not long ago, only beer and pizza would have satisfied his appetite. Now he was as keen for a shortbread as Hank was.

'Jesus,' he muttered to the dog leaning against his leg. 'I got old fast.'

*

The next day, Emily returned to the city, leaving Ravi with his grandma. As an adolescent and young adult, the thought of spending time alone with an old lady would have been daunting, but even then, Ravi had recognised that Edith was no ordinary woman. Only five years before, she had finally retired as Group Officer for the Country Fire Services, a position she held for over fifteen years. And before that, she had served as a Firefighter and Senior Firefighter for over two decades. Edith had saved more than a few lives and properties in this area.

As a farmer, she had excelled in a community previously dominated by men, earning respect along the way. She was tough without being ruthless and fair without being walked over. Their farm wasn't big enough to accommodate vast herds of sheep, but she and Ravi's grandfather made a decent living.

So it was with Edith, and his maternal background in mind, that Ravi woke the following morning feeling optimistic. Despite the chilly air, he wore his shorts, t-shirt and runners. He waved away his grandma's offer of tea and toast and jogged to the beach. The tide was receding, and the sand was littered with shells and the remains of sea critters. He pounded beside the surf, self-conscious even though the beach was empty. His paunch wobbled, and his inner thighs chaffed with the extra weight he carried. But he didn't let that dishearten him; instead, he ran further.

It was almost midday by the time he returned to the house. His grandma was in the front garden struggling with a heavily laden wheelbarrow. From a distance, she looked just like his mother, but the age differences were apparent as he drew closer. Finally, she paused in her pushing, worked her shoulder a moment and then continued.

'Let me do that!' he insisted.

She gave him a scowl, but he held up his hand before she could lecture him on her independence.

'Please, Grandma,' he said. 'I need to work off some of this flab.'

She eyed him up and down. 'We have a gym down at the depot.'

'At the fire station?'

'Yep. You can't use it unless you're a firie, or a volunteer firie.'

Ravi almost opened his mouth to ask, "What use is that?" Until he realised what she really meant. He shook his head. 'No, they won't take me, Grandma. I have a police record, and I can't hide it. I must check in at the cop station every Tuesday to see Officer Plackis, so the whole town will know I'm an ex-crim.'

Edith waved her hand in dismissal. 'You let me worry about that. Do you want to join or not?'

Ravi knew his job prospects in town were limited. But, while he was forced to rely on his grandma's charity to live, he was in her debt and should do whatever she suggested, even though there wasn't a hope in hell. He'd dreamed of being a firefighter when he was a kid.

'If they take me, then yes, I'd love to.'

Edith beamed. 'You just made me really happy, Ravi. You are a good boy.' She poked a finger at his gut. 'You need to lose this.'

'Don't I know it,' he agreed glumly.

'Okay. From now on, no more golden syrup dumplings with cream. Your treats are going to be spinach smoothies.'

'Grandma!'

'I know, I must be cruel to be kind. Now, you can empty that load of compost onto the veggie patch over there, and then I have some bricks that need moving.'

'Jesus, Grandma, when did you become a friggin' Nazi?'

'Since you turned into a marshmallow. Now, get moving!'

Ravi spent the remainder of the day working. It felt good to be outdoors, breathing the sea air and enjoying the company of someone who loved him. It felt good to be alive.

*

True to her word, Edith organised an interview with the local fire chief by the end of that week, and to Ravi's surprise, his volunteer training began two days after that. But it was more than a week before he attended his first call-out. A car had rolled over at the highway turnoff. Luckily, no one was injured. It was a fuel and glass clean-up job. It felt good to be part of a team and put his new skills to use. Ravi guessed the other three men and two women on call that day were aware of his circumstances.

Edith would have been upfront about Ravi's past. He received a couple of sidelong looks, which were to be expected, but overall, they treated him well. And the job provided a small retainer, making him less reliant on his grandma's charity.

Ravi used the station gym four mornings a week for the next couple of months and jogged daily along the beachfront. He avoided socialising. Attending his weekly fire station meetings was his only interaction with people, besides shopping for his grandma and parole visits to the police station. But despite his insular lifestyle, he was happy and getting fitter every day. Ravi was beginning to feel comfortable in his own skin.

Chapter Three

The day Ravi's grandmother was murdered was one of the hottest of the year.

After a muggy night with little sleep in the hot bedroom, Ravi hit the beach at daybreak. The rising sun turned the water into molten gold as it sluggishly emerged over the horizon. The only sounds were the splash of gentle waves and a few squawking gulls above a bin on the roadside.

Ravi jogged to the waterline and pulled off his t-shirt before diving into the clear surf. He'd lost almost five kilos and felt great. An optimism swelled within him, gaining momentum each day along with a feeling of certainty for a better future. Coming here had been the best thing he could have done.

Ravi emerged from the seawater just as the shots were fired. He shook his head and pushed his fingers into his ears, water squelching and popping. The first two blasts, he assumed, were from a car back-firing, but as the volley continued, he began running in the direction of home. Following each shot came the sound of crashes from within the house and howls from Hank out in the yard. Ravi counted at least ten shots and then saw a car as it tore away from the front of the house. At the speed it travelled, it was little more than a white blur. After that, he saw it again fleetingly before disappearing behind the dunes' cover. The next nearest neighbour was more than a block away, tucked in a clearing behind a tall iron fence.

Beyond that was sandy scrub and more sand dunes for a kilometre before the town proper began.

Ravi raced blindly over mounds of seaweed, cutting his feet on shells and cuttlefish bones. Hank was barking madly, clearly distressed, cowering in the doorway of his kennel but unharmed. Rounding the house, Ravi saw the chunks of wood blasted from the outer walls. A line of gunshots ran the length of the house at waist height. The back screen door had been blown off its hinges, giving him a clear view of the lobby inside. The far wall was awash with blood. His grandma lay slumped on the linoleum floor.

Ravi halted in the doorway and called her name. She was still oozing blood from a massive wound below her sternum, but she was already dead. Her pupils were huge, her lips pale and slack. He fell to his knees and hugged her to his bare chest. His tears fell onto her hair which still smelled of the vanilla shampoo she always used.

His mind was a turmoil of questions. Did he somehow cause this? Should it have been him?

In the distance, he heard a siren, so maybe the neighbour had reported the din too. That thought brought more questions. Did the neighbour get the car's number plate? Had the perpetrator been caught?

Ravi held his grandma even tighter and sobbed loudly. What kind of animal did such a thing to a sweet old lady?

He was still clutching her when he felt a hand on his shoulder.

*

Ravi didn't like Jesse Plackis when he first met him at the parole check. The cop's top lip had a way of curling slightly outwards when he was concentrating. It gave the impression of a sneer, perhaps a judgemental sneer. But over time, Ravi realised that was just his look and not a reflection of the man's personality. Jesse went to considerable lengths to help Ravi settle in Henderson and not draw out his compulsory weekly visits to the police station. Jesse still annoyed Ravi, but if there was any doubt about the man's character, it disappeared the day his grandmother was shot.

'Listen, Ravi,' Jesse said as he handed him a cup of sweet milky tea. 'There will be a Major Crimes team here by lunchtime. The Port Lincoln crew are comprehensive, so try to work with them. Sometimes the most insignificant seeming detail can be important.'

Ravi nodded and took a sip of the hot beverage. Despite the warm weather, he pulled the blanket tighter around his shoulders while Hank lay across his feet. Ravi had been sitting on the couch for more than two hours. His head was abuzz with gruesome images. At first, they made him feel sick, but after a long stint in the bathroom, retching and spewing, his stomach was empty and beginning to settle.

The front section of the house had been taped off, awaiting the arrival of a ballistics team from Adelaide, it had been badly damaged and required investigation, so Ravi and Jesse remained in the confines of the living room and sunroom. That suited Ravi because he couldn't bear to set foot out there.

Edith was taken to the local medical clinic before being transferred to Adelaide for a post-mortem. The ambulance crew who took her had asked questions, but Ravi couldn't remember Edith's date of birth, age, or any other detail they requested. He sat shrugging, mumbling and apologising.

Following a second round of prompting, Jesse had asked them to leave. 'I'll find out the particulars and get back to you,' he assured the crew as they departed.

The neighbour's teenage son had retrieved Ravi's shoes and shirt from the beach, but Ravi couldn't thank the boy. The words lodged in his throat but all he could produce were choking sobs. Jesse thanked the boy on Ravi's behalf. He told the kid that Ravi would come and see him when he was up to it.

The Major Crimes team, comprising a man and woman, arrived at three pm, and Ravi's mother arrived shortly after. The day and the process were a surreal blur for Ravi. Jesse stayed as his advocate throughout the interview, twice losing his patience when the questions were repeated. Eventually, the investigating officers called it a day but assured Ravi they would return the following morning.

Jesse ordered a pizza for dinner and stayed until nightfall. If his mother was surprised by this care, she didn't show it. Instead, they picked at the food in solemn silence.

Darkness had descended on their lives.

*

By the next day, Ravi's shock was morphing into anger. He didn't have the luxury of Jesse's support because the cop had been called away, but he didn't need it. His mother sat on the opposite side of the sunroom. She looked pale and fragile; her distress exacerbated his bad temper.

'How could the car just drive away? Why wasn't it stopped?' Ravi asked. His tone was incredulous, but the Major Crimes officer seemed dismissive of his sceptical rant.

The woman touched his hand, somehow confident he would not rebuff her sympathy. Her sharp features and severe bun were softened by her smile, and without wanting to, Ravi found himself warming to her.

Apparently, the two investigators were trying a different tactic today. The male cop, Ben someone or other, had been unsuccessful the previous day with his direct and occasionally brutal questions, so today, they were playing good cop, using the more empathetic of the two to obtain answers. But Ravi had more questions than they did.

'Someone must have seen something! Cars don't just vanish,' he cried.

'I understand your frustration, Ravi. Please be assured we are doing everything we can, but this is a remote town with little in the way of CCTV. Whoever was driving the car must have been aware of that. They avoided the local petrol station and its obvious cameras. Still, we are checking every other camera, both private security and dash cams, as well as traffic control on the highways.'

'My neighbour, Felicity, did she see the car?' Ravi asked.

'No. But her son Liam did. He confirmed it was a white four-wheel drive but couldn't give us the make or numberplate.'

Ravi glanced at his mother. 'And how many white four-wheel drives are there around? Only bloody millions! Every second car is a white four-wheel-drive in rural areas.'

Emily's eyes were red-rimmed. She looked empty and miserable, precisely the way Ravi felt. He knew his attitude was disturbing, but he couldn't control it. 'Do you know anything at all? Do you know why this happened?'

'Honestly, Ravi, at this point, we can't speculate. We need to have more details to build a picture.'

'Do you think it was meant to be me?' He blurted. The second the reality of the situation hit him, he was convinced he had caused his grandma's death, and he was pretty sure they were all thinking the same thing. 'Was I the intended target? I mean, it must have been me. No one guns down little old ladies. Especially popular ones. They got the wrong person, didn't they?'

'We are certainly open to all theories, Ravi. But, of course, they may not have been after you at all. This could have been a mistake on the part of the shooter. So, try to avoid jumping to conclusions. Having said that, we are taking your security very seriously. I have two constables coming from Port Lincoln this morning. They will stay in Henderson for at least five days, and then we will reassess whether they are still needed. They'll provide security along this road and escort you anywhere you need to go.

'But, I don't want you leaving the property unnecessarily because once the new wall cladding is in place, this house will be bulletproof and the safest space you could be outside the police station, and you have already indicated that you dislike that option.' The woman didn't give Ravi time to interrupt. 'As far as motive is concerned, we don't have much to go on yet, but these are early days, and we will build a comprehensive picture quite quickly. First up, we are trying to locate the owner of the car you tried to steal.'

Ravi dropped his head. 'Of course, that woman. Why am I so stupid. I'm just a fuck-up, and I probably did cause this.'

'Ravi,' the woman cop said in a harsher tone. 'No one has the right to take another person's life. You are not the guilty one here. Yes, you made a stupid mistake, and you've paid the price. The best way to help us is to try to think of anything that may be helpful.'

Ravi glanced at the male cop. His expression was hard and unreadable.

The woman stood and collected her notes and devices. 'We'll be checking in with each new development. Try to take it easy.'

'The funeral?' Emily asked. 'Do you know when we might have it?'

The bloke spoke up this time. 'You can't prepare for it yet; these things often take a few weeks at least.'

Ravi saw his mother clamp a hand over her mouth. He could hear the beginnings of a cry trying to escape, but before the tears started, the woman cop hunkered down in front of Emily and said, 'You will have plenty of time to gather photos, select music, and write your mum's eulogy. In some ways it's good not to have to rush that process. I'm sure you can understand that we must be as thorough as possible to avoid missing anything. I promise we will have her back to you as soon as we are done.'

Emily nodded for a few moments, perhaps not trusting her voice. Eventually, she said, 'Thank you, officer.'

'Molly,' the woman said as she extended her hand. 'I'll be in touch. In the meantime, don't hesitate to contact me if you need to.' She smiled at Ravi. 'Even the smallest thing, Ravi, okay?'

Ravi's questions had dried up along with his anger. Instead, a miserable numbness had settled over him. He glanced from cop to cop, eventually giving a grudging nod. His mother's sobs grew louder as the door closed, but Ravi couldn't move to comfort her because he found himself gazing at the ceiling. He had never felt so drained in his life.

*

Molly Hunter woke with a start when her boyfriend farted. The sound caused their German Shepherd to growl and their Maltese Terrier to yap. Both dogs leapt to their feet and raced outside. A cacophony of barking filled the yard. In seconds, Molly's sleep and the enveloping silence had been shattered. To make matters worse, the stench was eye-watering.

'Christ on a bike, Ferdi! You could kill someone with that stink!'

'Whatever,' he muttered as he rolled away from her.

She climbed out of bed without disturbing the covers. Then, wafting the air before her, she escaped into the ensuite bathroom. She showered under tepid water and dried herself vigorously. When she dressed and emerged from the room, Ferdi had made her a cup of coffee. He kissed her cheek as he handed it to her, but she sneered and said, 'You still stink!'

Ferdi grinned and said, 'Whatever.' Then he stretched out on the bed and read an article on his iPad. Shortie, the Maltese Terrier, had returned and sprawled across Molly's pillow, snoring. After a moment, Ferdi asked, 'Will you be late tonight?'

Molly straightened the collar of her shirt and asked, 'Why?'

Ferdi gave an overemphasised groan. 'Can you stop being a cop just for a while?'

'Why?'

'Because we're having dinner with Stevo and Rick.'

'Is that tonight?'

'Yeah. It's their anniversary. Fifteen years.'

'Oh shit. Um, I'm not sure.'

'We promised.'

'I know, but this case we're working on is in Henderson; just getting there takes two hours.'

'I'll wait for you,' Ferdi said.

'But if I get held up, it will spoil the evening.'

'Then don't get held up. Tell Ben to do some work on his own.'

'It's more complex than that. I could take my own car, but Ben won't be happy. He always insists that I drive.'

Ferdi scoffed. 'Maybe he doesn't have a license?'

Molly brushed her hair and then fixed her ponytail in place. 'Of course, he does.' She squeezed the blue dental gel onto her toothbrush and began brushing. 'I'll take my own car.'

'Thanks, baby. Try to be back on time.'

'Sure.' The toothpaste tasted weird. Ferdi had bought some unheard-of brand again.

'Ten to seven,' Ferdi called out. 'You're going to be late.'

'Shit!' Molly spat and rinsed. 'I'll text you during the day.'

But the bedroom was empty; even the dogs were gone. Ferdi was using the toilet at the other end of the house. 'Thank Christ for that,' she muttered as she picked up her phone and keys. 'See you tonight!' she shouted without waiting for a reply.

*

Ben was grumpy, so Molly was happy not to share a car with him. She remained about fifty metres behind him for the entire journey with the music up loud and the window down. She grinned at how annoyed Ben would be if he sat beside her now. He hated having his hair ruffled, and her choice of old grunge songs appeared to set his teeth on edge.

They finally pulled up, side by side, just after nine-thirty. Molly and Ben were using the Henderson Police Station as their base during this investigation. It was an old red brick building from the sixties that probably had asbestos in the ceiling and walls. The flooring was worn linoleum tiles, and the cells looked like something from Ned Kelly's era. Molly opened the refrigerator and was pleased to feel the cool air.

'Well, something works around here,' she said cheerily, placing her lunchbox on the top shelf.

'Better than the Internet then.' Ben was jabbing at his phone as if he could intimidate the Wi-Fi into working faster.

'Mmm. I'm using mobile hotpot.' She read through her emails on the SAPOL intranet site. 'Did you see this one from Adelaide?'

'Yep,' Ben said. 'Just reading it now.'

'So, Maryjo Katz owned the car that Ravi tried to steal. That's interesting.'

'I've heard that name before.'

'She was Amos Khalil's girlfriend.' Molly smiled. This was very promising.

'Khalil? The biker?'

'Yeah. He shot that pub owner as well as a rival biker. He got prison time.'

'Actual prison?'

'Yeah. Khalil missed out on the Criminal Ageing System sentencing. His offences were too serious.'

Ben shook his head. 'Good. They need to lock up maniacs like him. Age that bastard by twenty-five years, and you will get a dangerous older bastard.'

'Absolutely,' Molly agreed. 'But unfortunately, it also removes him from suspicion for the Edith Sanders' murder because we know where he was.'

'Well, we also need to look at whatever piece of garbage Katz is currently hooked up with. She must be an airhead to have been involved with Khalil in the first place.' Ben gave a humourless laugh as he glanced up from his device. 'Guess what she does for a living?'

'Exotic dancer?'

'Yep. Lap dances in some shitty dive in the northern suburbs of Adelaide.'

'Pure class,' Molly said facetiously. 'Get city onto that. We need to know if she was out for some sick revenge.'

'It seems a bit extreme.'

'We don't know how attached she was to her car. Plus, she was assaulted by Ravi. Maybe she has permanent scarring - perhaps something that hurts her career. We need her file.'

'I'm pretty sure nobody looks at strippers' faces.'

Molly rolled her eyes at his sexist comment but wasn't willing to start an argument. 'You're probably right, but it's worth checking.'

'Sure, I've requested a list of locals with firearms licences.' Ben shook his head. 'Not that I think it will yield anything. This looks more like a hit, and no criminal with half a brain would use a registered rifle.'

'Still, we need to follow the processes.' Molly shook her head. 'From the speed of those shots, it had to be a semi-automatic even though they're prohibited in this country.

The back door to the station opened with the squeal of ancient hinges. Molly glanced into the hallway and saw Jesse approaching.

'You call this morning?' Ben said, pointing to the wall clock.

'My morning started at six with a phone call from a farmer whose cow was struck by a semi-trailer down on the highway.'

Ben snorted. 'So what? You double as the local vet?'

'Is it okay?' Molly asked.

'No. Two smashed legs.' Jesse walked to the desk that Ben had commandeered. Jesse glared down at him.

'The nearest vet is in Port Lincoln and you should know how far away that is.'

Ben was on his feet, chest pushed out, and arms held rigid at his sides as he faced Jesse.

'Sit down, Ben. Stop being a jerk.' Molly stood and walked to the water dispenser. 'Did you shoot it?' she asked.

Jesse rubbed his brow. 'Had to. The owner was too distraught, and the poor animal was a mess.'

'Jeez. That's bad luck. Do you get jobs like that often?' Molly tried to shake the image of the cow from her mind.

'Often enough.'

'Poor thing.' After a moment she said, 'I'll update you on what we have so far.'

'No,' Ben said. 'He doesn't need to know. We can handle this ourselves. This is a Major Crimes case.'

Molly dismissed Ben with a wave of her hand. 'Jesse, you are probably the best person to liaise with the Sanders family. We'll give them any updates, but we want them to feel that we're doing something, even if we aren't progressing. Would you mind checking in on them daily?'

'Sure,' Jesse looked over at Ben. 'Be happy to,' he said smugly.

'Okay,' Molly continued before the atmosphere became any more macho. 'Please tell Ravi and Emily that we are looking at Maryjo Katz and her known associates but have no leads yet.

'Also, the preliminary post-mortem finding is death by gunshot. The projectile pierced the aorta resulting in massive haemorrhage and cardiac arrest. Remember to tell them it was quick; Edith didn't suffer. The coroner will examine the pathologist's final report, which should be ready in a week or so. Please don't give them any false hopes on timeframes. There are often holdups, and if the family expect it to take longer, they'll be pleased if it's shorter.'

'That's nice of you,' Jesse said.

Molly shot him a glance, wondering if he was being smart, but was reassured by his sincere expression. 'Thanks,' she said. 'I try to treat families like I'd want to be treated in the same situation.'

They both ignored the grunt that came from Ben.

'So,' Jesse said. 'I have a background on Edith Sanders. Nothing was on our files besides some vandal damage to her shed, but that was almost twenty years ago.' He placed a paper file on the desk he had set up for Molly. 'This is her CFS file.' Jesse shrugged. 'At a glance, I couldn't see anything helpful.'

'Oh, for Christ's sake,' Ben blustered. 'We have enough real work to do. Go through it yourself, Plackis.'

'Thanks, Jesse,' Molly said quickly. 'And Ben may be right. If you can look at Edith's file, that would help us greatly. And could you run through the list of locals with firearms licences?'

'Sure. I'll be happy to,' he said in a surly tone.

Ben smirked and then mumbled something incomprehensible, but his tone was sarcastic. As Jesse strode away, Molly rested her head in her hands. Keeping these two civil was going to test her patience. She hated this reek of testosterone. She swore under her breath, knowing this could be the first of many long and trying days.

*

The roller door rattled as it slowly opened. The street was quiet outside of the ambulance depot because most local workers had gone home for the evening. An older man walked his black poodle on the opposite footpath, watching Ruby Gill slowly back the ambulance into the depot bay.

'Keep the wheel dead straight,' Tash warned.

'I got it.'

'No, Ruby, you're pulling down to the left. Look at the top of the steering wheel. It isn't straight. You've only got a few centimetres of clearance for this side mirror.'

'But…'

'Whoa! Stop the truck. Let's change drivers before you do some damage.' Tash battled to keep her voice calm. New ambulance volunteers generally listened to the more experienced Ambulance Officers, but Ruby was an exception. 'Fucking Gen Zeds,' Tash mumbled under her breath. From the back of the ambulance, her partner sniggered. 'Shut up, Carl,' Tash warned. She rounded the vehicle and hauled open the driver-side door. 'Out.'

'No. I want to drive,' Ruby insisted. 'I must complete my training hours. I have to be able to park.'

'Sure, you can drive later,' Tash said, 'but I'm parking it right now. The last thing we need is our ambulance off the road because you've torn off the side mirror or worse.'

Ruby opened her mouth to complain when the mobile data terminal alert was activated. At the same time, Tash and Carl's pagers went off. Tash glanced at the screen. 'Priority two, hop in the back Ruby.'

Carl didn't wait for another protest; he clambered into the passenger seat and said, 'Hurry up and move. We've got to go!'

Once Tash was behind the wheel and had confirmed with communications that the crew were responding, she turned to Ruby, who sat in the air-way seat behind her. 'Ruby, why hasn't your pager gone off?'

'Oh, oops. I forgot to turn it on.'

Tash flashed an exasperated glance at Carl, who was shaking his head.

Carl hit the lights and siren as Tash pulled out onto the road. The calm of the summer's night was broken as the ambulance roared down the near-empty back streets of Tailem Bend.

'Sixty-year-old male threatening self-harm and violence.' Carl read from the MDT. 'SAPOL will be in attendance. No previous psychological diagnosis. Sudden onset.' Carl glanced at Tash. 'This is interesting – the address is Lavender Court.'

'What does that mean?' Ruby asked.

Tash glanced at Ruby. Her head had appeared over the barrier that divided the cab from the treatment area of the ambulance. 'Sit down and strap in, Ruby.' Tash rounded a corner and stepped on the accelerator. 'It means,' Tash shouted over the din of the siren. 'The patient is living in accommodation rented out to ex-offenders.'

'Sex offenders?'

'No. Ex-offenders. Lavender Court is housing for ex-criminals released from Mobilong Prison. The housing used to be for men who had served time for minor offences, but it may have changed.'

'Why?' Ruby asked, but Tash was too busy watching the screen of her GPS to answer.

'There have been overhauls since the Criminal Ageing System laws were legislated,' Carl said. 'Often people coming out of prison have lost their rental accommodation. Nowadays it's different because they don't spend time away. But,' he said, raising his finger in the air. 'Whenever we get called to this destination, remember that we always request police backup. Don't ever approach a patient there without it. If the cops are late, then you wait. These are, after all, ex-criminals, and we don't know what they were convicted of.'

'What if they're really sick?' Ruby asked.

'Then you hope to hell that the police get there fast. Your safety is a priority.'

Ruby began to ask something else as they stopped beside two police vehicles. Tash and Carl were out of the ambulance and lugging equipment from the side door. They had almost reached the front door of the house when Ruby finally clambered out.

Tash halted three paces into the front living area. An angry roar could be heard in the passageway, followed by the barking of orders. 'Stop. Hands in front! Drop it! Drop it now!' Then came the bumps and bangs of a scuffle, a few expletives and a shocked cry. A police officer suddenly appeared in the living area holding his head, his face red and eyes streaming.

'Help,' the man said. 'I've pepper sprayed myself.'

'And the patient?' Tash asked as she retrieved a litre bag of saline from her pack.

'Um, yeah. He copped it too.'

Tash nodded to Carl and threw him the saline. 'You sort him, and I'll deal with our patient.'

In the corridor were two officers standing and a man sitting. The bloke's head was slumped forward. The air was still sharp with the scent of pepper spray. Tash saw the man's hands were cuffed behind his back. She knelt, observing him with more than a metre buffer.

'His name is Murray Deakins,' the blond cop offered. 'He was wielding a knife. We got it off him.'

'Thanks.' Tash moved closer and tapped the man's shoulder. 'Murray! Murray! Can you hear me?'

The man slowly raised his head until Tash saw his swollen red eyes. His respirations were fast and laboured. His mouth twitched.

'Did you taser him?' Tash asked the cop.

'No. He was screaming and pulling the place apart. It took three of us to restrain him and get the cuffs on.'

'Do you know if he's taken any medication or illicit drugs?'

The cop shrugged.

'Have you checked his pockets?' Tash asked as she inched closer to the sick man.

'Hey! Don't get too close!' The other police officer warned.

Tash was more surprised by the cop's terrified expression than the warning, but she moved away just in time. The patient lunged, trying desperately to bite her ankle but instead latched onto the bottom of her trousers. His teeth were gnashing, and he growled furiously.

'Jesus,' Tash exclaimed as she edged further away.

The handcuffed man thrashed his head from side to side, belly crawling to get closer to Tash, before being stopped by Carl, who stood astride the man and lifted him by his belt buckle. He hauled the livid bloke back down the hallway, letting him down with a thud.

Carl touched Tash's elbow as he passed by. 'I'll get the net and face screens for us,' he said. 'And I'll warn the hospital.'

'Carl!' she called before he disappeared. 'Get that student out of the truck. She can ride with the police.'

Carl gave a slight grin. 'That's for bloody sure.'

Tash hunkered down and gazed at the man. He looked more like a cornered beast than a human being. She wondered what drug had induced such violent behaviour. There were always new products on the streets, and they seemed to be getting worse and worse. And then she wondered how hard it would be to restrain him on the stretcher.

The answer turned out to be hard, very hard. It took almost forty minutes to safely load him.

Chapter Four

Ravi hadn't wanted to leave his grandma's house but had to. Despite a section of it being the scene of awful carnage, it had become his haven, his safe place. The area where his grandma was gunned down had been repaired and scrupulously cleaned. It looked nothing like the place in his nightmares anymore, but Ravi's newfound confidence had vanished since the shooting.

Floral tributes now lined the wall of the back lobby. And there was a deep calm Ravi felt within the walls of this home. It was a feeling that bolstered his fragile self-confidence, a sense that his grandma's essence was still there, looking out for him. The outside world was a different matter. He was a nervous wreck.

It had been four days since Edith passed away, and Emily had returned to work and life in the city. His sister, Samantha, had spent a sombre day with them, but she too had returned to Adelaide. During the past two days, Emily had phoned several times, asking Ravi to speak to the local computer repair man, AJ. Emily needed to access her mother's photo and music library to assist with the funeral service arrangements. Because Ravi had insisted that Emily stay away from Henderson until the police either caught his grandma's killer or proved that neither she nor Ravi were the intended targets, the computer arrangements now fell to him.

Edith was tech-savvy and had password-protected her laptop. Ravi had tried hundreds of combinations of names and birthdates but had failed to open it. So that morning, Ravi loaded the small computer onto the passenger seat of his grandma's utility. He peered towards the roadway. A young constable was sitting in his car out the front. The man momentarily glanced up from his phone as though aware he was being watched. Ravi guessed the cop was bored. Long shifts, sitting and watching an empty street must have been mind-numbing, because when Ravi asked the cop if he would escort Ravi into town, he agreed immediately.

The main street of Henderson was the central hub, with a few crossroads incorporating businesses rather than stores. AJ sold toys and sporting goods in a shop on one of the side streets. Repairing devices was a hobby that supplemented his income, and he was more than happy to take the job.

'Yes, no worries. I can access it for you. Give me a day or two,' AJ said as a kid barged past Ravi with a new edition of Call of Duty. The boy waved his parent's debit card at the shopkeeper. AJ grunted, and Ravi took the opportunity to escape into the street, down the block and then home.

Although he hadn't noticed anyone glancing in his direction, not even the cop sent to watch him, Ravi felt scrutinised. He supposed some of those feelings were due to the guilt of being a lawbreaker, but primarily because of his grandma's fate. Surely, if someone had been out to get him and failed, they would try again.

Ravi arrived back home again within twenty minutes. The sweat had soaked his t-shirt, sticking him to the car seat despite the efficient air conditioning. He took deep breaths and tried to ignore the swiftly throbbing pulse in his neck; he wondered grimly if it was possible for his head to explode.

These were the same feelings he had when he met with the cop, Jesse Plackis, at the station for his very first weekly check-in. That time, the urge to run had been overwhelming, and his heart ticked away like a hyperactive watch. It was a sensation that had all but disappeared before his grandma died, but now it was back and becoming more intense. The twinges in his chest felt like a panic attack or worse, and worrying about that intensified his panic. It was a crazy hamster wheel that he could see no way of escaping from.

When Ravi arrived at the toy and sports shop two days later and saw the front door was locked, his anxiety levels escalated again. He supposed part of his nervousness was due to not having a police escort. The security around him had been scaled back because Major Crimes had reassessed the risk as low. But low didn't mean nil, and standing in an exposed position on the street was terrifying.

Ravi rattled the handle half a dozen times to be sure, but it didn't budge. He glanced in the window. The store was dark, and he couldn't see much beyond the window displays. Then, from across the street, someone called out.

'Hey! AJ's closed for lunch.'

Ravi turned around and saw a kid on the other side of the road.

'Do you know when he'll be back?' Ravi asked.

The kid looked both ways, though it was hardly necessary given the infrequent dribble of passing traffic and walked to Ravi's side of the street. But as the kid drew closer, Ravi realised it wasn't a kid. Instead, it was a young woman, and she was short. The top of her head came up to his shoulder. She was slim, pretty much straight up and down, but when she removed her sunglasses and smiled at him, he realised she was beautiful. Ravi was so surprised that he was momentarily lost for words.

'Sorry mate, I couldn't hear you.' The woman said as she leaned against a veranda post and adjusted her leather sandal.

'I – um – not sure. Um – when does he get back?'

'Whatever it says on the note,' she replied.

'Note?'

'Yeah. In the window.'

She passed by Ravi and pointed to a scrap of paper taped beside the shop's opening hours list. Ravi had to tear his gaze from her perfect arm to read it.

She spun around and gave a dimpled grin that threatened to stop his heart. 'Half an hour,' she said.

'I – um.'

'Are you okay? You look a bit strange. Not a diabetic, are you?'

'A what?'

'You don't have diabetes? Not hypoglycaemic?'

Ravi shook his head and looked desperately up and down the street. He wanted to run to the car, but he could not for the life of him remember where he'd parked it.

She cocked her head. 'Hey, don't I know you?'

Ravi began shaking his head and took a step backwards.

'It's okay. I know what you've been through.' Her face was suddenly solemn. 'I was at your grandma's the day she died.'

But Ravi shook his head. Surely, he would have remembered this woman.

'Yeah, I was helping the ambos. I drove for them that day. We came and took your grandma away. I'm so sorry. She was a brilliant person. I've known her all my life. She meant a lot to my family and me.' The woman wiped her hand against her denim shorts and then extended it.   'Bailey Donovan.'

'Oh, um, Ravi Sanders.'

Her hand was soft and small, and he knew he held it for too long, but she didn't seem to mind. She moved closer and put her other hand on his upper arm. She smelled amazing, and the effect was dizzying. 'Listen,' she said. 'I'm waiting for AJ to get back too. I'm picking up a pair of runners for my sister. Do you want a get a coffee or something while we wait?'

She could have asked him to jump into a fire pit, and he would have nodded. He followed like a puppy, almost bumping into her when she stopped at the cafe entrance. When she turned, they were nearly face to chest. She looked up and grinned.

'Are you alright?' she asked with a giggle. 'You haven't been smoking weed, have you?' But when she saw his appalled reaction to her comment, Bailey laughed again and said, 'I wouldn't care if you had. I don't mind the odd cone myself.'

At the counter, she ordered them both coffee without asking how he took it, then pointed to a table by the window. 'Sit down,' she said before turning back to pay.

Ravi angled his chair towards the street, but his gaze was drawn back to Bailey after just a few seconds. He saw the concentration on her face as she navigated the cluttered cafe with two steaming mugs. Her fair hair had fallen over one eye, and she chewed her bottom lip as she moved.

Her bare legs were tanned, and now that he had time for a better look, she wasn't as straight up and down as he'd first thought. Ravi's head was spinning, but not with anxiety. He licked his lips and focused on the plastic table number. He wondered if he was coming down with something. Surely this reaction was not just to a pretty woman. Piper had been quite a looker, but she'd never had this effect on him.

'Are you okay?' Bailey asked as she sat opposite him.

Ravi nodded before answering. 'Yeah, I mean, no. I'm mean, I'm not exactly sure.'

'I get it. You're still in shock. The whole community is. Your grandma was so loved. She spent her life helping people. There isn't a person in town who's not indebted to her in some way.'

'I – I guess.'

'I mean it. If it weren't for your grandma, Edith, I wouldn't have been born.'

'Really?'

'Absolutely! When my mum was just a kid, her house burnt down. It was your grandma who dragged her and her baby sister out. Without Edith, they would have died.'

'Wow!'

'So, you and I have a big connection.' Despite her cheerful words, her expression was sad.

Ravi had a dim memory of the story. 'Not everyone made it?'

'No. Mum's elder brother, my Uncle Colin, was killed. But I never knew him.'

'No, but still, it's upsetting.'

'Yes. Also, my grandmother died just a couple of months ago.'

'Oh no. I'm so sorry. You're worried about me, but you have your own grief.'

She gave a brave smile. 'It's okay. It wasn't unexpected. She had been sick for some time. I guess it's a bit of a relief for my grandpa. It was tough nursing her at home, especially at the very end. I helped when I could. It was pitiful, cruel.'

'Cancer?'

'Yeah. Pancreatic.'

Ravi shook his head. 'So, are you a nurse?'

'Sort of. I work as a personal carer at an aged care facility, but I've been accepted to study physiotherapy. I start my course in the new year. I can do some of the studies externally, but most will be in Adelaide.'

'Oh.'

'It's not so bad. I went to college in Adelaide, so I still have some friends I can board with down there.'

'Adelaide's a long way from here.'

Bailey shrugged as though she hadn't given it much thought. 'I'll get home every weekend and help Mum with Grandpa. So, how's the police investigation going? Oh!' She slapped a palm against her forehead and shook her head vigorously. 'Sorry, that was insensitive. I didn't mean to pry. I just wondered if you had any answers yet. It will be important to help you move on.' She dropped her gaze and chewed her bottom lip. 'It's probably too soon for you to talk about, I guess.'

All this talk of death seemed to be affecting her. If her smile caused an unwanted response, then her distress was almost crippling. He held out his hand to her while his chest bunched in pain. A moment later, Ravi was mortified when his own unwanted tears flowed. He covered his face with his free hand. Bailey moved closer and hugged him, brushing her hand over his hair. Ravi realised he wasn't suffering so much from love at first sight as acute loneliness. Bailey had managed to release the floodgate on the emotions he had bottled up for days.

'I'm so sorry,' he muttered.

'No. Don't you dare. I feel privileged to be here for you.' She gently kissed him on the cheek and dabbed her eyes with a napkin.

Ravi wiped his face with his sleeve and sat taller in his chair. He glanced around the room, once more concerned about onlookers or gossips. His eyes were drawn back to Bailey, and he saw that their hands were still clasped. She began to pull away, and he released her.

He opened his mouth to apologise, but she shushed him, predicting his response. Instead, she took his hand once more, the returning smile making her face radiant. 'Well, Ravi, I have some good news,' she said.

Ravi stared into her eyes for a full five seconds before asking, 'What?'

Bailey grinned and gestured to the pavement outside just as a man walked out of view.

'AJ's back.'

*

Ferdi pulled into the drop off area of Port Lincoln Airport just before eight-thirty. Molly knew by his silence that he was unhappy about her departing for Adelaide. She was going to miss their tenth anniversary. Ferdi had planned a surprise party for the occasion, a large venue, private caterers and a local band, but now his plans had been scuttled. He had also booked a weekend away in the Flinders Ranges, which she could make, but not the secret soiree for more than fifty guests. Molly was amazed that Ben hadn't let the cat out of the bag before this, but he never showed much interest in other people's lives. He was too busy moaning about his own.

Ferdi sighed as Molly took her small suitcase from the back seat.

'I'm sorry,' she said for the twentieth time that morning.

He shook his head and looked the other way. Molly walked around the car and opened his door. She crouched down, peering up at him. Ferdi didn't look at her until she rubbed a hand on his knee. 'I really am sorry,' she repeated. 'You know the job.'

'I know the job. Sometimes I hate it.'

'I know baby. I hate it too. But we'll have the weekend.'

'Yeah.' He looked miserable.

'I gotta go.' Molly lunged forward and kissed him. By the time he reached to grasp her, she was turning away. 'Try to be good,' she said.

He had no reply to that; if he had, she wasn't sure she wanted to hear it.

Ben was already waiting in the small departure lounge, sipping a takeaway coffee. He mumbled something as Molly sat beside him.

'What?' She asked.

Instead of repeating himself, he handed her his phone. The text message from SAPOL Adelaide informed them that Maryjo Katz would have a lawyer present during her interview that day.

'Interesting,' Molly said. 'What reason was she given for this interview?'

'The usual,' Ben said. 'We want to ask her some questions about an ongoing investigation.'

'The murder has been headlining news. But the media reports about Edith Sanders' death don't mention Ravi Sanders or his past misdemeanour. So, hiring a lawyer could be construed as guilty behaviour. How else could Katz know about Ravi's relationship with the victim?'

'She probably wouldn't unless she's involved.'

Molly glanced at Ben as she handed the phone back. 'It would be too easy, wouldn't it? So maybe she doesn't know anything. Perhaps she is just being cautious.'

'Yeah. But maybe we'll get lucky, and she'll miraculously confess.'

'Mmm. I don't think it will be that simple.' Molly stood up and said, 'Time to go.'

They waited for the other passengers to board the small plane and then took their seats. Molly read files on the first half of the journey and dozed for the remainder.

*

Ravi swam that morning. It was the first time he'd been in the water since the shooting, and he felt guilty for enjoying it, so he followed up with a punishing five-kilometre run to the distant bluff and back. As he neared home, he saw a woman standing ankle-deep in the swell. It was his mother. She looked lost, forlorn, and Ravi felt another stab of remorse. His mum had spent time comforting him, and he had done nothing for her. Emily had lost her mother, a mother who had been dear to her.

'Hi, mum.'

'Oh Ravi, how are you?'

'I'm – okay. What about you?'

She gave a slight shrug and an even smaller smile. 'Oh, you know.'

'You can talk to me, mum.'

Emily gave him a hard stare. 'Sure. I know I can.'

'I picked up grandma's laptop yesterday.'

'I know. I saw it on the kitchen bench. Did you find any photographs?'

'Yeah, quite a few. I also found some old Polaroids in the laundry cupboard. They were in an old biscuit tin.'

'Really? Does it have an English fox hunting scene on the lid?'

'Ah, yeah, it does.'

'Gosh, I remember that tin from my childhood. My mum had it forever. We used to love seeing it come out on special occasions, like Christmas and birthdays. "Memories in a can", dad used to call it.'

Ravi was pleased to see her smile. 'We can have a look at them now if you want. Over a cup of coffee?'

'That sounds lovely.'

Emily led the way over the small dune and into the back garden. Hank bustled about as they opened the gate, his tail wagging furiously, and then snuffled at their feet while he made high-pitched cries of joy.

'I think he misses Mum. You should have taken him with you for a run.'

'No. I'll take him later. I went for a swim to clear my head. The run just kind of happened, and I went too far for him. The old boy would have conked out.'

'Sure.' Emily knelt and gave the dog a hug. 'Maybe I should take him back to the city with me.'

'You're at work all day, mum. It won't be much of a life for him; besides, he knows this place. It's home.'

'Well, if you're sure, Ravi. I don't want you stressed. You have enough on your mind already.'

'Seriously, mum, you must stop worrying about me. Are you eating properly? You look thin.'

'I'll be okay, honey.'

But Ravi could see the tears welling. 'Mum. You must take care of yourself.' As he said it, her face crumpled, and she walked to the garden bench, gathering her skirt as she sat. He moved beside her and put an arm around her shoulders.

'I need to be strong,' she said.

'You are strong. You and Grandma were so alike. You got your strength from her.' Ravi squeezed her shoulder. 'I wish I wasn't so piss-weak.'

'You aren't weak Ravi.'

'I'm like my dad, aren't I? He was pathetic.'

Emily sniffed loudly and sat up straight. 'No, Ravi, that's wrong. Your dad wasn't weak. He was sensitive.'

'Well, that sounds pretty lame.'

'No. His problem was he felt too much and let other people's worries become his own.'

It struck Ravi that they had never discussed his father and his shortcomings. They only ever discussed the good years, the wholesome memories. Somehow his mum's defence of his father didn't surprise him.

'You loved him, didn't you?'

'Of course. But I couldn't help him. He didn't want to stop drinking, he got neglectful and selfish, and I had to put you and Samantha first.' She shrugged. 'That's what mums do.'

'It must have hurt to give up on him.'

Emily nodded, and Ravi was sad for her, sad too that he had started this conversation.

'Let's go look at some photos.' He suggested.

She gave a smile and took his offered hand. Hank followed them into the kitchen, making a beeline for his bed by the stove. Once the kettle had boiled, they settled at the table and sorted through the mountain of polaroids, sipping coffee and reminiscing. They made piles of their favourites, which would later be digitised and added to those already selected for the funeral service.

'I met a young woman yesterday,' Ravi said after a while.

'Really? Is she nice?'

'Mum, it's not like that.'

'Like what?'

'Like, I don't know. But, anyway, she knew grandma.'

'What's her name?'

'Bailey, Bailey Donovan.'

'Oh yeah. The Donovans. I went to school with Donna Donovan, although back then she was Donna Winters.'

'Yes, that's her mum. Bailey said her grandma recently died.'

'Oh no. The poor thing. She would have been about grandma's age but always sick. Did you know her house burned down back in the seventies?'

Ravi nodded. 'Bailey told me that grandma saved Donna and her sister.'

'She sure did. I remember it. I was just a kid. We went to her brother's funeral. It was the first funeral I'd ever been to. It was so sad.' Emily took a long drink and asked, 'So what's Bailey like?'

'Um, pretty nice.'

'You're smiling! I think this lady has made an impact.'

'No, mum. She's too young for me.' Ravi felt a wave of self-pity. 'Maybe in another life.' He saw his mother flinch at his wretched tone. 'Sorry, mum. I'm not complaining, I just…'

Emily reached over and touched his elbow. 'You're allowed to feel pissed off, you know. Your sentence was far too harsh. If that woman hadn't harped on about you assaulting her when it was clear you were trying to run away, well, the punishment wouldn't have been so severe.'

'I don't blame her for trying to stop me. I was the idiot who was trying to take her car.'

'Yes, I know, but there is deliberate assault and accidentally colliding with someone.'

Ravi put his hands in the air. 'That's enough, mum. It's a useless discussion and one I have had far too often with myself. At the end of the day, I'm the dickhead, not her.'

'Okay, but I want to hear more about this girl, Bailey. She sounds interesting. Do you have anything more in common than recently deceased grandmothers?'

Ravi smiled at his mum's gallows humour. 'You really are amazing, mum.'

She waved his compliment away. 'Tell me about the girl. Obviously, you like her, and don't give me any crap about you being too old. You two were born around the same time.'

Ravi spent the next twenty minutes reliving the previous day. He was pleased to notice his mother's eyes shone brightly the whole time.

*

Maryjo Katz did not look anything like what Molly had expected. In fact, Molly raised an eyebrow when Maryjo first entered the room. She glanced at Ben and found they shared the same reaction. Maryjo wasn't hardened nor tarty. If Molly had first seen the woman out on the street, she would have thought – a kindergarten teacher.

Maryjo was slight but sinewy, with a mass of red curls and pale blue eyes. She had turned up without her lawyer but didn't explain why.

'Thank you for speaking with us, Maryjo. Please, have a seat.' Molly introduced Ben and then asked,' You're wondering why we've asked you to come in this morning?

'Well, I assume it has something to do with Amos Khalil. The police are always asking me about Amos. It doesn't matter that I haven't seen him in months. I mean, the dumb bastard is in prison, and he was my ex when he was put away.'

'I understand Maryjo. My questions today may or may not concern Khalil. However, they do concern, Ravi Sanders.'

'Ravi Sanders? The man who tried to steal my car?' Maryjo asked. 'Why do you want to talk about him? I don't even know him.'

Ben leant closer across the table, staring but not speaking. If Maryjo was intimidated, she didn't show it.

'Maryjo, someone may have tried to kill Ravi Sanders. Last week, a drive-by shooting occurred, and Ravi's grandmother lost her life, but we suspect Ravi was the real target. We need to know if you had any knowledge of this attack.'

'Oh my God, that's awful, but I had nothing to do with it, and I doubt Amos did either. I mean, the bloke, Ravi, he just tried to nick my car.'

'And he assaulted you?'

Maryjo's eyes dropped to the tabletop, and she shook her head slightly.

'Didn't he?' Ben asked.

'Well, yeah. He gave me a concussion.'

Molly frowned. 'He struck you?'

Maryjo fidgeted with the strap of her handbag and gazed towards the door. She gave the impression of wanting to be else ware.

Ben read out the police statement made at the time of the assault. He stared at Maryjo as he read the final sentences. 'You were sent to the emergency department for examination. An x-ray confirmed a contusion to the occipital bone, and you were kept under observation for the day.'

'What did he hit you with?' Molly asked.

'His head.'

'He headbutted you?' Molly's face screwed up in disgust.

'No.' Once more, Maryjo's fingers worried at her handbag strap. 'It wasn't like that. He didn't see me come up behind him. I yelled at him when I reached the car, he got out and tried to run. Our heads crashed together. I saw stars.'

'So - it was accidental?'

'I had a hell of a black eye!' Maryjo said in a defensive tone.

'Yeah, sure, but Ravi Sanders didn't strike you on purpose.'

'Well - no.'

'So, was Khalil angry when he saw your face, your black eye?'

Maryjo nodded. 'Yes, he was furious, but that was then. Now, he doesn't give a shit about me. I had to be harsh to get Amos out of my life. I had to tell him some home truths that weren't very pleasant. I know I damaged his ego. Men like Amos don't take kindly to that sort of treatment.'

'And why did you decide to "get Amos Khalil out of your life?"' Ben asked.

'Because he was bad for me.'

'In what way?' Molly asked.

Maryjo rolled her eyes. 'How do you think?'

'We don't know. That's why we're asking.' Ben copied her sarcasm.

'Please,' Molly said in a quiet voice. 'We would like to know.'

Maryjo stopped fiddling with her handbag and let it drop onto the floor. 'Look. I've made some bad decisions, but I'm not a bad person. I thought Amos was nice, maybe misunderstood, but still a decent bloke. I realised that he was living a biker's life and enjoying it. I don't like the police.' She paused and gave Ben a deadpan look. 'Present company accepted, but I was getting too much attention from them. At first, I thought it was harassment. I mean, we couldn't go to a bar anywhere without the cops showing up. But then I found out things Amos had done. Not just stealing and drug stuff, but things he had done to ex-girlfriends. At first, I thought he would never treat me like that.' She shook her head. 'It wasn't until I broke up with him that I saw his other side. So when I heard about the biker shootings – well shit, I wasn't even shocked by then.'

'Did he hurt you? Physically?' Molly asked.

'No. Although I could tell he wanted to.' Maryjo's eyes were wet, her voice tremulous, but she kept speaking. 'As I said, I'd heard things about him. I confided in one of my friends at the club I worked in. She knew things between us were bad. I told her I was going to break up with Amos, but not until after his sister's wedding. It was a big event, and I had promised to go.' Molly took a noisy breath and cleared her throat.

'Anyway. My friend wasn't exactly looking out for my best interests. She told Amos what I was planning. I should have ended it with him, but I thought it was kinder to wait and better for his family to see me there. Otherwise, he would have hated all the negative attention on the day. "Oh, where is Maryjo? What happened?" I thought I was saving him from that kind of thing, but he already knew, and I was wrong. When I went to pick him up the afternoon of the wedding, he had two women with him. He was half naked – and so were they.'

'Bastard,' Molly whispered.

'Yeah. I wanted us to break up, but I never set out to hurt him. I felt humiliated. I ran off.'

'Have you seen him since?'

'Yes, I saw him after my car was stolen. I shouldn't have, I guess. But I was distressed, and it was reflexive to turn to him. He was upset that I was hurt; in fact, he was nice to me. Then, only a few days later, he was arrested for the Sydney shootings.' Maryjo threw her hands in the air. 'What was I thinking going out with him?'

'Have you had contact with him since?'

'No.'

'So, the court thing with Ravi Sanders was a - distraction?' Molly asked.

Before Maryjo could reply, Ben asked, 'You wanted to hurt someone, didn't you? So Ravi Sanders was that person.'

Maryjo didn't raise her eyes. Instead, she nodded while gazing at the tabletop. 'I'm not proud of that.'

Molly let out a huge sigh. 'Thanks for being honest with us, Maryjo.'

'That doesn't make me feel any better.'

'That's your problem,' Ben said as he stood.

Maryjo slung her handbag over her shoulder. 'You don't have to believe it, but I am sorry for Ravi and his grandmother.'

Molly touched the woman's upper arm. 'I know, and there is something you can do about it.'

*

Ben's phone pinged with a delivered email as they walked through the airport terminal, but he waited until he and Molly were seated on the plane before opening it. Beside him, Molly fussed with her jacket, draping it over her shoulders in anticipation of the drop in temperature, even though the cabin was uncomfortably warm.

He nudged her with his elbow and spoke softly. 'New results from ballistics. The projectiles came from an older style SKS assault rifle.'

'A Soviet rifle?'

'Yeah. It was superseded by the AK-47, but they're still manufactured today.'

'Didn't one of those recently turn up in a drive-by shooting in Sydney?'

'Yeah. The biker gang paybacks.'

Maybe we are looking at Khalil?

'They were not the same bikers, and I don't see why he'd risk a revenge shooting for a girlfriend who dumped him.'

'I know, but who else would shoot someone with an illegal firearm? The average person would have trouble accessing that kind of weapon. Think about it. A shooting happens in a quiet little town where crime is usually non-existent, but where Ravi is living, plus the fact that Khalil, courtesy of Maryjo, had a grudge against Ravi, come on, Ben, I don't think it's a coincidence.'

Ben rubbed his sweaty brow and said, 'You're probably right, Molly.'

'What calibre ammunition do they take?'

'7.62 millimetres.'

'Jesus, no wonder it did so much damage. Edith Sanders never stood a chance.'

'Wrong person, wrong place?' Ben shook his head.

'It could just as easily have been Ravi if he hadn't slipped out for a swim. Someone had been watching the house, but not close enough.'

'Ten shots in total hit the house. No other projectiles were found in the surrounding shrubs or on the lawn.'

'No casings?'

'Nah. Forensics think the shooter had the barrel resting on the passenger-side window; all the casings should have fallen inside the car. Whoever it was, they were confident with that sort of rifle.'

'So, someone pulled up in a car and let rip with a random spray at a timber walled house. You're bound to hit something.' Molly stared out the small window at the sky. 'Have we heard anything from Jesse Plackis?'

'Yeah, he asked what time we were due back today.'

'Does he have something for us?'

'He didn't say. Although he came up blank on any unregistered firearms in Henderson and surrounding towns.'

'Hardly surprising,' Molly said.

'No, but the place isn't gun-free. Farming communities never are.'

'I guess, but you aren't going to pick off the odd fox with an SKS. You can't obtain them legally, and you risk jail by possessing one.'

'Mmm. Have we checked for any ex-army personnel living in the area?' Ben asked.

'No, but Jesse Plackis will have some idea. He can investigate that.' She was silent momentarily and then said, 'You don't like him, do you?'

Ben cleared his throat and thought for a moment. Molly was okay, but she was a stickler for the rules. He had to watch what he said. 'I hadn't really thought about it. I guess he's okay, but he's playing a cop in a town where nothing ever happens. So, he should stay out of the way when the real police are working.' He looked away but could feel her gaze.

'I like him,' Molly said. 'If he seems a little soft, well, that is a good thing. The world could do with more placid people.'

Ben felt a pang of jealousy which he dismissed with a grunt and sat deep in his chair. Then, after a moment, he closed his eyes, waiting for the image of Plackis to clear from his mind and sleep to take him.

Chapter Five

The small church nestled in the heart of town was packed and uncomfortably warm. The surrounding streets were choked with farm utes and four-wheel drives. Most of the local shops and businesses had closed for the morning. Everyone in the area seemed to have made time to say goodbye to Edith.

Andy Ruthers, the current Group Officer for the Country Fire Service, seemed at home in front of a crowd, but he did go on in too much detail. Even Ravi, who enjoyed hearing about the accomplishments of firefighters, found the speech tedious after fifteen minutes, but still, the man droned on for another ten. By then, the audience was squirming, and the scattered children in the room were complaining of boredom. So, it was a relief when Ravi's mum was finally asked to step up and speak.

There had been mention of Ravi reading a eulogy, but he had soon declined. Public speaking was a nightmare for him, and probably always had been, but all his fears worsened since his life-shortening sentence had been imposed.

Emily spoke of her mum's influence over her life, not in a dominating way, but her support and constant guidance through good times and bad. They obviously shared a closeness, a friendship that went beyond child and parent. Ravi was a bit envious. He figured he would never share such a bond with his mum because she was a woman or perhaps because he was too selfish. He wondered if he would always be more of a burden than a help to her.

He was shaken from his reverie by a tap on his shoulder. He began to turn when Bailey whispered in his ear. 'I just wanted you to know I'm here. Stay strong Ravi.' She sat back in the pew before he could respond, which was just a well because her proximity and intimacy made his head reel. He gave her a brief grin which she answered with a beaming smile.

Ravi abruptly turned to watch his mother return to her seat beside him. His heart was racing, and despite the bleakness of the circumstances, he was guilty of feeling a thrill. Bailey's effect on him could no longer be ignored or seen as a symptom of his anxiety.

He knew he was falling for her.

Two of Edith's fire service colleagues spoke briefly, and then Edith's niece, who had come down from the NT, told of her experiences in Edith's company. The two had travelled together since Edith became widowed and formed a firm friendship. Ravi tried to concentrate on the woman's anecdotes and memories of his grandma, but he hardly took anything in. When the eulogies were over, everyone converged on the pub where the local CWA ladies had cooked up a storm of scones, cakes and savoury pastries.

Ravi was pleased to see his mum smile as old friends greeted her. Some of the tension in the build-up to this day had dissipated, and Ravi felt it too. Jesse Plackis came over to speak to them but didn't mention the case. He was there, he said, just as another mourner, to pay his respects to an exceptional lady. Ravi was a bit surprised when Emily hugged Jesse. Ravi wondered if he felt resentment because this man controlled him and would for another twelve months while he was on parole. Ravi reluctantly shook Plackis' hand and muttered a thank you.

Emily handed Ravi a pint of beer, raising her eyebrows as he took it.

'What?' Ravi asked, trying to fathom her meaning. But instead of replying, his mum inclined her head, staring past his right shoulder.

'Hi, Ravi. Hi Jesse. Hi Mrs Sanders.' Bailey extended her hand to Emily. 'I'm Bailey Donovan. I'm so sorry for your loss. Your mum meant so much to our family – I guess you already knew that.'

'Yeah, sure I did. Nice to meet you, Bailey. Ravi has said nice things about you.'

Ravi felt his face flush, and to make matters worse, they all turned to face him.

Emily smiled. Obviously, finding his embarrassment amusing and then said to Bailey, 'I was sorry to hear about your grandmother. I didn't know her well, but I went to school with your mum, so I remember seeing your grandma on sports days and at other school events.'

'Mmm. Grandma got a bit reclusive in her later years, being so sick. Grandpa never wanted to go places anyway. I think it suited him.'

'How is he coping?' Emily asked.

Bailey shrugged. 'I dunno. I think he's turned into a grumpy old man. Maybe he always was, but we didn't realise it. Anyway, he's managing on his own.'

'Is he still out on the farm?'

'Yes. We've tried to get him to move into town, but he won't hear of it.' Bailey looked down at her shoes. 'It's horrible to say, but I bet we find him dead one day. He won't complain if he's sick. He'll suffer and die alone because he's just so stubborn.'

'Ravi's grandfather was the same. It was the way that generation was brought up. So there isn't much you can do about it apart from offering help if you notice he's struggling.'

'I guess.' Bailey reached out and placed a hand on Ravi's chest. 'How are you doing?'

But before Ravi could reply, his mother butted in.

'Oh, sorry, Bailey, but Jesse and I must talk to Andy and Gloria.' She was already waving to the fire chief as she turned towards him. 'Come on, Jesse,' she said, yanking the cop's arm.

'Well, that was a little too convenient,' Bailey observed before turning to grin at Ravi. 'But I don't care. Now I have you to myself.'

Ravi returned the smile despite the flurry of butterflies in his gut. 'It's good to see you,' he said before turning away. He placed his empty glass on the nearby table, using the moment to collect himself.

'You look better than I expected.'

'Thanks,' he said. 'This is a hard day, you know, the final goodbye. Well, you know all about losing your gran. But we've had some time to get our heads around it.' He shrugged. 'Small mercies. Anyway, I'm glad you came.'

Bailey took his hand. The feeling of its warmth cheered him, emboldened him.

'Would you like to catch up sometime soon?' Ravi asked.

'Do you mean like a date?'

He flinched at the word. Dating sounded serious, and he wasn't sure if he was ready. His reply seemed to catch in his throat, so he nodded instead.

'Yes. I would. I like you, Ravi.'

'I like you too. A lot.'

The words were out before he could think. Perhaps he appeared a bit shocked because Bailey took both his hands, her dimpled grin once more making his head spin. Then she stood on tippy-toes and kissed him on the lips, long and slow. When he opened his eyes, she was three strides away, and without turning around, she raised her arm in a wave. But before he could react or call her back, he felt someone nudge his upper arm. It was the cop. He was holding a fresh beer.

'Oh. Hi, Officer Plackis.'

Jesse gave a sharp laugh. 'Please, leave the officer stuff for the station. Call me Jesse.'

'Sure. Jesse.'

'I hope you don't mind me being here. Like everyone else, I was a big fan of your grandma. She helped so much in this community and encouraged others to do the same. Plus, she was a cool lady. We've suffered a great loss.'

Ravi's eyes momentarily stung. 'That's nice of you.' He coughed to clear his throat.

'I have some good news. Unfortunately, it's not about your grandma's killer, but we're still working hard on that. This news is about your assault case. Maryjo Katz has made a new statement. She has admitted that you accidentally slammed into her. She denied you attacked her, so you can appeal against your sentence.'

'But it's already been dealt with.' Ravi held his hands out at his sides. 'This is me now. It can't be reversed, can it?'

'Apparently, it can. I've never heard of it being done. But when the Criminal Ageing System was implemented, one of the biggest arguments against it was the chance of falsely accused people being punished, so they made it reversible. So it seems the ageing process can be transposed.'

'But surely Maryjo can be in trouble for changing her statement? I mean, she testified under oath.'

Jesse nodded. 'Yes, but given the mental abuse she was suffering from Khalil at the time, any judge would forgive her for overreacting. It wasn't perjury so much as a misinterpreted memory due to mental stress.'

'She took a risk though.'

'She certainly did.' Jesse took a sip of his beer. 'And she was distressed about your grandma. Perhaps that's what swayed her. Either way, it looks good for your future.'

'Wow,' Ravi said quietly. He gazed around the room, but no one was looking at him. He wondered if people would see him differently now. He was guilty of trying to steal a car, but the stigma of assaulting a woman would be gone.

'Ravi!' Jesse robbed him of his wool-gathering. 'You've been given a helping hand. Don't blow it.'

Ravi stared at the cop and knew he was right. 'No way. I've been an idiot for the last time.'

'That's good to hear. So, what about the CFS? Will you keep firefighting?'

'Yeah. I will. I need to get a proper paying job too.'

'It seems like your life is looking up.' Jesse gave a knowing grin. 'And Bailey Donovan is a lovely girl.'

The corners of Ravi's mouth twitched before he could clamp his lips shut. 'You don't miss much, do you?'

Jesse shook his head slowly. 'No Ravi. I don't. That's why I'm a cop.'

*

'Ben!' Molly called as she reread the email. There was no reply, only the sound of the toilet flushing and Ben zipping up his fly.

'Oh great,' she muttered as he stepped into the office.

The Henderson police station comprised three spaces; the reception area flanked by a long desk that stopped public access to the rooms beyond it, the office where she now sat, and a locked room with two holding cells. Outside was a fenced courtyard, probably only used by smokers over the years. And beyond the fence was a prefabricated home. It was built as accommodation for the officer in residence but was currently rented out to an elderly lady.

The bathroom was an afterthought, plumbed into the corner of the office space, and it was very blokey. The lack of a mirror, lock on the door, or sanitary receptacle enhanced this theory. And the thin walls of the cubicle did nothing to dim any sounds. Molly had taken to using the public toilets near the town library. She valued her privacy.

'What is it?' Ben asked as he sat at his desk.

'Does the name Jerry Wainwright mean anything to you?'

'Wainwright? The biker?'

'Yes.'

'Didn't he get done for sexual assault or something?'

'He did. The girl disappeared halfway through the trial. She went back to her community near Ceduna. Apparently, she feared for her life.'

'But they found him guilty, didn't they?'

'Yes. They had enough evidence. He got fifteen years.'

'Prison?'

'No. The Criminal Ageing System had just been passed into legislation.'

'Bastard.' Ben spat. 'He should have had his balls cut off.'

Molly cocked her head. She wouldn't have said that, but she had to agree.

'So how old does that make him?' Ben asked.

Molly scanned through the document. 'Fifty-three. And now he has a heart condition.'

'Good. I hope it explodes on him.'

'Anyway, there are two interesting things about Wainwright; he is an old friend of Amos Khalil - and he lives in Cummins.'

Ben screwed up his face. 'I don't think that means much. Cummins is close to Port Lincoln but still about two hundred and fifty kilometres from here. And probably lots of bikers are friends with Khalil.'

'I think he's worth looking at. Two fifty k's of travel around here is nothing. It's practically the next suburb.'

Ben walked over to where the kettle and cups were kept on a bench. He flicked the switch on the wall and turned to stare at Molly. She flinched. His amorous gaze was creeping her out.

'We should see what he's been up to,' Ben said casually. 'At least we can rule him out.'

'Thanks.' Molly directed her eyes back to the screen, but when she looked up again Ben was leaning over her monitor, staring at her intently. 'What?' she asked.

'You know what,' he said quietly.

'Ben! Don't start that shit again.'

'I can't help it. I really like you, Molly. I mean it.'

Molly's hands balled into tight fists. 'You must stop this kind of talk Ben. I never want to hear it again. I've told you before. I love Ferdi and am not interested in you or anyone else.' Her face felt hot, and she wondered if it was from embarrassment or the lie.

'But – I just had to know. I mean, what if you'd changed your mind? What if I missed an opportunity because I was too scared to ask?'

Molly sat taller in her chair, not bothering to curtail her growing displeasure. 'This is not a conversation to be had in a professional environment. You listen to me, Ben! This is the last bloody time I want to hear this kind of shit. You're my working partner, and that's all. If you harass me again, I'll report you. There are plenty of other cops just as good as you, so don't push it.'

Before Ben could reply, Jesse Plackis coughed from the reception doorway. Ben spun around and glared at the man. 'Can't you fucking knock?'

Jesse gave a compliant open palms gesture and said, 'This is my working space. It's not usually the setting for soap operas.'

Despite the situation, Molly laughed loudly, which inflamed Ben further. He grabbed his car keys and mobile phone, striding dangerously close to Jesse as he departed.

'I'm sorry you had to hear that,' Molly said.

'I take it you've been fighting off his advances.'

'Only a couple of times. He's only ever been like that after a few drinks. This is the most serious he's got.'

'You should report him,' Jesse said.

But Molly shook her head. 'He's a friend. He's a massive jerk but a good cop. And we have a lot of history of good police work together. We get results.'

'Well, it better stop because this is my station. I must report sexual harassment.'

'Fair enough.' Molly conceded. She hurriedly changed the subject. 'Anyway, I have a possible contact of Khalil's to investigate.'

'Cool.' Jesse handed her a paper file. 'And I have a list of names from the rifle range log.'

Molly leaned back in her chair and used the file to fan her heating face. She wanted this case finished and to be back in her hometown.

Chapter Six

E mily had sorted her mother's possessions into three groups; clothing and items for the op shop, bags destined for the refuse bin, and drawers from various places around the house that held paperwork and knick-knacks. Any essential papers had been removed, so it was up to Ravi to sort and distribute the remaining items. The piles took up most of the sunroom floor.

Ravi began loading his grandma's old Triton utility with recyclable items and then filling the garbage bin. It was almost eleven when he sat down to sort the drawers. When he hefted the third one onto the table, he immediately saw the old green Babushka. He picked it up and smiled; it evoked happy memories. It had once been his favourite plaything at his grandma's. As a toddler, he spent many hours taking it apart and putting it back together. For a moment, he recalled the joy of first revealing yet another perfect doll and wondering how many more would be discovered.

Ravi rattled the doll, but somehow it didn't sound right. When he dismantled it, the first three layers were just as they had always been, but instead of the other miniature dolls inside, an envelope was stuffed into the centre. Ravi frowned as he withdrew the letter, laid it flat and smoothed it against the tabletop. He immediately recognised his grandma's neat and flowery cursive. It was addressed to Ravi. After a quick glance around the room, he opened it.

Dear Ravi,

I have written you this letter in case your mother doesn't disclose the truth about your father.

Ravi suddenly had a bitter taste in his mouth. He took long sips of his lukewarm coffee until his gut unclenched and read on.

There is a good reason for your father's absence from your life, and you need to know why. It is a topic that your mother and I have never agreed upon, but you have a right to know.

When you were almost three, your mum took Samantha to Melbourne to watch a Disney stage production. I can't remember which one, but you were left in the care of your dad. His drinking had been problematic, but he had been sober for at least a month at that time.

It was a sheer fluke that I arrived at your house that day. Your Pop and I were delivering a stud ram to a property north of Adelaide. I also had some papers for your mum; her school reports for a CV she was preparing. I had meant to post them, and Pop was not too happy about driving into the city with a sheep trailer in tow, but I insisted, and as you know, Grandpa always did what I asked.

Anyway, we arrived at your house in the early afternoon. It was summer, so we had plenty of daylight hours to drive home again. The day wasn't scorching hot, but warm, maybe in the low thirties. There was no answer when I knocked on the door, so we assumed you and your dad were in the back garden. His car was in the drive, so we knew someone was home.

You were in your playpen on the back lawn. When your father put you in it, it was probably shaded by the mulberry tree, but it was in full sun when we got there. You were lying so still, but you weren't asleep. We couldn't rouse you. Your skin was red and hot. Your lips chapped and split. If it wasn't for the fact that you had partially covered your face with your teddy, the burns might have been much worse.

Ravi paused and ran his fingers over the bumpy skin of his right forearm. His mother had told him it was scarring from Chicken Pox, but perhaps it wasn't. He continued reading.

I yelled at your Pop to phone for an ambulance. When he ran into the house, he found your dad sitting with his head on the kitchen table in a drunken stupor. I think both Pop and I wanted to kill him just then.

You had a couple of convulsions in the ambulance and another when we arrived at the hospital. The doctor said it was a grave prognosis, but you made it. In the following weeks, I asked you about that day, but you seemed to have no memory of it. Perhaps that was shock or some coping mechanism; either way, it was a blessing.

And I guess it was because your mother wasn't there to see how close to death you came that made her play down the situation. She didn't leave your father immediately because she was still hoping for a miracle, but it never came. The thought that you could have died, which was his fault, pushed your dad further over the precipice. In the end, it was he who chose to leave.

Your mother and I are guilty of overprotecting you, but maybe now you can understand why. We should have let you be a kid and take the risks, within reason, that other kids got to take, but we couldn't. I know you got bullied at school, and I wish I could take that back. The truth was, I knew it was a miracle that you survived that day, but you probably wouldn't get a second chance. We had to keep you safe, but we did you a disservice.

We hoped when you met Piper that, our worries would be over. But, unfortunately, she wasn't the girl we prayed she would be. Perhaps she used you, sensing your vulnerability, having always been protected. Again, we were to blame.

Ravi, you are smart, and you are stronger than you know. Your perceived weakness grew from our fear. Please forgive us.

Love you always.

Grandma.

'Jesus,' Ravi muttered.

He walked to the bathroom and splashed cold water on his face. Then, looking up, he saw his older self; crows-feet around his eyes and grey hair at his temples. His eyes narrowed as he considered himself. He might have aged prematurely, but given what he'd just discovered, it was miraculous that he'd survived until now. The shock of the revelation quickly vanished, and Ravi felt strangely numb.

But a few minutes later, a niggling irritation at being left in the dark for all these years grew. His annoyance was suddenly focused on his sister. Throughout childhood, Samantha had been the first to dob him in or be the happy bearer of bad news. It seemed she delighted in his suffering. Sometimes her behaviour towards him had been so spiteful that now, as adults, they rarely spoke. So how had she held her tongue all this time? Surely, she would have relished telling him of his near-death event. Or did she even know? Ravi guessed it was easy to keep the truth from her. She had only been six at the time.

But then Ravi had another thought – what about his father? Because with the benefit of this new knowledge, Ravi realised another possibility. If it wasn't for his grandmother, Ravi might have died and been lost to his father, but paradoxically, if it wasn't for her he may have died and his father may still have had a family, minus Ravi.

Did his dad hate Grandma because of his marriage and family breakup?

Ravi's mouth felt dry. He reran the tap, scooping water onto his tongue.

Again, his father's face forced its way into his thoughts. He peered up at the mirror and realised how similar they were. Perhaps his dad had heard about Ravi's conviction and punishment. But could his dad still have clarity enough for anger against a woman who had influenced his son's life? Did his father hold her responsible because Ravi's life had gone terribly wrong? Grandma played such a big part in Ravi's upbringing that she had almost been a father figure.

The water tasted metallic. Ravi grimaced and spat it into the sink.

Surely his father was too incapacitated by alcohol to carry out a murder. And could he have the wherewithal to obtain an illegal gun?

Ravi stood for many minutes while questions crowded his mind. Did the cops have a suspect if they believed his grandmother was the intended victim? If they did, could it be his father? Should he talk to Jesse Plackis about this? Should he try to see his father? If he did, what would he say to him?

Ravi stared at his reflection. 'Did you, Dad?' he asked. 'Did you kill grandma?'

*

Ben ignored Molly on the drive to Cummins the following day. At first, she had tried cajoling him, making light of his inappropriate come-on, but after five minutes, she gave up. If he wanted to sulk, then he damn well could.

Ferdi had been livid when she told him of the indiscretion. He was not so angry that Ben had tried to hit on a married woman; after all, Ferdi had said to her, you are pretty hot. Instead, it was Ben's disregard for their friendship that riled him. He and Ben had fished, golfed and drank together over the years, and although far from best buddies, Ferdi felt they were close enough not to shit on each other. He believed that only decent indiscretions occurred between strangers. Ferdi used quite a few choice phrases to describe Ben, and Ferdi also told her what he would like to do to Ben. Some of the things were humorous, and some sounded downright painful. Molly had to stifle a grin, but the funny side of the situation turned sour as Ben continued to fume from the passenger seat.

Jerry Wainwright lived about one kilometre out of town. There were few neighbours, and the local Cummins cop, Sean, told them the man mainly kept to himself. Sean handed Ben a piece of note paper with Wainwright's address, landline number and a map.

'I see him around the place occasionally,' Sean said. 'Either at the supermarket or the bottle shop. He's always the same, keeps his head down, gives you the nod but doesn't converse with anyone.' The young cop put a finger to his temple and said, 'Except maybe Mari at the Bottle-O. I have seen him chat to her once or twice.'

'Well, what is it, once - or twice?' Ben snapped.

Sean shook his head, obviously confused by Ben's hostile reaction. Molly butted in before the situation escalated.

'Sorry mate,' she said. 'Ignore that comment. Someone's having a bad day. We'll drop by the Bottle-O on our way back from Wainwright's. Thanks for the info. Come on, Ben, let's go.'

'Don't apologise on my behalf,' Ben said moodily as they approached the car.

'I'm apologising on behalf of SAPOL. You don't need to be reported for rudeness. You're already on thin ice.'

'What's that supposed to mean?'

'It means Jesse Plackis is not some pushover that you can bully. He's ready to see you in trouble, so you'd better curb your temper.'

'I'm not worried about that jerk.'

'Oh, for God's sake Ben, grow the hell up. You've had your feelings hurt. I get it; I do. But it's over, and it needs to be forgotten.

Ben remained silent until they arrived at Wainwright's property.

The acreage looked like a dust bowl with no garden or lawn visible as they approached. A few straggly peppercorns grew along the perimeter, but they were the only greenery. The house was an old transportable surrounded by scattered outbuildings fashioned from corrugated iron. They were rusty and flimsy. In fact, the place looked like a good wind would blow it away. There were at least six cars in the yard at the front of the house, but only one looked road worthy.

'A bit of a hoarder,' Molly noted.

Ben gave a grunt and walked one pace behind her, swearing at buzzing flies and cursing the heat. They followed a rock-lined path to the house. The wooden steps were rickety, and the veranda wasn't much better. The fly-screen door groaned as Molly opened it, then knocked on the closed door behind it. When Ben tapped her shoulder, she brushed him away. But when he spoke, she spun around.

'Look, Molly!' His voice was strained, and his eyes were narrowed as he pointed to the two advancing Rottweilers near the sheds.

'Jesus!' Molly said as she fumbled for her taser.

The dogs growled and snapped at each other as they crossed the yard, ambling at first but then picking up to a fast clip. They were at least fifty kilos each and didn't look friendly. Ben had drawn his pistol, and Molly held her breath as they grew nearer.

'Look, over there,' Ben said.

Molly followed his line of sight and saw a man appear at the door of a large shed. He wheeled out a motocross bike, moving fast despite a noticeable limp. He slung his leg over it and started the motor. The dogs were momentarily distracted by the engine noise, so Ben aimed his gun into the air and fired. The dogs pulled up abruptly, and Molly growled at them, ordering them to "stop it." Ben took aim, but the Rottweilers were now watching the motorbike. As the man tore off towards the exit gate, one of the dogs ran after him. The other slunk towards the shed the man had come from, giving one last look behind as it disappeared through the doorway.

'Come on,' Ben said. There was still a worried edge to his tone.

They strode to their car, frequently glancing behind, but the dogs ignored them. Whatever protective urges had overcome the dogs, had now vanished. Ben finally holstered his pistol as he opened the car door. Molly fell back against the headrest and took a few long breaths, staring at the car roof lining.

'I thought you liked big dogs?' Ben asked.

'I do, usually. But not when they growl like that. Growing up watching Cujo wasn't such a good idea.

Ben gave a weak imitation of a smile and said, 'Let's get after him.'

Molly started the engine and floored the accelerator. They drove off in a cloud of dust. Soon they bumped along in the opposite direction they'd come for about two hundred metres, but the road suddenly shrunk to a narrow track winding through dense scrub. Molly could hear the distant whine of the dirt bike's motor, but the vehicle was nowhere in sight.

'We lost him,' she said.

'It seems like he was tipped off.'

'Really?' Molly wasn't so sure. 'Who would do a thing like that?'

'I don't know, but he had enough time to lock up his house and find a vehicle to outrun us, so I'd say he was.'

'Maybe. Let's go and talk to that woman at the Bottle-O.'

Ben grunted in the affirmative.

The drive back to town was as silent as the trip out had been. Ben didn't make eye contact with Molly. Instead, he gazed moodily out the side window. When the adrenaline from the threatening dogs and the subsequent car chase subsided, Molly was vexed with Ben's childish behaviour. She bit down angry words and stared straight ahead. It was well past lunchtime, and her unfed stomach protested, which didn't improve her disposition.

They reached the Bottle-O as a woman in her mid-forties flipped the sign on the entry door to "open."

'Well, there's a stroke of luck,' Molly muttered as she exited the car.

The shops air conditioning was welcoming, and it made her skin tingle. The woman behind the counter greeted them with a smile, but it vanished when Molly produced her SAPOL ID.

'Hi, I'm Senior Sergeant Molly Hunter, and this is Senior Sergeant Ben Richards from the Port Lincoln Major Crimes Unit. We heard from your local police officer, Sean McMurtrie, that you're an acquaintance of Jerry Wainwright.'

The woman stared at Molly, her face set. Only the rubbing of her thumb and forefinger at her side gave away her agitation.

'So, do you know him?' Ben wasn't giving the woman time to concoct a story.

'I – um. What's this all about?'

'Answer the question.' Ben took a step closer to her.

'Yeah. I know Jerry - a little. He comes in here at least once a week.'

'What's your name?' Molly asked.

'Mari, Mari Preston.'

'Okay, Mari, what things do you discuss with Wainwright?' Molly asked.

'Drinks mostly. He buys beer all the time, but sometimes he splashes out and gets a spirit or a liqueur. He asks me about them.' She shrugged her shoulders. 'He wants to know about flavours. I let him know about special offers when they come up. Sometimes we chat about music or tv shows.'

'Did you know that he's a bad man?' Ben asked.

Mari's eyes widened.

'Ben!' Molly said gruffly before addressing the woman. 'There's no need to panic. It's just that you should be careful around him. But then, you should always be careful of people you don't know.'

'What's he done?' Mari held her hand to her throat as though unsure she wanted to hear the answer.

Molly glanced at Ben, who raised one eyebrow. 'Okay,' she said with a sigh. 'Jerry Wainwright was accused of rape, although he was convicted of a lesser charge.' Molly watched the disgust transform Mari's features. A moment later, she began trembling.

Molly continued. 'He has served his sentence, but…'

'Oh, my God,' Mari whispered. 'That's sick. I mean, he lives here now. Right in our town!'

'As I said, he's served his sentence, so he has the right to freedom. With luck, he's been rehabilitated. I need to know what else he discussed with you; friends he's mentioned, places he goes, anything at all.' Molly handed her a SAPOL contact card and said, 'Have a think, please. This is important. My direct number is on the back.'

Mari took the card without looking at it. Then, after a moment, she said, 'he has spoken about a fella named Rabbit a few times. Apparently, Rabbit had a still and made his own whisky, but I had a sense of that being some time ago.' Mari suddenly held her hand over her face. 'Oh, God. I went to his house!'

'When was that?' Ben asked.

'A few weeks ago. Jerry came in to buy his usual beer, but the deliveries were late that day due to some hold-ups from one of our interstate suppliers. Jerry seemed a bit stressed about not getting his drinks, so when they arrived, I dropped them off on my way home.' Mari's voice was growing shrill with panic. 'I went there alone!'

'Mari,' Molly said in a firm voice. 'Jerry obviously likes you. I don't think he would hurt you, but you must stay safe.'

'Did his dogs harass you?' Ben asked.

Mari shook her head. 'No. He didn't have any dogs.'

Molly and Ben exchanged glances.

'He didn't mention getting some dogs?' Ben asked.

'No. Nothing.'

'Okay. Then perhaps they aren't his, or he got them from someone,' Molly said. 'Can you think of anyone around here who keeps Rottweilers?'

'There is a dog rescue out on Port Lincoln Road, about five kilometres out. There's a sign with the name of the rescue on it. "Muddy Feet" or something.'

'Oh, "Muddy Paws"? We saw it on the way in. That could be really helpful, Mari.'

But Mari wasn't listening; she was still trembling and beginning to weep. 'How can I work in the Bottle-O now? If he was to come in, I don't know if I could face him!' She wrung her hands and stared at Molly. 'He comes here every Thursday!' Hysteria made her voice shrill. 'That's in two days time!'

Molly glared at Ben as she tried to comfort the woman. 'Nice one!' she hissed at him.

Ben gave a smirk and headed for the door.

Molly took Mari's hand, which was still clutching the business card. 'We will find him.'

'And then what? He'll come back here, won't he?'

'If we find he's done nothing wrong, then yes, he will come back. There is no reason to believe he's dangerous. Since the – treatment, he's aged fifteen years and isn't healthy. Just don't go to his property again. I'll speak with Sean, and he can talk to your manager. Try to stay calm, Mari.'

As Molly departed, she could hear Mari weeping again. Molly swore under her breath. This was because of Ben's stupidity; scaring the life out of the woman wasn't necessary or productive. During the drive to the dog rescue, Molly said nothing, but her anger bubbled just below the surface.

*

Jesse sent emails to Ravi's court-appointed lawyer, who was taking on the case to overturn part of Ravi's conviction. Although the Criminal Aging System had been adopted in dozens of other countries, Jesse hadn't found a single instance of the process being reversed, but there was one case pending in America where the convicted woman had been proven innocent. Unfortunately, that process was set to drag on for months, or more likely years, before reaching an outcome. Jesse let out a grumbly sigh.

When his phone rang, it was not the usual Timba beat. Instead, it was the quacking of a duck. Jesse smiled. 'Hello, Emily. How are you?'

'Hi Jesse, I'm okay. Ravi told me about Maryjo Katz's new statement. Is it true that Ravi's treatment might be reversed? I've Googled the process but couldn't find evidence of it being carried out. I don't want him to have false hopes.'

'Well, I'm looking up the process too. The legislation says it's possible, and I have yet to find any evidence of it being executed either.'

'Then maybe it's risky. Poor Ravi. I knew he wouldn't have hurt that woman intentionally.'

'Emily, you must stop babying him.' Jesse shook his head; she needed persuasion, not a lecture. 'Did you know there was an electrical fire in the Meals on Wheels building last night when Ravi was on call?'

'What? No.'

'Unfortunately, most of the building was destroyed. But, according to Andy, Ravi did an excellent job. He stayed until the site was cool, half the night. So, he's a lot tougher than you think.'

'I know. I suppose you think I'm a fool, but I can't help it. I'm sorry.' Her voice was wispy, and Jesse could picture her sad face. He knew she was going to cry.

'You should be proud of your son. He's really proving himself.'

'I am so grateful to you, Jesse.'

'Then come and see me, please.'

'I can't just now. I haven't said anything to Ravi about us. I don't know how he'll take it.'

Jesse pursed his lips. It was always the same. Every time things began to develop between him and Emily, something went wrong, and it usually involved Ravi. Of course, not everything was Ravi's fault, but Emily's son had become a thorn in Jesse's side. 'I gotta go,' he said abruptly.

'No, please, Jesse, I'm sorry. I will talk to him, but it must be face-to-face, and I'm only off work on weekends for the next month. It's such a long drive – I – I'm not making excuses. I promise I will; it's just – his grandma too, you know, it's too much for him, all these changes.'

'For Christ's sake, start treating him like a man! I really must go. Bye.'

It gave him no joy to hang up on her. Jesse didn't doubt her sincerity. They had real feelings for each other and, on many occasions, immense passion, but it was constantly tested by her emotional distractions. Bloody Ravi!

Jesse made up his mind; he would tell Ravi about the situation.

Edith had told Jesse, months before her death, that a relationship with Emily would be fraught with problems. She had also told Jesse about Ravi's upbringing and the maternal guilt that fed Emily's overreactions. Jesse sighed again. He missed Edith because she was a straight-up person, no bullshit. Sometimes her blatant honesty got her into hot water, but she was thick-skinned and could bear it. Emily was not made of the same stuff, but perhaps her gentleness and vulnerability drew him to her. The son, on the other hand...

Jesse cursed as he stood up. He raked his fingers through his hair and straightened his collar.

'Okay Ravi. Time for a little chat.'

He picked up his keys and strode to the back door.

Chapter Seven

Ravi pulled into the small car park beside the old church. The building was recognisable as Lutheran, from the square design to the A-line roof, which comprised half its height. It showed signs of age but wasn't doing too bad for a church built in the early 1960s. The sign over the doorway confirmed it as "Raymond's Shelter", a home for destitute substance abusers for over two decades.

Despite Ravi's recent revelations and the resulting anger directed at his sister, Samantha, she had supplied him with his father's address. Ravi and Sam had hardly spoken since their grandmother's death, but Sam had not seemed in the least bit surprised when Ravi phoned her for information about their dad. To Ravi, it felt like she had been expecting this enquiry.

Since his rapid ageing, Ravi was now the elder of the two. This alteration in the family dynamics left him questioning the reason for their ongoing sibling rivalry. Sam had been a nasty pain in the arse as a child, but was that enough reason to continue hostilities? Would they ever get past the animosity and become friends? An image of her face came to mind. That sneer which voiced her disdain for anything Ravi did or said. The eye-rolling and bored exhalations whenever he spoke. Yes, she really was a bitch, but instead of angering him, Ravi gave a chuckle. He guessed he had found his answer.

Nothing would ever change between them.

The ticking sound of the car's engine as it cooled distracted Ravi from his wool-gathering. He regarded his image in the rear-view mirror, smoothed down a tuft of hair and tried out a smile. 'You can do this,' he whispered before opening the car door. As he stretched, his joints popped in protest. The six-hundred-kilometre trip was quite a chore, and he was already dreading the return leg, but that thought disappeared as he neared the church.

Ravi was ushered into a small alcove which at one time must have served some religious purpose, but he had no idea what. He remained seated while his request to see his father was considered by Raymond Settler, founder of the charity and ex-alcoholic by the sound of it. The same man who had welcomed him returned in only a few minutes. He was smiling, which Ravi took as a good sign.

'Your dad is sleeping, but considering how far you have come, we are happy to wake him for you,' the man said. 'Raymond is in a meeting but sends his regards.'

'I really appreciate that. Thank you.' Ravi said.

A middle-aged woman appeared in the doorway, making the space go from crowded to sardine-tin, but she didn't stay there long. 'Follow me,' she said as she strode along the worn carpet.

The main area of the church had been divided into small rooms accessed by a corridor that ran the length of the building. The woman stopped at the third doorway on the left. She gave a gentle knock and peered into the room. Then, she stood back after a moment, holding the door open.

'He's ready for you.' Before she moved away, she touched Ravi's upper arm. 'You look so much like him,' she said.

Her face was unreadable, so Ravi wasn't sure if her comment was a compliment or an insult. But when he glanced over at his father, he figured it was the latter.

The older man grasped the table beside his bed for support. His whole body shook as he moved, and after just a few steps, he cried out in pain. Ravi dashed to his side, steadying and guiding him back to the bed. His father collapsed and began to sob.

'I'm sorry Ravi. You shouldn't see me like this.'

His father's voice was just a whisper. His vocal cords were shredded by years of booze and cigarettes. His skin was crinkled like an old leaf. Ravi wondered how years of excessive fluid intake could make a person look so dried out. His father's eyes were the only lively part of him. They were darker than Ravi's. But like Ravi's, they seemed to reflect his emotions. Right now, despite his initial despondency, they brightened with happiness.

'It's so good to see you son. I hoped – prayed you might visit. But your mum and your grandma want what's best for you.' Randy began to cry again. 'And that isn't me.'

Ravi put an arm around his dad's shoulder and shook him gently. He was little more than a bag of bones, and those eyes were clouded in misery once more. The sight of them made Ravi's eyes sting. He swallowed down salty tears and cleared his throat.

'Dad. When did you last see Mum?' Ravi asked.

'Your mum? I guess, Christmas time.'

Christmas was still a month away. 'Do you mean last year?'

'Yes. She always calls in around Christmas.'

'And Samantha, when did you last see her?'

'Um, Father's Day. She brought me cake and a new shirt.'

September. Ravi smiled. 'Dad, has anyone told you about grandma?'

The older man tried to rub his eye, but his palsy was so intense he jabbed himself in the eye, causing more tears to run. 'I – I don't know. What would they tell me? Did something happen? Is Edith alright?'

Ravi hugged his father, holding the embrace while relief washed over him. The only thing this man could murder was a drink.

'Are you alright, son?' His father's eyes were heartbreakingly sad.

'Yeah Dad. I'm just sorry I haven't been to see you for so long.'

'You live such a great distance away.'

But despite the words that justified Ravi's negligence, his dad's eyes continued to tear up, and a trail of snot dangled from his nose. Ravi handed his father tissues from a box by the bedside, looking away as the older man blubbered for a few minutes. When his dad finally regained his composure, Ravi asked, 'Would you like to drive somewhere? We could go to the beach and get lunch or ice cream if you like.'

'We could go to the pub,' his dad suggested.

Ravi shook his head. 'No, no pub, Dad. I'm sorry.'

'Chocolate ice cream would be nice.'

'Okay. Here, let's put your shoes on.'

The older man's eyes were smiling once more. Ravi took his hand and led him outside, realising this would be a bitter-sweet day.

*

At first, Ravi thought the thumping sound was a branch from the large Silky Oak hitting against the eaves, but when the fog of sleep began to diffuse, he saw the world outside his window was sunny and windless. The banging continued as he pulled on his shorts and t-shirt. He tripped on Hank as he headed for the door. The dog glanced up at him and soon returned to dozing.

'All right, all right!' Ravi said as he pulled the door open.

Bailey was grinning at him, the dimples more seductive than sweet today. One strap of her floral sundress had fallen from her shoulder, and Ravi's eyes were drawn to her creamy skin. He groaned and slowly shook his head. 'I don't think you should be here; it's dangerous.'

She gave a laugh and crushed herself against him. 'That's what I was hoping for.' She kissed him, short and wet, but with the promise of more.

He quickly glanced at the empty street beyond and pulled her inside. When he tried to speak, she kissed him harder. He realised whatever he was going to say wasn't necessary. He allowed his primal needs to dominate his mind. For once, shutting the door on his anxiety. Their clothes were discarded, and soon they lay naked and entwined beneath the cotton sheets. She repeatedly whispered his name, urging him on, staring at him in awe. He felt like a man who was loved. He felt like a god.

After, they lay side by side, sweat drying on their skin. Ravi's breathing slowed while he reflected on the madness of the act. Finally, Bailey turned to face him. He held her chin and stared at her face, but they didn't speak until Hank began barking at the front door.

'No!' Ravi groaned. 'What now?'

'Don't answer it.'

He smiled and kissed her on the nose. 'I said I'd help at the depot this morning. It's probably Andy. He offered me a lift.'

'If you stay, I'll cook you breakfast,' Bailey suggested.

There was only a moment of hesitation. 'Deal,' Ravi said as he dressed. 'I'll tell him I'll meet him there.'

Bailey gave a dimpled grin before covering herself with the tangled sheet. 'Just get rid of him.'

But Ravi's smile vanished when he opened the door. It was Jesse Plackis. Despite his disappointment, Ravi opened the door wider. 'Come on in,' he said unenthusiastically.

'Where were you?' Jesse asked just one step into the house.

'What? Yesterday?'

'Yes, Ravi. I called around here four times, and you weren't here. Weren't you on the CFS call last night?'

'Yes, I was. I didn't go on until midnight. I told Andy I was going to be late back. He said that was okay. Am I under arrest?' Ravi asked.

'No. You know you're not. But people are worried about you, that's all. You shouldn't just disappear like that.'

'I went to see my dad.'

'In Adelaide? Why?'

'Aren't I allowed to visit my father?'

'Well, sure. But isn't that a bit out of the blue?'

'Yeah. Unfortunately, it was, but I intend to go and see him more often. He's not very well, and I don't know how long he will be around for.'

The cop stared at him for a long minute as though assessing the credibility of Ravi's story. Finally, Jesse shrugged and said, 'Fair enough.' He glanced down at the trail of clothing in the hallway. 'Am I interrupting something?'

'Yes. You are.' Ravi picked up Bailey's sundress and bra, flinging them through the spare bedroom door. 'I'm due to go to the depot soon.'

'Did you plan to wear those?' The cop had a grin on his face.

Ravi laughed and said, 'Maybe. So, what is it you want? Do you have news?'

Jesse shook his head and said, 'Nothing about the case; sorry, I was hoping to talk to you about a personal matter, but I can see this isn't a good time. So, I'll tell you what, I'll buy you lunch tomorrow if you're free, nothing flashy, just a burger. What do you say?'

'Is it regarding my CAS reversal?'

'No,' Jesse said. 'It's personal.' He shot a glance at the coffee table beside him.

'You aren't going to give me a hint?'

'No. I'm afraid it may be upsetting for you.'

Ravi frowned and stared at Jesse. 'Is it because you have the hots for my mum?'

'Um – I...'

Ravi laughed at the cop's stunned expression. There was a feeling of satisfaction at causing his embarrassment. 'You seriously think people haven't noticed?'

'They have?' Jesse looked genuinely bewildered. 'But, we haven't – told anyone.'

'I picked up on it ages ago. People see things whether you want them to or not.'

It was at that moment that Bailey chose to emerge from the bedroom. She wore one of Ravi's T-shirts. It came almost to her knees.

'Hello Jessie,' she said.

'Hi, Bailey. Um, listen, I'm going to go now. If you're up for that chat tomorrow, call me.'

Ravi considered the invitation. 'Yes. We probably should. I'll text you.'

Bailey came and stood at Ravi's side; hand in hand, they watched Jesse leave.

'Is there a reason he appears to have his tail between his legs?' Bailey asked.

'Oh yes. There certainly is.' Ravi was smiling. He put his arm around her waist. 'Come back to the bedroom, and I'll tell you about it.'

*

The sweat trickled, channelling along Molly's collar bones and running down towards her cleavage. She took a couple of heaving breaths. This had been as strenuous as her infrequent visits to the gym. She clutched the sheet, using it to swab away the perspiration. She could taste the salt on her lips. From behind her, the mattress groaned as Ben rolled onto his back. His hand was hot against her buttock.

Molly couldn't turn to face him, much the same as she knew she couldn't face Ferdi that evening.

'Regrets?' Ben asked.

At least he had the decency not to sound arrogant. Molly glanced around the budget motel room and tried to recall how they got there. 'The bullies,' she muttered. But thankfully, Ben hadn't heard her. She lay back against the pillow, her face angled away from his and remembered the story he had told her.

'Why are you such a jerk?' she had asked him shortly after they left Cummins.

It had been their second visit to the town, and they were returning to Port Lincoln. Mari from the Bottle-O had been right about the dog rescue; Wainwright had purchased two dogs only days before they visited his property. But there was no sign that the man had returned to his home, so the rescue owners were called to go and retrieve the Rottweilers. Aggressive or not, Molly had no desire to see them starved.

On the way back to Port Lincoln, Ben had asked her to stop at the bottle shop, but his purpose hadn't been to call in on Mari. Instead, he purchased a six-pack of Bundi and Coke cans.

At first, Ben had sat silently, occasionally sipping on his drink and staring out the window. Then, when Molly asked her question, it seemed he wouldn't answer, but minutes later, he began to speak.

'If I'm a jerk, and I guess I am,' he said. 'It may be because of my childhood.'

Molly gave a tiny shake of her head. It seemed people always had something other than themselves to blame for their personal faults.

'I dunno if I ever told you,' He continued, 'but I was a prem baby.'

She frowned but said nothing.

'I was born at thirty weeks, and my mum said no one expected me to live. I caught up to the other kids when I was around twelve, but I was a squib at ten. A pathetic little thing that couldn't knock the skin off a rice pudding.

'I had a best friend; his name was Adam. He was a good kid, two years older than me, and the son of family friends. At school, he always looked out for me. It was his last year at primary school, and I worried I would get picked on without him being around.' Ben paused and shook his head. 'I was so stupid. Adam asked me who was bullying me, and I told him. One kid was the principal's son, and the other was a prefect. That should have raised alarm bells, but Adam, the nice guy he was, walked straight up to them and asked them to stop harassing me.

'It worked. They stopped picking on me. Instead, they launched this retribution against Adam. It went on for months, almost seven months. He had the usual; dog shit in his school bag, library fines for books he'd never taken out, punctured tyres whenever he rode his bike to school, and his homework would always go missing. But it was okay. He could cope with that.

'It was the end of the nineties, and lots of kids had their own email addresses, and that's how they got to Adam. I'm not sure to this day, but I think the kid who helped them was Aaron Hall. He was a nerdy kid with a lot of talent in photoshopping. The photos – I guess if I saw them today, I'd probably laugh. It was obvious they weren't real, but they worked perfectly back then.

'When it started, even Adam got a laugh out of them, but then they got worse. They got disgusting. So, when Adam would go to school, he'd get called a dog fucker or a sheep fucker. Man, they were sick. I remember his dad coming to see the principal, trying to get to the bottom of these emails, and that seemed to make things worse. There would be new pictures every few hours instead of daily. They were being distributed to every kid in school.

'Adam got teased so badly. No girl at school would talk to him; some kids thought those pictures were real. So, I tried to talk to him.'

Ben took a long slug of his drink, crushed the can, and opened another. Molly was shocked when she realised, he was fighting back tears. When he offered her a drink, she took it.

He cleared his throat before saying, 'I didn't know how to help, but I went to see him the night before he died. We were sitting in his room listening to Pearl Jam, and he put his hand on my head and looked me in the eye. He was smiling, but he looked sad. I think he knew what he would do then, but he didn't say anything. Instead, he told me not to worry and that everything would be fine. He said I needed to stick up for myself and never put up with shit from anyone.'

Ben was silent for more than a minute. Then, finally, he said, 'The next morning, I was told Adam had hung himself.'

Molly almost choked on her drink. She coughed and covered her mouth.

Ben continued. 'I got sad; losing Adam was the worst thing that had ever happened to me. Then I got scared, terrified, and then - I got really fucking angry. I didn't go to the same school as those arseholes who had bullied Adam, but I was bullied by different bastards regardless. I did what Adam told me; I stayed angry, and it was the only thing that kept them away from me. I guess I had a reputation as a bit of a psycho, and I was and still am, but at least I'm alive.' He glanced at her with tear-filled eyes. 'I'm so sorry, Molly. I am a jerk but can't help how I feel about you.'

She pulled the car over onto the dusty shoulder of the road, and they hugged for a long moment.

But when did the kissing start? She wondered about that as she lay on the bed beside him. Ben moved closer and rubbed her shoulder, kneading her flesh, making her mutinous body react again. Molly raised her hand to push him away because this was crazy. He caught it and put her fingers to his lips.

'Please don't hate me, Molly,' he whispered.

She couldn't answer; she could only let him cover her mouth with his. She didn't want him to stop.

Chapter Eight

The previous night's storm had left the sand littered with seaweed. A brisk breeze still battered the coast, the houses on the foreshore and the beachside café. On days like this, Ravi would rather have sat in the sunroom watching the sea than go out for lunch.

He pulled his beanie over his ears as he ran from the car but paused when he saw his mother's sedan parked beside the police four-wheel drive. Ravi wasn't expecting her. He groaned when he considered the discussion he was about to endure, and he was still scowling as he entered the café.

He spotted his mum right away. She was half standing, her fingers forming a tentative wave, her expression teetering between fear and relief. Plackis was reading the menu, his expression one of self-satisfaction. It irked Ravi.

'Hi, mum. Hi Jesse.' Ravi was saved from saying any more by the café attendant, who moved swiftly to the table, biro poised.

Jesse offered Ravi the menu, but Ravi's appetite had fled.

'Just a flat white, please.'

'How are you feeling, honey?' His mother asked.

'Fine, mum. But I know why I'm here, so why you don't just cut to the chase?'

She clasped his hand and shook it, forcing him to look at her. 'Son, I never meant to keep any secrets from you. I just…'

'Did grandma know?' Ravi interrupted.

'Um, yes. She did.'

Ravi turned his attention to Jesse Plackis. 'Grandma liked you, I know, but what did she think of your relationship with her daughter?'

Jesse held out his hands, palms up. 'She was pleased. I told her we were taking it real slow. She agreed that was best.'

'So, what speed is it at now?'

'Ravi!' His mother was blushing.

'Come on Ravi. I know you're a bit pissed at not being told, and that's a fair enough reaction, but we have put things on hold until we fill you in.'

Jesse and Emily were sitting on opposite sides of the table, keeping their distance from each other. Ravi knew that if he and Bailey were in the same situation, they would at least be holding hands, showing solidarity. So did these two feel they couldn't support each other right now? Was the spoilt son standing in the way of their happiness? Ravi shook his head. 'You two don't have to explain stuff to me. Whatever you do is your own business.' Ravi turned to his mum. 'I want you to be happy.' He pointed his thumb at Jesse. 'If this guy does it for you, then great.'

Jesse smiled and held out his hand. 'I appreciate that, Ravi.'

'No problem,' Ravi said as he shook it. He was about to say more, but his mother dissolved into noisy tears, blubbering that he was such a kind and understanding boy. While Ravi hugged and tried to calm her, Jesse gave a laugh that sounded a lot like relief.

'As long as you know what you are getting yourselves into,' Ravi said to no one in particular.

Lunch was a pleasant affair of burgers and fries. Only after they'd finished did Jesse discuss the newest findings in Edith's murder case.

'According to the logbook from the local firing range, there had been two men using the facility leading up to your grandma's shooting on a frequent basis, one of whom has a criminal record. I spoke to this man, and I'm trying to confirm his alibi, but it seems solid.'

'You can get a gun license if you have a criminal record?' Ravi asked.

'In some cases.'

'Was he convicted for a serious crime?'

'Fraud. So certainly not a violent crime, but he spent time in prison some years ago.'

'What about the other man?' Ravi asked.

'No. He's an older bloke and quite harmless. I think he may have a touch of dementia and perhaps doesn't realise how much time he's spent there.'

'Should he be at a firing range if he's not right in the head?'

Jesse shook his head. 'No. The range officer has been alerted, and the man will be spoken to, but I don't think he is our killer.'

Ravi nodded. He was grateful for the updates, but there had been little progress in all this time. He guessed that was the way these things went.

'There was something else I discovered at the firing range,' Jessed added. 'It may be nothing, but I noticed some large bore holes in the target posts of the original range. It's unused these days, but they appeared to be recent. I spoke to the range officer, and he couldn't tell if they were new or historical. Apparently, back in the day, the army reserves from Port Lincoln once used the range for training. So, I've asked ballistics to come and examine the holes and search for projectiles.' Jesse shrugged. 'As I said, it could be nothing.'

For the following hour, Ravi sat and listened to Jesse's police stories and his mother's account of how their romantic relationship had blossomed. It was more information than he wanted to hear, and Ravi felt everyone was relieved when it was time to depart. His mum hugged him tightly, and Jesse gave him a firm pat on the back.

As they turned to walk in separate directions, Emily doubled back. 'Hey, son! Next time it will be your turn.'

'Huh?'

'We want to hear about you and Bailey and *your* plans. Maybe I'll get to be a grandmother soon!' She grinned and walked to her car.

When Ravi turned, he spotted Jesse leaning against his car with a smug look.

'Arsehole,' Ravi mouthed.

The cop laughed.

*

If Ferdi noticed Molly's strange moods, he didn't let on. On the contrary, he seemed to ignore her, and she was grateful. Perhaps he put her distraction down to the pressure of the Edith Sanders case, which was going nowhere. Ferdi knew the distance she and Ben were required to travel each day. Perhaps he thought it was wearing her down. Molly suffered some fatigue, but it was due to the physical motel visits rather than drawn-out working days.

It was Friday afternoon, and Ferdi had planned two outings for them over the weekend. Molly would rather have escaped to the seclusion of her home office and continued research on the case. At least while she was working, it was easy to avoid interacting with Ferdi. The late finishes during the week were convenient; home, dinner and then early bed, gone at first light, sometimes gone before he woke, but now the weekend was here, and there would be an opportunity to talk. It was the last thing she felt like doing.

So, when Ferdi appeared at the back door and glanced around the patio, clearly looking for her, she took a deep breath. But he had not come for conflict or even conversation; he held out her phone. It was Ben.

Molly rose from her chair, took the mobile and walked towards the path that flanked the lawn.

'Ben?'

'I had a call from Mari, the woman from the Cummins Bottle-O.'

Molly hadn't realised that she was holding her breath. She exhaled loudly and instantly regretted it.

'I'm sorry, Molly,' Ben said upon hearing the sound.

'No! You must stop.' Molly glanced back to the patio, but Ferdi had retreated indoors. 'This case is our priority. I don't want to think about us and the mess we've created.'

'I do. I think about it all the time. Nothing has ever made me happier.'

Molly scrunched her eyes closed. 'Stop it. Just stop it right now.' There was a long silent pause. 'So, what did Mari have to say?'

'She said she was tidying the bottle shop cupboard behind the serving counter and found a raffle book.'

'Yeah?'

'It was from a Melbourne Cup raffle, drawn back in November. When she saw the book, she remembered that Jerry Wainwright had bought a ticket. The prize was two thousand dollars. Apparently, he was banging on about what he would like to do with the winnings whenever he came into the shop.'

'Did he win?'

'Well, no. But she recalled that he scribbled down a mobile phone number on the ticket stub. Apparently, she had once asked him why he didn't have a cell phone, but he didn't answer her.'

'So, *did* the ticket stub have his number on it?'

'It sure did, and I.T. has given me a triangulation.'

'Oh wow! That's great work. Where is it?'

'On a property just outside of Bradbury. It belongs to a farmer who lives on another homestead. The area the phone signal is coming from is his old family farmhouse, listed as an Airbnb. We have the farmer's permission to search the property.'

'Bradbury? Isn't that on the coast?'

'It certainly is, and it's only thirty kilometres from Henderson.'

Molly smiled as the butterflies began churning in her gut. 'This could be our lead!'

'Shall I pick you up?'

'No. I'll meet you at the station and we'll drive from there.' Molly glanced down at her track pants. 'Give me fifteen minutes. I'll see you there.' She hung up before he could reply.

*

Jesse was washing his police vehicle on the street outside the station when Ben called. There was not the usual vitriol in the Port Lincoln cop's tone today, but that may have been because he was requesting backup. But more realistically, it was probably because Molly was driving the car he was travelling in, and they were on speakerphone. Jesse was sure that Molly wore the pants in the partnership, and lately, she kept Ben tightly harnessed. So, Jesse could hardly say "no," to the request, although he did hesitate before agreeing.

'How sure are you that Wainwright is our guy?' Jesse asked.

'We're not, but he ran from us, so he has something to hide,' Ben said.

'Fair enough,' Jesse said as he rolled up the garden hose. 'I can follow you up there or lead the way. It's up to you. I know Bradbury pretty well.'

'We'll follow you, and then we'll take the front entrance to the farm. There are only two access doors to the house. So you can cover the rear.'

'Do you think he'll be armed? Were there weapons on his property?'

'No. We only received a warrant for the day the dogs were removed. The place was clean then, but Wainwright could have taken any firearms with him.'

'So, he could be armed.'

'Yeah, maybe,' Ben conceded. 'Any sign of trouble, and we hang back and wait for special ops.'

'That will take a while.'

'They're on standby. A chopper will have them to us in around forty-five minutes. It's the most we could ask for without evidence that Wainwright has weapons or is a threat.'

'He is a convicted felon,' Jesse said.

'I know, but preying on young women is a far cry from instigating a shootout. At least, that's how the hierarchy sees it.'

'Yeah, but it isn't the hierarchy who will be trying to question him.'

'I agree, but that's just the way it is.'

Jesse rubbed his bristly cheek and asked, 'What about bringing the woman from the bottle shop? She may be able to calm him if things get heated.'

'I wondered that too, but Molly says the woman is too freaked out, and they weren't close friends, so he may not listen to her anyway.'

'All right, how far away are you?'

Jesse could hear a mumbled conversation before Ben said, 'ETA to you, twenty minutes.'

'Good, that still gives us a couple of hours of daylight. I'll be ready.' The phone went dead. Jesse smiled as he strode inside to get his sidearm and flak jacket. It was probably wrong to enjoy this adrenaline buzz, and if Emily knew of the possible danger, she'd have a fit, but these were the jobs he lived for. He guessed that was why he'd stayed a cop all these years.

The drive to the property was uneventful. The two police vehicles bypassed the town of Bradbury and took a sandy track that led through an adjoining property towards the farmhouse. They had followed it for almost two kilometres when they reached a fork in the road.

Jesse pulled up for their briefing, leaning against the car in the last of the afternoon sun. Molly parked beside him.

They examined the satellite image of the farm on her iPad, and she pointed to the eastern road. 'That's the route to the back of the place. It's winding, and you will have no visual until you reach these trees.' She pointed once more. 'Just beyond that is the gateway. Once you're in, shut the gate in case he tries to flee. We'll take the track straight ahead but won't enter until we get a text confirming you're in position at the back door. Okay Jesse?'

Jesse nodded. 'Sure.' And then asked, 'No radios?'

'No. Too noisy. Texts are better and put your notifications on vibrate. If there is any sign of a threat, we leave. If other people are on the property, we will assess the risk and probably leave. Understand? The last thing we want is a shootout.'

'Yep. I got it.'

'Let's go!'

Molly's mouth tightened. She adjusted her dark baseball cap, ramming it tight on her head. Her right hand touched the butt of her pistol and then her spare magazine – she appeared to be taking a mental inventory. As she walked away, Jesse thought he saw Ben touch her left hand, but perhaps he was mistaken.

Jesse drove down the bumpy track with the window down. He went slowly to minimise the tell-tale dust plume behind the car. He passed the trees and saw that the entranceway was fully open. The air was deathly still, and the only sound was the buzz of insects. Jesse closed the gate and glanced down at the old farmhouse. A low stone wall surrounded the bungalow veranda, shading the windows, which looked dark and ominous.

Jesse cruised within twenty metres of the house and parked by an old lemon tree. He quietly shut the door, running crouched over towards the porch. He ducked below the veranda wall and listened. The sound of a tv or radio was coming from inside, so he texted Ben and waited.

Only a minute later, he heard the police cruiser crunching its way up the gravel drive. He heard car doors close, one, two, and a loud rap on the front door shortly after. From inside, Jesse heard the scrape of a chair and then running footfalls. He cocked his head. Someone was coming in his direction. He ducked to the side of the door just a second before it opened. The bloke flung himself through the doorway but hadn't seen Jesse's foot. The man tripped and fell headlong down the steps and onto the dead lawn.

He was much older than Jesse expected and judging from the way he struggled to sit up, he wasn't exactly fit. So, Jesse didn't need to aim a gun at him. Instead, he offered the man his hand and hauled him to his feet. A second later, Molly and Ben burst from the house, out through the back door with guns drawn.

'It's okay,' Jesse said. He rested his hand on the man's shoulder while Ben cuffed the bloke. Pushing him aggressively back towards the house.

'I haven't done anything!' Wainwright protested. 'What's this all about?'

Once inside, Molly pointed to an armchair in the lounge room and said, 'Sit!' She sat opposite Wainwright while Jesse and Ben stood, both with hands on hips. 'We came to speak to you last week, and you ran. Why?' Molly asked.

'I was scared. I've been beaten up by cops before.'

'Really?' Ben asked. 'I've seen no record of a report.'

Wainwright gave a bitter laugh. 'Report? What's the point. You cops all cover for each other. You're a bunch of dogs cun....'

'Not true,' Jesse butted in. He shook his head. 'Be honest with us, mate, and things will go much easier.'

For his comment, Jesse received a harsh glance from Molly. Apparently, she wanted to run this show. So Jesse walked across the room to the couch and flopped down. She could have it her own way.

'Was there something you didn't want us to see at your house?' Molly asked.

'Yes!' Wainwright said belligerently. 'Everything! I don't want any bastards snooping around my house and invading my privacy; I doubt any of you pigs would like that either.'

Jesse sniggered under his breath. The bloke had a point.

'We only came to ask you some questions,' Molly said.

'And I was only taking my bike for a ride.' Wainwright's tone dripped with sarcasm. 'But when I saw the guns come out, I panicked!'

'Why such aggressive guard dogs?' Ben asked.

'They don't like intruders either.'

'We were visiting,' Molly said.

'You weren't invited.'

'What were you hiding?' Ben yelled. 'Just answer the bloody question!'

Wainwright cowered overdramatically, and Jesse laughed. He earned two scowls and a grin from Wainwright.

'Come on, Jerry,' Molly said. 'The sooner you answer our questions, the sooner we'll be out of your hair.'

'Was it drugs?' Ben interrupted.

'No!'

'Guns?'

'Do you think I'm crazy? I'd get ten years for possession of a firearm.'

'Kiddie pawn?'

Wainwright dropped his head. 'No!' he said emphatically.

'What then?' Molly asked.

'A still, okay. A fucking still! But I wasn't selling any of the booze. It was just for me – for my own use.

The only problem is – it tastes like shit. I haven't quite perfected it yet.'

Ben and Molly stared at each other. Jesse shook his head and stood; after a moment, he paced to the window.

'Okay, forget the still. Where were you on the fourth of December this year?' Ben asked.

'Jesus. I dunno? How's a bloke supposed to remember something like that?'

'Think!' Ben shouted.

Jesse glanced at Wainwright's phone sitting on top of a low cabinet. The cover pattern was familiar. An orange and red-crested logo.

'Where were you?' Ben repeated.

'I dunno what day that was?' There was desperation in Wainwright's voice now. 'I don't have a job! I'm too sick to work, so I don't know which day is which! They're all the bloody same to me.'

Ben was clenching his fists at his sides. His face was florid, nostrils flared.

'I know what day it was, Wainwright. It was the day Manchester United played Tottenham,' Jesse said. 'It was a fundraising game.'

Wainwright stared at Jesse. His brow creased, and his jaw worked from left to right. 'Oh, um, I do know then. I was at a mate's place in Lincoln. We went to the pub during the day and then to his place to watch the game. So yeah, I was there all night. Man United's my team. He was a Spurs fan. We've been watching games together since we were kids.'

'Soccer, really?' Ben's tone was pure disgust.

'It's football.' Wainwright's expression was truculent. 'Not like that weird shit that dumb Aussie's play. It's my favourite game, and I never miss one.'

Ben took a step towards Wainwright. 'We'll find out if you're lying,' Ben said, but his hostility had dampened. Wainwright's confidence in his alibi was too authentic to be contrived.

Wainwright sat straight in the chair, his expression now righteous indignation. 'Go on then! And when you find out I *was* there, I want a fucking apology.'

Ben and Molly exchanged a bemused glance.

'We'll check the CCTV in the hotel and speak to your friend, so I hope you aren't lying,' Molly said.

Jesse tuned out for the remainder of the interview, gazing instead out at the yard. Wainwright was clearly not the shooter, so they had a problem. There was still a killer to catch and no real clues.

Chapter Nine

The temperature was rising and would be in the high thirties by early afternoon. Ravi and the other CFS volunteers were on high alert. Although there were no forests to catch fire on this part of the peninsula, grass fires were common and potentially devastating. The crops had been harvested, and the paddocks were full of dry stubble. There was so much out there for fires to feed on. Farmers sometimes accidentally ignited fields by driving over them; the hot exhaust pipes created sparks. And thunderstorms with lightning strikes were not uncommon. Once, in the early nineteen hundreds, almost half the town had been lost to fire, and it was the same for many other nearby areas. The local community took the fire risk very seriously.

But today, the crew's only callout was an extrication with the ambulance team. Their patient weighed almost two hundred kilos and had fallen, injuring his hip and possibly his spine. It took six staff to manoeuvre the fellow safely onto the stretcher via a longboard. Given the enormous girth of the man, it was a tricky procedure, and the narrow hallway of his home made the process even more challenging.

Ravi drove his grandma's ute home along the coast road. The water looked peaceful and inviting after the physical workout, so as soon as he arrived home, he changed into his shorts and went swimming.

Just minutes later, Ravi floated on his back, adrift on the still water, gazing at the cloudless blue sky. He checked his position every so often. It was safer to stay in the shallow clear water, away from the blue line where the sand and seagrass merge and which could potentially conceal sharks. Great whites were not infrequent visitors around the Eyre Peninsula, and swimmers were attacked yearly. Most didn't survive, so it paid to be vigilant.

It was with sharks in mind that Ravi let out a scream when something touched his leg. He saw the dark shadow beneath the water and thrashed wildly.

When he heard Bailey giggle behind him, he was torn between laughter and the desire to throttle her.

'Not nice,' he said breathlessly.

'Sorry, I know that was cruel, but I couldn't resist.' She floated on her back beside him, wearing a black one-piece swimsuit. Her short-cropped hair was plastered to her perfect head. Ravi gave a sigh of amazement.

'What?' Bailey asked as she splashed water at his face.

'You,' he said with a smile. 'How did I get this lucky?'

A shadow seemed to cross her face, or did he imagine it? Then she cleared her throat and grinned. 'I think I've done okay too.' She paddled closer, put her arms around his shoulders, and kissed him.

'Are you okay?' Ravi asked. Again, he saw a flicker of something; worry perhaps? 'I really do care, you know.'

She ran a finger over his cheek and along his lips. He gently bit it, and she said, 'I know you do. I guess I worry because this has all happened so fast.'

Ravi nodded. 'I know what you mean. I can hardly believe it, but I'm pleased.'

Her lips were salty, and they kissed for a long time. The sun was hot and relentless, and neither of them wore a hat. Ravi touched Bailey's nose. It was hot.

'You're getting sunburnt,' he said. 'Let's go back to the house.'

They jogged side by side through the waves, holding hands. Once home they hosed each other off in the back garden while Hank sniffed around in the bushes. Then, to dry off, they lay on the small stretch of lawn under a Jacaranda tree. Bailey rested her head on Ravi's shoulder as they stared at the dappled sunlight.

'What do you think of the cop, Plackis?' Ravi asked.

'Jesse? He's a great guy.'

'Really?' Ravi screwed up his face.

'You don't like him because he's a cop. But he's more than that. I've known him all my life.'

'I think he's a smartarse.'

'No, he isn't, and he hasn't had an easy life. His wife was a patient at the nursing home when I first began working as a carer about six years ago.'

'He was married?' Ravi frowned. He hadn't imagined Jesse with a wife. 'Has he got kids?'

Bailey shook her head. 'Julie had multiple sclerosis. She was first diagnosed in her mid-twenties. I guess they decided not to have a family.'

'Wow, that sucks.'

'Yep. Jesse cared for her at home for many years. He's a bit of a hero to me.'

'And she died?'

'Yeah. Maybe a year or so after she went into care. Aspiration pneumonia. Sadly, it's a common condition for patients who can't swallow properly. Food goes into their chest, and they get an infection.'

'That's awful.'

'Maybe you should cut him some slack?'

Ravi exhaled loudly and then twined her hair around his fingers. He loved the feel of her breath on his neck and chest.

'I went to see my granddad this morning,' Bailey said.

There was a sadness in her voice. Ravi kissed her forehead and asked, 'Is he okay?'

She chewed at her bottom lip and then shook her head. 'He has some medical problems. I thought talking to him about Christmas lunch might cheer him up. He's always so angry lately. I guess his illness makes him grumpy.'

'He lost his wife.'

'I know, but – it's something else. I don't know what to do.'

'Take him to see someone; his doctor can talk to him. It might help.' Ravi suggested.

Bailey gave a sharp laugh. 'Easier said than done. When I told you my granddad was stubborn, I mean pig-headed. I don't think he's ever been made to do something he didn't want.' She shrugged. 'He's not about to start now.'

'Can you try convincing him? Make it seem like it's his idea?'

'Mmm. If I can think of a way, I will try to talk him into it.'

'Would it help if I came with you? Maybe he would open up to another bloke?'

'Maybe.' She gave a wicked smile. 'Or are you just angling for an invite to Christmas lunch?'

'I could be.'

'Are you sure you want to put up with my crazy family?'

Ravi grinned. 'I would, but I'm rostered on over Christmas. I figured it would be a good chance to study since Mum isn't coming. She's spending the time with her sick aunt in Perth.'

Bailey was about to reply but screamed instead. Ravi sat bolt upright as Hank dropped a shingle back lizard onto his groin. The reptile opened its mouth wide as Ravi shuffled backwards. It hissed, displaying a gaping pink mouth and blue tongue. It whipped its head from side to side.

'Jesus Christ!' Ravi said as he leapt to his feet. 'What are you doing, Hank?'

The dog took off, and a few seconds later, Ravi heard the screen door slam.

Bailey was standing too, laughing and slapping her thighs. 'Your face!' she said. 'I can't believe the look on your face.'

'Hang on a minute! You're the one who screamed.'

'Did not!' Bailey called as she ran towards the house. But Ravi caught her before she reached the doorway. He picked her up, cradling her like a child while she flapped her arms and legs.

'Put me down,' she squealed.

'Never,' Ravi said as he reached his bedroom door.

'You can put me on the bed.'

'If you ask nicely, I might.'

Bailey put her hands on either side of his face, holding him still and drawing his lips closer. 'I'm asking nicely,' she whispered. 'Put me on the bed?'

As Ravi placed her down gently. He silently prayed for no callouts because he knew he wouldn't leave her, not for fire or any other catastrophe. Right now, he wasn't going anywhere.

*

Tash and Carl had been tasked to back up another crew who were having problems dealing with a psychiatric patient. Tash turned off the siren as Carl swung the ambulance into the driveway. Three police cars and the other ambulance were parked askew on the sidewalk. Across the road, a small group of rubbernecks had gathered. Tash and Carl ignored them as they grabbed their kits and ran to the rear garden entrance. It sprung open when they drew closer to the gate, and two police officers emerged.

'Be careful,' a dark-haired cop warned. 'This bloke's off his chops.'

'Okay,' Tash said as they rounded the corner and ducked under an ivy-covered arbour.

'Those cops looked pretty spooked,' Carl observed. 'This could be tricky.'

But Tash didn't reply. She ignored the din and scene playing out at the rear of the house, and instead, she went to speak to the first ambulance crew. The two ambulance officers were in their early twenties, and they appeared as shocked as the retreating cops had. Then, as if to prove her theory, one of them jumped as the screaming began again. They were clearly out of their league.

'Hi Tom, hi Gino,' she said, reading off their name badges. 'I don't want to tread on any toes, but we can take this job if you like. I'll call comms and sort it out.' Tash paused as they looked at each other. 'I mean, I'm sure you can manage, but Carl and I have dealt with many psychiatric patients and restraining them is our specialty.'

The two men nodded eagerly and were packing their kits before she'd finished talking on her radio. Tash gave them the thumbs up once she received the okay, and they hastily departed. She didn't blame them; such confrontations could be challenging.

The group of cops stood a few metres back from the man who was wearing nothing but a torn singlet. He stood on the rim of a vast concrete plant pot. Blood was running down both his arms but the injuries appeared superficial. Bits of decimated palm fronds were scattered over the pavers. The man wielded a long kitchen knife in his left hand, slashing mindlessly at the air and screaming unintelligible words. As one of the cops stepped closer, the man spun, bending at the waist and raging into her face. She stepped back in line with her colleagues and then turned to Tash.   'Any ideas?' she asked.

Tash gazed at the man and shook her head. He appeared more confused than angry, but either way, he was unhinged. 'Those cuts aren't deep, so luckily, he hasn't lost much blood. It would be impossible to successfully sedate him without someone getting hurt.'

'Sure,' the cop agreed. 'And he's too high up to pepper spray; the stuff will go everywhere except where we want it to. So, we'll have to taser him and then secure him.'

'Have you contacted any family members who could help to calm him?'

The cop nodded. 'There's only one daughter as far as we know, and she's interstate. Unfortunately, this guy was a loner.'

'You really don't have much choice then. Taser it is,' Tash said. 'Just make sure you break his fall. I'll get an IV line in once he's restrained.'

Tash gathered her equipment for the cannula insertion while the police conversed. The two cops they had met at the gate returned with a couple of blankets and a mattress they'd sourced from somewhere. They threw them on the ground in front of the man as he babbled and spat at them. Carl parked their stretcher by the fence and stood beside Tash. They watched as one of the cops crept closer to the man. The bloke paid no attention to the officer. Instead, he made howling noises and urinated down his leg.

'Jesus,' Carl muttered.

'Do you think this is drug-induced?'

'Maybe. Probably been smoking crack or bingeing on some stimulant.'

Tash frowned; something about the man's movements didn't fit with drugs, but she said nothing. Then, finally, the cop closest to the man yelled for everyone to stand clear. The taser struck just below the man's chest, and he bawled briefly before falling. The knife clattered onto the patio tiles while the man hit the blankets. The cops all rushed forward to restrain him. They rolled him onto his stomach and zip-tied his arms behind his back. Tash came and checked his carotid pulse; it was rapid but strong, so she stood back while the cops hauled him onto their stretcher.

Tash and Carl quickly secured the netted restraint once the zip ties were cut. Tash managed to place the cannula while the man was still stunned enough to lay still, and then two of the police officers helped to push the stretcher and load it into the ambulance.

'I'm coming with you,' the woman cop said as Tash sat in the attendant's seat beside the moaning patient.

'Sure.' Just as Carl started the engine, she pointed to the airway seat beyond the man's head. 'Sit there.'

'Ready?' Carl asked from the cab.

'Absolutely,' Tash replied with a noisy breath.

The man was twitching slightly and beginning to look around. Tash moved closer and said, 'Hello.'

The man blinked a couple of times but said nothing.

'Do you know this fella's name?' Tash asked the cop.

The woman glanced at the notepad in her hand. 'Loris Tivollo.'

Tash moved closer and said, 'Loris? Loris?'

The man glanced at her and frowned.

'Do you prefer to be called Lorrie?'

This time he gave a slight shake of his head.

'Hello, Loris. Are you sore? Pain? Do you have pain?'

He muttered something that may have been "pain."

'He's responding to you,' the cop said.

Tash touched Loris' arm gently and asked, 'Is there pain somewhere?'

Again, he shook his head and then muttered something. It was hard to hear over the sound of the moving ambulance, but Tash thought he said "no."

'Are you saying you have no pain, Loris?'

He stared at her for a long moment and then nodded.

'You were angry, Loris. Why?'

His mouth worked, but there was no sound. Tash reached out and held his hand, acutely aware that the inside of her glove was full of sweat. Loris' eyes crinkled and filled with tears. Tash grabbed a tissue and dabbed at them.

'Everything is okay, Loris. You're safe now, okay? I'm right here with you.' He closed his eyes and sobbed silently.

The handover at the hospital took longer than usual, and by the time Tash and Carl cleared from the job, Loris was tranquilised and sleeping peacefully.

'I don't think that was drugs,' Tash said. 'Think about how he was reacting, Carl. If you had to compare his behaviour with another patient, who would it be?'

Carl took a moment to answer. 'You mean apart from the last guy we picked up in Lavender Court?'

'Yes, *apart* from him.'

'Then I'd have to say the old fella in the nursing home a few months back, who caused the whole place to be locked down.'

'Yeah, that man was so agitated that he blocked the lobby access, wielding his walking frame like a weapon. He acted violently and insanely until his niece showed up, someone he trusted, and then he changed into a kitten.'

'So, you think this man, Loris, has dementia? If it is, it's a sudden and acute onset, which is highly unusual unless he's suffering from a raging infection, which his vital signs didn't reflect.'

Tash shrugged. 'I know, but dementia is what it seems like to me. You heard what that cop said, the guy's a loner. Maybe he's had these symptoms for some time, but no one picked it up.'

'I'll radio comms and see if we can access his medical history because there was no record of visits to that hospital. It seems he's new to the area.'

'If he's residing in Lavender Court, he may be an ex-con. If so, he may have received treatment in prison. See if comms can send his institutional medical records to us.' Tash paused as she turned into the depot driveway. 'They may give us some answers.'

The requested file came through as Tash and Carl sat eating their lunch. Carl read it while picking at his vegetable bake, which smelled like boiled socks.

'Did you cook that, Carl?' Tash asked.

He grinned and shook his head. 'Nah, it's a tv dinner. But I bet you didn't cook yours either.'

'You're right. Angela cooked it for me.'

'Wish I had a missus who could cook like yours.'

Tash smiled and pointed to his plate. 'I bet you do. You need to find yourself a lucky girl one day.'

Carl ignored her quip and swallowed a mouthful of food. After a moment, he cleared his throat and read from his tablet screen. 'Listen to this. You were right about our patient being in prison. It looks like he spent a good part of five years in there. He was only released two months ago. Hang on – what the hell is CAS?'

'CAS, really? The other patient from Lavender Court had that on his file, too, didn't he?'

'Yeah, but what is it?'

'Don't you ever read your memos? It means that both men were treated under the Criminal Ageing System.'

'Isn't that when they mess with your cells?'

'Yeah, so you do read your memos.' Tash spooned chicken pasta into her mouth and chewed. 'Although "messing with your cells" is dumbing it down a bit.'

'Maybe.' Carl sat back in his chair and said, 'I guess if the prisoners are predisposed to developing dementia, then the treatment accelerates those diseases.'

'Sounds barbaric.'

Carl shrugged. 'It would have progressed in time anyway.'

Tash dropped her spoon. 'What we saw today was horrid. If the disease had progressed under normal conditions, his problems would have been dealt with as they cropped up instead of him becoming some raging beast with no clue what was happening to him. It's bloody cruel.'

'So how long ago did he have the CAS treatment?' Tash asked.

'Just before his release. Two months ago.'

Tash pushed a piece of mushroom across the plate. 'What about the other Lavender Court patient?'

'His treatment was about nine months ago.'

'You sound pretty sure,' Tash said.

'Mmm, that's because I am. I remember the date on the paperwork; it was Saint Patrick's Day.'

'Why would you remember something like that? You aren't catholic, are you?'

Carl laughed throatily and said, 'No, my parents were Lutheran. But you see, my grandfather lived with us when I was little. He was a wizened older man with no teeth and didn't speak much English. My mum was the last of eight children, and he looked old enough to be her grandfather.'

'Wow!'

'Yeah. He fought in World War Two and rarely had much to say, but every year on Saint Pat's Day, he'd have a toast to a dead soldier.'

'Was it a friend of his?'

'No. My granddad fought for Germany. The dead man was English.'

'He fought for Germany, really? How did people in Australia react to that?'

'No one knew. He moved here in the eighties after my mum married Dad and immigrated. It was okay to be German by then.'

'So, who was the dead soldier?'

'Some bloke that he shot on Saint Patrick's Day.'

'And he celebrated that?'

'Yeah, weird, I know. He used to say, 'It was him or me. I shot first and lived, so I owe him a drink.''

'That's messed up!'

'I know. Like I said, he was elderly.' Carl shrugged. 'People were different back then.'

Tash pondered the story momentarily and then took a swig of coffee. 'Well,' she said, 'if that first patient's CAS treatment was so long ago, then it may not have anything to do with his recent psychotic breakdown.'

'I guess not, but we should report it to the Health Department anyway.'

'Good idea. We'll report both cases.' Tash dropped her spoon onto the plate. 'I'm full.'

She glanced at Carl, who was eyeing off her leftovers. 'I still have more in the fridge,' Tash said. 'And I'm sure Angela would be pleased if you ate it.'

Carl grinned and said, 'Cool!'

*

Molly had spent nights away from home before, usually for work-related training, hardly ever because of sex. Now this was the second night in a week that she and Ben had stayed in a motel overnight, and Molly was feeling less guilt rather than more. Some of her lack of feeling was due to Ferdi's blasé attitude towards her absenteeism. He hardly batted an eyelid anymore. Ferdi hadn't been upset when she didn't return from Henderson for Christmas Day or Boxing Day. He seemed pretty content to spend the time with his horrid sister instead.

Molly wondered if Ferdi would be so complacent if he knew she and Ben had spent the holiday break holed up in the Henderson Motel eating cold barbeque chicken, drinking wine and having sex.

On the other hand, Ben had undergone a total change in character. He was warm and loving, so far removed from the careless arsehole persona he had mastered. And he wasn't just concerned about Molly either; he had become thoughtful of other people too. It was one of the reasons that Molly found it so hard to say "no" to him. Of course, the main reason was the great sex, but it wasn't the only motivation.

The case had hit a brick wall despite what seemed to be early positive breakthroughs. And while that should have been enough to encourage the cops to redouble their efforts, it had the opposite effect on Molly and Ben. They spent more time on intimacy.

'Jesse Plackis has sent us an email,' Molly said as she lay back against the pillows.

Ben rolled over and brushed strands of hair from her cheek. 'It can wait.' His hand slipped down to her breast.

'Ben, we need to get up and leave.' She checked the time on her phone. 'It's almost nine. We should have been at the station by eight-thirty.'

Ben groaned before throwing back the bedcovers. 'I have to shower.' He stomped to the ensuite and shut the door. When Molly looked up from her phone screen, he was gone.

'Jesse is going to interview some farmer this morning.' She shouted over the sound of the running water. 'And he's requested a meeting with us.'

There was no reply, but Ben appeared only a few minutes later, clad in a towel. 'We can phone him.'

'No, not this time. Jesse specifically requested that we meet him at the station. If we aren't there, questions could be asked.'

Although the mention of Plackis no longer aggravated Ben as it had previously, he did appear peeved. He gave a grunt of displeasure as he pulled on his trousers.

'Besides, we need to touch base with Ravi Sanders.' Molly added.

'I thought Plackis was our liaison with the victim's family.'

'Yes, but as you frequently point out, this is our investigation.' Molly zipped up her skirt and ran her fingers through her hair. She tossed her head and grinned.

'Why are you smirking?' Ben asked.

'Because I heard on the grapevine that Jesse is taking his liaison work seriously.'

'Huh? What do you mean?'

'I asked Andy Ruthers to keep me posted on Ravi's progress within the CFS. It seems old Andy is a bit of a gossip. He let on that Ravi's mum, Emily, is more than a friend to Jesse.'

'Do you mean he's banging the victim's daughter?'

'Ben! Is that what we're doing? Banging?' Molly's face heated as Ben fumbled for a reply.

'No, of course not. I'm sorry.'

'A bit of decorum, please.' But his remark had stung. She turned away so he couldn't see her catch her breath and wipe her eyes. Were they more to each other than just sex? Or was she kidding herself? Was this merely sly sexual gratification? More to the point, did she want them to be more than fuck buddies? Was this fling becoming serious?

Suddenly Ben was beside her. He clasped her shoulders and turned her to face him. 'I'm sorry.'

Had he read her thoughts?

'I have deep feelings for you, Molly. Very deep.'

'Well, you shouldn't. You know this can never evolve into anything meaningful.'

But it was as though he didn't hear her. He kissed her for a long time, and it took all her resolve to break away.

'Okay. We've got to leave now,' she said. 'We can talk about this later. Right now, we focus on the case.'

Ben held her gaze for a moment and then shrugged as he walked away, a hint of the sulking, short-tempered beast he had been. Molly felt a pang of sadness and wondered if this was the death knell of their affair. She had to admit, she'd been enjoying it.

*

Jesse nodded to Maury Winters as he entered the police station. The farmer had mud around his trouser bottoms, and instead of a belt, the pants were fastened with baling twine. His white shirt had yellowed with age, and the button-down collar was frayed, but it was an apparent attempt at dressing up for this visit.

After being ushered into the office space, they shook hands. There were two chairs facing each other which Jesse gestured to. He was glad Molly and Ben were not around because this old bloke was not the most outgoing of men, and strangers would probably make him clam up. Jesse had known the old boy for years but had probably shared only a dozen words with him.

'Have a seat Moe. Would you like some water or a coffee?' There was a whiff of body odour as the man passed. 'Or tea?'

'Nup.'

'It's been a while, Moe. I haven't seen you around since Gwen's funeral.'

Maury gazed at his hands clasped on his lap. He shook his head. 'That was a bleak day, one of the worst.'

'Of course. I'm so sorry.' Jesse tried to sound cheery. 'I thought I might have seen you at Edith Sanders' memorial. Most of the town turned out. Pretty sure you weren't there.'

Jesse noticed Moe stiffen in his chair, but the man's face gave away nothing, and he didn't reply.

'You've been out at the rifle range a lot recently.'

'I didn't realise that was a crime. I'm a paid-up club member, you know. And I have been for years.'

Jesse leaned back in his chair, fingers drumming on the arms as he scrutinised the man. He let the silence build in the hope that Moe would say more. He didn't have long to wait.

'I've had some fox problems out on the farm. Don't like using those poisons, so I needed to sight in my old shotgun to twenty-five metres, so it's ready in case I catch one red-handed. From my tractor shed, I got a good line of sight to where the bastard got in last time. Lost eleven chooks, you know. If it weren't for the Alpacas, I might've lost lambs too.'

'Do you own an SKS rifle?'

'A what?'

'Do you have problems with your hearing?'

'I heard you say some kind of bullshit, but I dunno what it was.'

'I'm pretty sure you would have heard of an SKS.' Jesse leaned closer, staring hard.

'What the hell would a sheep farmer living in the middle of nowhere want with an old Russian army weapon?'

'So, you *do* know what an SKS is.'

'Course I do. I've just never seen one. And I certainly don't own one.'

'Have you ever seen anyone using the old part of the firing range?'

'Down towards the highway?'

'Yeah. Someone's been down there firing a big bore weapon.'

Moe raised his hands, palms up. 'Never seen no one out there.'

Jesse watched Moe. He gave a few slight shrugs and glanced around the room. His attempt at nonchalance was believable until he rubbed his eye and cleared his throat.

'So,' Moe said. 'Is that it? Are you done with your questions yet?'

Jesse slowly shook his head. 'Nowhere near it, Moe.' He left the threat hanging in the air to unsettle the farmer.

'Well, I got stuff to do. Sheep to feed and fences to mend, so make it snappy.'

'These things take time, Moe. That's why I told Bailey I would call her when we're done. You can only leave once she picks you up, and I'm not calling her until I get the answers I need. I'm going to find the person who killed Edith Sanders, and I'm hoping you'll help me.'

'I didn't see nothin'.'

'The forensic team have dug the large bore projectiles from the hill on the old range. They match perfectly with the ones taken from the Sanders' crime scene.'

Moe scratched his stubbly cheek and picked something out of his top teeth.

'That means her killer was out on that range, the same place you frequently visit. If you saw something that could help me, I may be able to catch a killer before they hurt anyone else.' Jesse intensified his stare once more.

'If I told you something, I'd just be making it up, coz I didn't see nothin'.'

'So you said.'

Moe's attitude had never been obliging, but Jesse found his refusal to help infuriating, so he tried another tack. 'It must have been hard losing Gwen,' he said with controlled neutrality.

'Course it was,' Moe growled.

'I know it was hard when I lost Julie.'

'Sorry,' Moe said flatly.

'And I imagine it was damn hard for Emily and Ravi to lose Edith.'

Moe shrugged. 'I guess it was her time.'

'What? Her time to be gunned down by some maniac?'

Moe hung his head and said, 'I just meant, you know, God wanted her, I guess.'

'I don't think this had anything to do with God,' Jesse said with more venom than he intended.

Moe fidgeted with the baling twine that held up his pants.

'Gwen and Edith were friends, weren't they?' Jesse asked in a calmer tone.

'Yeah. I suppose.'

'But I noticed Gwen didn't attend Edith's retirement party when she finished with the CFS all those years ago. That was a big event. I'm pretty sure most of the town turned out for that too.'

'She was probably crook. Gwen was crook for a long time, you know.'

'Yeah. But I know she had her good days too. After all Edith did for your family, I expected to see her there.'

Moe's hands bunched into tight fists.

'I mean, if it wasn't for Edith, you would have lost all your children.'

'I lost my boy. I lost Colin.'

'Edith saved your two daughters.'

'Yep.' The older man's lip was trembling. 'I know.' His eyes were moist.

'Okay Moe. Can you promise to watch out for anything odd at the rifle range?'

Moe coughed and nodded.

'And if you think of anything, or remember something, even something small, let me know?'

'Yeah. Are we done?'

'Yeah Moe. We're done. Take care of yourself.'

'Call Bailey. I'll wait for her outside.'

Moe walked from the room, leaving nothing but stale air. Jesse sat back in his chair, letting his head tilt back to stare at the ceiling. But the vast white space offered nothing in the way of help or comfort for his swirling thoughts. There was something wrong with Moe's reactions, something more than irritation at being summoned to the police station. He knew more than he was letting on. Jesse could feel it in his gut.

Chapter Ten

Bailey was in one of her reckless and playful moods. Most of the time Ravi found it endearing but today it was driving him to distraction. There was a dull ache in his head that two paracetamols hadn't been able to ease. He had multiple bills made out to Edith that required transferring into his name, so he already wasted two hours on hold with different billing departments. The amounts owing needed to be paid before their due dates, and Ravi also had a couple of local job application forms to complete.

When Bailey first arrived, she chattered constantly, totally sabotaging his concentration. Ravi had pointed out his need for quiet, and although he'd used a diplomatic tone, it seemed she was peeved at the dressing down. Since then, Bailey had been teasing Hank out in the yard, dragging his toy rope along, urging him to grab it and then pulling it up and away from him. Each time the dog fell for it, he would sit back on his haunches and howl in protest.

Perhaps, Ravi thought, it was funny the first thousand times, but now it was getting old. He understood her need to burn off some energy and that he was probably coming across as a bore, but he was determined to finish what he'd started. Ravi turned up the volume on the speaker and pulled the sunroom blinds closed, but the Highly Suspect song didn't help his concentration, and he soon stopped the music.

'Hello! Hello!'

'What the hell?' Ravi tore at his shirt collar. 'Come in!' The pen in his left hand snapped in two.

'Ravi, It's me.'

Ravi swore as he rose from his desk chair. 'In here, mum!' he called.

'Oh, sorry, you look busy,' Emily said.

'It's fine.' But despite his words, he groaned when Hank began to howl again from out in the yard. 'Bloody hell,' he muttered.

At that second, Bailey burst through the back door with Hank at her heels. She threw the dog's rope, and Hank slid across the floor to grab it. The dog almost toppled a pedestal with a vase on top of it. Bailey caught it just in time and then stood there grinning. 'Oops,' she blurted.

'For Christ's sake Bailey, can you just stop that!' Ravi yelled. 'Isn't it time you bloody well grew up?'

Emily and Bailey both stared at Ravi. Hank was impervious to Ravi's outburst and took the opportunity to make off with the rope. Emily was the first to speak.

'Really Ravi! I think you need to calm the hell down. You don't speak to people like that.'

'Yeah, Ravi,' Bailey agreed. 'Who pissed in your cornflakes?'

But Ravi didn't laugh or calm down. Instead, as he spoke, saliva and sweat flew from his top lip. 'I am trying to better myself by doing grownup shit, like paying bills and applying for a job, but I can't concentrate because you can't stop acting like a fucking two-year-old!'

He watched Bailey's face. First, her grin disappeared, then her brow furrowed as she made sense of his words, her bottom lip trembled, and she glanced at Emily, perhaps for support, then back to Ravi as tears began to flow.

'You pig. Don't you ever speak to me like that again?' She stalked to the sunroom and picked up her bag. 'Goodbye Emily, Goodbye Ravi.'

Emily moved to follow her, but Ravi held his arm out to stop her.

'Let her go,' he said.

'She's right, you know,' said Emily. 'What the hell has gotten into you? You were very rude.'

'I don't care, mum. I must start getting serious. This isn't kindergarten; this is my life, my future. Bailey needs to grow the hell up or move on.'

'Oh, I'm pretty sure you just saw her moving on. So, I hope you're happy.' Emily took her car keys from her handbag and walked to the front door. 'You'll be lucky to ever find another girl like her again.' Emily's face was flushed with anger. 'I'll talk to you later when you stop being an arsehole,' she said over her shoulder.

'Mum!'

'Shut it, Ravi!'

She didn't give him a backward glance. Ravi's anger suddenly dissipated, leaving him with an unspoken apology trapped in his throat. When the door closed, the encompassing silence failed to give him peace.

'What the hell just happened?'

But there was no one to answer him, and the only sound was Hank barking in the backyard.

*

Bailey pulled up in the driveway of her family home, but instead of parking at the rear, alongside her flat, she reversed back to the roadway and stopped. For a long moment, she stared at the house. Bailey could imagine the conversation with her mother when she described Ravi's awful behaviour. Of course, her mum would be sympathetic, upset even, and Bailey would feel like a failure during that display of emotion.

She had never wanted to return here when she finished college. Her roommates were moving to Sydney once they graduated, and it was a foregone conclusion that Bailey would join them. That had been two years ago, and she was still here. At first, her mother had talked her into staying for the summer break, but then her gran became sick. Grandpa kept having meltdowns and wasn't coping with his terminally ill wife, but any mention of carers entering their home set him on a rampage. Sometimes it seemed like Bailey's mum, Donna, was afraid of her father. Of course, she denied it, but Bailey had seen her reactions when he raised his voice in her presence.

So yes, Donna would take it badly when she heard that Bailey had been shouted at by Ravi. And Bailey could add a failed relationship to her list of flops. She had botched her escape to Sydney and bombed in her efforts to appease her grandfather. So what could she stuff up next?

With no real plan of what to do or where to go, Bailey drove out onto the highway. She thought she should up-stumps and leave Henderson for a while. Ravi deserved to be abandoned, but did she really want to?

She passed a huge green road sign and thought about the distance to the destinations on the board. Another few hundred kilometres north, and she would be in Ceduna, but she didn't like the place. Two thousand kilometres east would take her to Sydney, or two thousand west, and she'd end up in Perth. The fact that Bailey had choices didn't make her decision any easier.

There was her cousin, Abby, who lived in Perth. Bailey was close to her, and the warmer climate would agree with her, but there were mates in Sydney too, and the greenery would make a nice change.

Without thinking, Bailey put on her left indicator and turned automatically onto the dirt road, which led to her grandfather's property. She gave a humourless laugh as she realised what she had done.

'Damn autopilot! Oh, well, it will cheer up the old bugger to have some company,' she muttered. But she couldn't help but wonder if he would be happy to see her. The last time she saw him was after Jesse Plackis asked to speak to him at the police station. Grandpa had been in a black mood on the drive home and Bailey had not stuck around. These days he was either moaning or ropable. There was nothing in between.

Although she'd seen her grandpa in ugly rages, Bailey had never been scared of him. She realised as a small child that his bark was his way of communicating his frustration at the world and circumstances beyond his control. He'd become more vocal since losing his wife. Sometimes Bailey wished she could so bluntly demonstrate her feelings; perhaps it was cathartic. She should have given Ravi a bawling out instead of fleeing.

'Perhaps I'll be a cranky old lady one day,' she said as she lowered her driver's window and let in the dusty air.

As she drew closer to the homestead, she noticed her grandpa's work ute was gone. With his driver's licence revoked, he couldn't have gone far. Bailey glanced at the time on her dashboard. It was just after eleven, so he was possibly out checking the water troughs before lunch. She parked her car and walked to the shearing shed. The steps creaked as she entered, and she was immediately hit with the evocative smell of sheep, pine and lanolin. Bailey loved this place. It brought back her childhood.

Most of the season's wool bales had gone for sale, but a couple remained, so she lay across them and closed her eyes. Sometimes during school holidays, she had been permitted to watch the shearing in progress. It was thrilling to be amongst the action, although *her* job was sweeping up mud and sheep shit while staying out of the way of shearers and roustabouts.

But the first time she watched the shearing, she had cried. So many of the animals suffered lacerations, and the blood was sickening. Her grandpa had handed her a can of purple antiseptic and told her to spray the cuts. He'd also told her to "quit your bloody bleating!"

It had been a grownup's world, and she fell into it. Funny how once the wounds were covered in purple, they seemed to lose their impact.

'Well, look who it is!' Grandpa boomed from the doorway.

Bailey gave a start before rolling off the bales and greeting her grandpa with a hug.

'Hi, Grandpa. I thought you'd be back soon.'

'You expect lunch, do you?'

Bailey laughed and said, 'No, I just came for a visit, but I'd love a cup of tea.'

'Well, you know where the bloody cups are, don't you?' he said gruffly.

But Bailey could see the laughter in his eyes, and although he tried to push her away, she threw her arms around him again and hugged him even tighter.

'Well, what's all this nonsense for? Go on, get off me and make us a cuppa.'

She grinned, took his hand and led him back to the house. While she boiled the kettle in the kitchen, she could hear him struggling to remove his work boots, but she knew better than to offer assistance. So instead, she waited until his feet were bare before bringing out the tea and biscuits.

They sat at the dining room table. The rosewood was buffed to a gloss, and the silver cruet set was gleaming too. Bailey reached out and touched the cut glass bottles.

'They were your grandma's favourites,' Grandpa said.

'I can see why. It always felt like you were royalty when we visited for Christmas lunch and birthdays. Having such fancy things.'

He gave a harrumph and sipped his drink.

'You miss her, don't you?'

He gave a shrug, intended, Bailey thought, to be blasé but missing its mark when his eyes misted up. She reached across and took his hand. He pulled away, which she expected, so she clung on tight until he eventually tolerated the gesture.

'I miss her too.'

There were minutes of silence, but that was to be expected because the conversation never flowed around Grandpa, and over the years, Bailey had grown used to him. She suspected that he enjoyed her company all the more because of her willingness to embrace quiet.

'You didn't go to Edith Sanders' funeral.'

Grandpa shook his head.

'And neither did mum.'

'That was her choice.'

'We all should have been there.'

He chomped into a biscuit without glancing at her.

'Grandma idolised Edith. Our family should have been there to show our respects.'

'I don't see why.' Grandpa immediately shook his head as though realising a mistake.

'Well, I'm grateful to her,' Bailey said. 'Without her, I would never have been born.'

'Yeah. That was a good thing,' he conceded.

'She couldn't save everyone,' Bailey said.

She watched his reaction, but there was none apart from a slight flaring of his nostrils. Bailey didn't want more silence. She hadn't come here to think about dead relatives but to purge her mind of Ravi and his furious outburst.

'How is Belle? And the foal?'

'I put the yearling out last week. The greedy bastard wasn't gonna wean, so I had to separate them. Belle's out in the yard.'

'Could I go for a ride?'

'Yeah, of course. I'd lunge her for a bit first. Hasn't had a saddle on her since last year.'

'Sure. I'll be careful.'

'If you want to make yourself useful, check the back paddock. There's this ewe that keeps lying down. I'm gonna butcher her if she's still on the ground today.'

'What if she's got an infection? You can't eat her if she's sick.'

'Nah. It's nothin' like that. She's old and got arthritis. She usually comes good in the warmer months, but not this time.'

'Okay. I'll check her out.' Bailey drank down the last of her tea.

Grandpa pointed to her shorts and asked, 'You got proper clothes?'

Bailey shook her head.

'Have a look in the tack room cupboard. I'm sure your mum's old jodhpurs and boots are still there. Just watch out for redbacks before you put 'em on.'

'Sure.' Bailey stood from the table. 'I'll see you before dark.'

Grandpa grunted and began picking at his toenails.

The chestnut mare flattened her ears when Bailey first approached her, but despite the horse's antsy appearance, she remained placid while saddled. Bailey led her to the driveway and lunged for a few minutes. When she was younger, the mare would have bucked and pig-rooted, but today it was hard to get her moving.

'You've turned into a lazy old sausage,' Bailey said as she gathered the reins.

She put her foot in the stirrup and hoisted herself up, holding the pommel, but waited a moment before throwing her leg over. This was the time when Belle might react, but after a few seconds, it was clear there would be no fireworks. Bailey settled into the saddle and gave slight pressure through her seat. 'Oh, come on,'

Bailey laughed when the mare failed to respond. It took a few taps of her heels before the mare began to move and a few more to trot, but once they reached the sandy firebreak on the eastern border of the property, Belle broke into an eager canter.

This is what I need, Bailey thought as they loped along. Clear air, a good horse and some time to forget about Ravi.

*

It was almost dark when Emily returned to her mother's house. There were no lights inside, so she opened the front door and called to Ravi. Hank came running from the rear of the house to greet her. He spun on the lawn a couple of times and then took off the same way he came. Emily followed him out to the back patio. One flickering candle in a lantern was the only light. It illuminated Ravi's face. His expression was maudlin. Emily felt a tug of sadness as she walked towards him.

'Ravi, why are you sitting out here? It would be best if you were inside. Perhaps watching some tv would cheer you up.

'I blew it with Bailey. She won't answer my calls. She hates me, and I don't blame her.'

'Well, you were out of line. I could see how much you disturbed her.' Emily switched on the patio light. She glanced at the takeaway pizza box. 'Eating that crap isn't going to do you any good.'

Ravi flicked up the corner of the box. The pizza was untouched.

'Oh, Ravi. How about I cook you something? What about some seafood pasta?'

'I can't stomach food just now.' He put his head in his hands. 'I'm such a loser.'

'Oh, for God's sake Ravi. If you talk like that, you *will* be a loser. So stop feeling sorry for yourself.'

'I behaved like an idiot.'

'Have you told Bailey that?' Emily asked.

'How can I if she won't speak to me?'

'Have you tried texting her?'

'Not yet,' Ravi admitted.

'Call her again, now that she's had some time to calm down,' Emily said.

Ravi levelled his gaze at his mother. She flinched at his misery and took a deep breath. Her son had been through so much, but then again, life was tough for everyone. At his age, Emily had managed to escape a destructive marriage, get a career and raise two children. Sure, she'd had the support of her mother, but Edith had lived hundreds of kilometres away. Emily got her life on track single-handed, and Ravi could too, but not by sitting around and wallowing in self-pity.

'Call her and tell her how you feel. There's no point guessing how she's feeling. Ask her, and say you're sorry while you're at it. If you've blown it, well, move on.' Emily didn't give him time to argue. 'Come on Hank. I see you haven't been fed either.' She pointed to her son. 'Get up Ravi. Put that pizza in the fridge or the bin. Your dinner will be ready in twenty minutes. I want you showered and in a better bloody mood by then!'

Emily didn't wait for a reply but didn't hear the grumbling she'd expected either. Her days of doting on her son were finished. It was no good for Ravi or her, and if that wasn't enough reason, it was certainly no good for her relationship with Jesse. And besides, it was what her mum would have expected.

'Twenty minutes Ravi, or I'll feed it to Hank!'

*

Carl strolled back from the kiosk, pausing twice to sip his takeaway coffee while Tash drummed her fingers on the ambulance steering wheel. Her stomach was rumbling, and although she had expressly requested a croissant with ham and cheese, she noticed her partner only held two takeaway cups. She looked at her watch. Four hours until their crib break and the opportunity of eating without disruption. But as Carl hauled himself into the passenger seat, Tash could smell food.

'Well?' she asked.

Carl gave a grin and, from his top pocket, delivered a brown paper bag by way of a mock handball. Tash caught the package, tore the paper apart and bit into the pastry. Then, through the flaky crumbs and steam, she mumbled, "Thank you", to which Carl laughed and produced a chocolate bar for himself.

Her stomach settling, Tash eased back in the seat while Carl scrolled through news articles on his phone.

'Wow!' he said.

'What?'

It was more than a minute before he answered. 'You should read this.' He paused to glance at her. 'The Australian Medical Association are demanding an investigation into the Criminal Ageing System due to the number of violent incidences affecting medical staff and ex-felons.'

'Like the Lavender Court men?'

Carl nodded and read from the small screen. 'There are estimated to be 21,000 men and women, who have so far been subjected to the mandated punishment in the year since its implementation, and over two hundred violent episodes have been recorded in Sydney alone. In all but two cases, it is suspected that the treatment had precipitated dementia. Doctors who have examined these patients agree that the speed of the disease's progress is causing the victims to be overwhelmed, confused and therefore volatile.'

'That's exactly like those two cases we saw.' Tash agreed. 'So, what are they doing to prevent more occurrences?'

Carl shrugged and said, 'It's being dealt with state-by-state. Victoria has put a hold on all CAS treatments. Western Australia is likely to go the same way. New South Wales has set up a task force.'

'Are they halting the treatments too?'

'No. Still waiting. South Australian government officials are collating data.'

'Great. Collate away while we get our heads kicked in.' Tash drank down the last of her coffee and was about to say more when their pagers sounded.

Tash confirmed the job with Comms and hit the accelerator pedal.

'Your turn to treat,' Carl said as he kept reading, oblivious to the siren or the fact that they had mounted the curb to bypass a traffic snarl. The only time he peered around was when Tash groaned.

'What?'

Tash pointed to the MDT screen. 'The bloody job is at Lavender Court.'

Carl grinned and said, 'You're right, it's "bloody". It's a haemorrhage case.'

She saw him glance at her from the corner of her eye, but instead of appreciating his dumb joke, she looked away. Images of their CAS patients had haunted her dreams for the past two nights. Maybe today, there would be another chilling face to envision in the dark. 'You got any coffee left?' she asked as she rounded a corner. 'I'm a bit parched.'

'Don't worry Tash. We aren't going in until SAPOL arrive.'

'You got that right.' She felt her lips tremble as she drew in a breath.

Tash turned off the siren before they reached the arched entranceway. The Lavender Court area consisted of around thirty homes and two small parks with their own playgrounds, picnic areas and toilet blocks. Today the road was surprisingly empty of cars and people.

'Number sixteen, eighteen,' Carl called out the street numbers as they drove by. He pointed to a red brick home with an open front screen door. 'That one there is number twenty, but the cops aren't here yet. Pull up further, under that tree.'

Tash parked and turned off the engine.

'Look at that,' Carl said, pointing to a laneway on the GPS screen.

'Yeah.' Tash nodded. 'There's back access around the entire court. I guess it was put in to encourage walking or bike riding.'

'I'll stroll along there and see what I can spot in the back of the property.' Carl said as he slipped a radio into his shirt pocket.

'Be careful,' Tash warned.

She watched him stride along the length of the path and then duck behind the houses. Then, only a few minutes later, he reappeared, jogging towards the ambulance. He pointed to her window, and she lowered it.

'There's a man in the rear yard of the house. There's a lot of blood, and he's clutching his upper leg. It looks like he was pruning trees. There's a small chainsaw on the ground beside him.'

'Oh, Jesus! Radio comms and find out how long until SAPOL get here.'

Tash exited the ambulance and retrieved their kits while Carl was talking.

'Any luck?' she asked.

'Ten minutes, there's been a traffic accident. Three-car pile-up at an intersection south of here.'

Tash shook her head furiously. 'Let's take a look at this bloke. He could be dead if we wait any longer.'

'Okay,' Carl agreed.

The driveway led to a two-car garage; the roller door on the right was open. Beyond the late-model sedan was a long bench covered with neatly placed tools. To the left, a doorway opened onto an expanse of lawn. The man lay facing away from them. He was unmoving but breathing.

'Hello, hello, ambulance,' Tash called as they approached.

Carl grasped her by the elbow with just two metres to go. 'No closer,' he warned.

The man gave a weak cry and rolled onto his back. His hands were red with blood, clutching his leg just below the groin.

'What happened?' Tash asked, but the man gave a pleading cry and began to sob. Tash glanced at her latex glove, where she habitually wrote patients' names. 'Terrance? Is it Terrance, or do you prefer Terry?'

The man gave a nod.

'You cut yourself, Terry? Up high on your leg?'

Another nod.

'Carl, please get me a tourniquet.' Tash looked back at the man. He was sweating and breathing heavily. She couldn't be sure what his normal complexion was, but he appeared pale. When Carl tossed her the windlass tourniquet, she took a step closer. 'Terrance! I need you to wrap this around your leg, higher up than the cut, do you understand?'

It took a moment, but he eventually nodded. Tash threw him the tourniquet and watched as he fumbled with it.

'There doesn't seem to be any fresh bleeding,' Carl observed.

In the distance, they heard a siren. Tash gave a noisy exhalation just as the man stopped moving. He stared at the sky, his mouth slack and his fingers moving weakly.

'Come on, Terrance, you need to tighten that thing.'

Tash turned to look at Carl, who shrugged. They could hear cars pulling up from the street and boots on the ground. Tash knelt by the man's feet and leaned towards the discarded tourniquet, her fingers only centimetres from it, when he sat bolt upright and grabbed her by the hair. He pulled her towards him, crushed her against his body, and then rolled on her, pinning her to the ground.

'Carl! Carl!' Tash whipped her head back and forth. She saw a fleeting image of the newly arrived police, one of whom was drawing a weapon, and a pile of clothing by the back door of the house. But another peek revealed it to be a person, unmoving, and with such a halo of blood pooled around them, likely dead. Tash opened her mouth to warn them when Terry covered her face with one massive hand. Her eyes peered at him over the meaty palm. She shook her head, willing him to let her go. Her tears punctuated her desperation, but he glared back with eyes as lifeless as stone.

'Let her go! Get away from her now!'

Tash wasn't fooled by the authority in the cop's voice, and it seemed Terry wasn't either. When she felt the blade bite her neck, she tried to pull away, but the crushing weight on top of her prevented her from moving. Tash whispered Angela's name and mouthed the word "sorry". She jumped slightly when the taser arced through their joined bodies, but by then, the knife had finished severing, and Tash's colours were fading to black. The last thing she saw was Terry's blood-spattered cheek - that and his smile.

Chapter Eleven

Ravi opened the door and stood as far back as he could. Bailey wasn't smiling today; she looked miserable and wary, which made his heart sink. He ushered her into the sunroom and pointed to the jug of iced tea with glasses beside it.

'Half black and half green tea, just how you like it,' he said.

Bailey perched on the very edge of the couch with her elbows on her knees. She appeared ready to bolt. Maybe she anticipated disappointment or, even worse, more angry words. Ravi gave a sad smile, and she looked away from him. Again, his heart bottomed out.

'Oh, Bailey, I'm so sorry. I don't know what came over me.'

'Then find out,' she snapped. 'Don't put other people at risk. You need to be diagnosed before you hurt someone.'

Ravi was shaking his head, his mind full of arguments. He wanted to vehemently deny that he could be capable of violence, but his voice was too fragile to back it up, and besides, he wasn't one hundred per cent sure.

'You do read the news, don't you?' Bailey asked. 'You heard about the ambo who was killed? The poor woman was doing her job. That man had the same therapy as you, Ravi, and it turned him crazy.'

'I know. I saw the news.' The story had stolen his sleep from him last night. He'd seen images of himself being that madman. The light of day couldn't come soon enough.

'I don't want to be the next victim of an attack because you did nothing about getting yourself well.' Her voice softened. 'I have real feelings for you, Ravi.'

Ravi's shoulders slumped, and he moved to the armchair opposite her. 'What do you want me to do?' He said once he'd cleared his throat. 'I'll do anything you ask.'

Bailey didn't reply, and the silence was unbearable. Communication between them had been a strong point of their relationship, it had to be to get him over his lack of confidence, but it seemed that was over now. He'd ruined everything. Ravi's head hung down. The gloom enveloped him, and he let his dark hair fall, hiding his welling eyes. Finally, Bailey moved in front of his chair, knelt at his feet and pushed back his hair.

'Ravi,' she said. 'You need to see someone and find out if you've been affected by that treatment. It's not like you to lose your temper like that, and I don't want to be afraid of you.'

'I know.' Ravi's hands gripped the sides of his chair, and although she was only inches away, he made no move towards her. 'I think we should distance ourselves – until I know the outcome.'

'That's probably the safest thing,' Bailey agreed.

'Jesse came to see me this morning,' Ravi said. 'The health department has set up special clinics for CAS recipients. The closest one is at the Whyalla Hospital. So

Jesse's going to take me there tomorrow.' Ravi sniffed. 'I have an appointment at eleven. I must have a brain scan and other tests too.'

'Then we'll know.'

'Then we'll know,' he agreed.

But she didn't move away or take her eyes off him. His skin felt prickly, and his brow was covered in icy sweat. Her stare was intense, and his heart reacted by beating faster. He felt panicky because he didn't know if it was due to having her so close or the return of his rage.

'Please, Bailey, you're making this really hard for me.'

'Am I?' She gave her mischievous grin and touched his knee.

'Oh, don't. Please, Bailey, this isn't a good idea. What if – what if I lose it? What if I hurt you?'

'Are you going to hurt me, Ravi?'

'No. Of course, I don't want to, but what if I'm not in control?'

Her hand moved up his leg, and he gasped, clutching her fingers. 'Please don't,' he begged.

Her stare was blatantly wanton, silencing his protests.

Ravi drew her hand to his mouth and kissed the back of it. With her other hand Bailey caressed his face and pulled him closer. When he began to speak, she covered his mouth with her own. He groaned and wrapped his arms around her, breaking the kiss for a moment to ask, 'Are you sure about this? I'm scared I'll lose control.'

Bailey broke the embrace and stood. Wordlessly she led him to the bedroom, kicked off her shoes and dropped her shorts. Any thoughts Ravi had of self-control vanished as he watched her. He yanked off his shirt and fell on the bed beside her, squeezing his body against hers. Their kissing grew furious, teeth clashing, and lips crushed in the frenzy. They were both caught in the madness of their needs, seeking out each other's bodies.

Outside in the yard, Hank was barking at birds. The sound brought Bailey back from the brink. Ravi lifted his mouth from her breast and stared back at her.

'You can lose it a bit Ravi, but in a good way,' she said as she straddled him.

He felt the heat of her body on top of him, and it overcame his senses. Soon his desire was all that mattered. Her desperation spurred him on until there was nothing else in the world.

Then Ravi lost it, but this time, in a good way.

*

Molly had been contemplating this meeting with Jesse Plackis on the long drive from Port Lincoln. It was a sensitive situation because now they had to consider that Ravi Sanders may have suffered a psychotic breakdown and murdered his grandmother. It seemed unlikely, or at least it had, but now, with the growing number of reports in the media of violent attacks from offenders subjected to the CAS treatment, it made Ravi's involvement an actual probability.

So given the relationship between Jesse and Emily, Molly would have to rely on her diplomatic skills to broach the subject. This was also the reason she had left Ben in Port Lincoln today. She didn't need his bull-at-a-gate approach derailing her interview. And, of course, she didn't need the distraction of her lover being in proximity. God knew her job had become ten times harder when he was around. There was a chemistry between them that controlled her body and clouded her judgement. It was almost easier when he acted like a jerk, because now, with his caring façade, she couldn't free her thoughts of him.

Molly liked Jesse, another good reason not to have Ben in the same room. The rivalry between the two was obvious enough without the unwanted sexual tension adding more drama to their interactions. She had never wanted her professional life to become so complicated, and she cursed her lack of self-control.

Molly jumped when the station's back door slammed but smiled when Jesse appeared at the doorway. Forcing herself to appear calm, she said, 'Hi Jesse. Come on in.'

His expression was stony. One look told her that this was not going to be easy. However, he was a clever bloke and had probably guessed why she requested this meeting. Molly rose from her chair and walked to the bench, switching on the kettle.

'I can't stay long,' Jesse said. 'I've got to take Ravi Sanders to the Whyalla Hospital by eleven. So why did you want to see me?'

While the hum of boiling water drew to its climax, Molly chose her words, but she waited until she had poured their coffee before speaking. She placed the cup in front of him and sat in the chair beside his desk.

'I know you've read the reports sent by SAPOL on the Criminal Ageing System recipients,' she said. 'And I guess after they check him over today, we will have some answers, but you know Ravi Sanders far better than I do, so I need to know if he has displayed any signs of violence so far. Do you think he's been affected by the treatment?'

'You want to know if I think he murdered his grandmother?' Jesse glared at her.

'Yes.' Molly stared back at him and gave a slight shrug of her shoulders. 'Yes, that's exactly what I'm asking, and I know you don't like it, which is fair enough, but I still have to ask the question.'

Jesse dropped his gaze. 'I know you do.' He paused and sipped from his cup. 'I have had to ask myself the same question, and while I haven't asked Emily outright – she knows what's been happening. She has assured me that Ravi has been behaving as he normally would. So no, I don't believe that Ravi killed Edith Sanders.' He steepled his hands in front of him while he chewed the inside of his lip. 'And it wasn't possible for Ravi to pull up at the house, fire all those shots, dump the car and rifle somewhere so well hidden that we couldn't find them, and return to his grandma's in the fifteen minutes it took me to arrive there that day.' Jesse slowly shook his head. 'To be honest, Molly, the guy is a bit of mum's boy. I reckon he'd cry if he found a dead bird. He just couldn't have – you know, killed her.'

'Sure.' Molly made a few notes and then put down the pen. 'I don't think he did either. From what I've read about the violent outbursts in the CAS files, these people haven't been able to turn off their rages. It's like permanent insanity has kicked in. If Ravi had gone mad…'

'He'd still be mad,' Jesse finished for her.

'So it seems. All the same, I was hoping you could keep a really close eye on him. SAPOL had word this morning that the government are fast-tracking reversal therapy for some ex-felons, and the CAS has been halted in South Australia pending an enquiry.'

'So, it's back to prison for the criminals,' Jesse said.

'For now.'

'And Ravi?'

'His case is up for reassessment, but things are a little crazy right now. So we must be patient.'

'What do you think of the CAS?'

Molly shrugged and took a sip of coffee. 'They implemented it too early. I mean, that's obvious now. I guess the government were more concerned with cutting costs, but this should have been trialled over decades, not a couple of years.'

'Yeah, I thought it was too soon.'

'Anyway,' Molly stretched back in the chair. 'Where are we with the large calibre projectiles found at the rifle range?'

'Well, we know whoever shot Edith was using the rifle range because the projectiles were a match, but apart from the club logbook, there is no way of telling who fired them. I guess if you're sighting in a gun you plan to murder someone with, you wouldn't do something so stupid as put your name down in an attendance book, and there are no security cameras at the range.'

'Really? Is that normal procedure for a gun club?' Molly asked.

'If no firearms are kept on the property, then there is no need. They might have a few targets stolen, but there isn't much there to steal or vandalise.'

'Have you spoken to anyone living near the range?'

'There are some farmhouses nearby, although nearby is a few kilometres. None of the farmers recall seeing or hearing anything odd outside the normal practice days. But on windy days,' Jesse shrugged. 'They probably wouldn't hear anything from that distance.'

Molly let out a noisier sigh than she intended. 'Any news from the Firearms Taskforce?'

'Apart from the SKS found after the biker shootout in Sydney, reports of that type of gun these days are rare, and only three were ever registered in South Australia. Two of those were handed in during the amnesty, and the third was last listed to a bloke in Ceduna who has passed away.'

'And the rifle?' Molly asked.

'According to his son, the old man's gun safe was empty when they cleared his house.'

'How long ago did he die?'

'Just after the 1996 gun buyback began.'

Molly groaned. 'After so many years, there's probably no chance of tracking that one down.'

'As I said, those were the only registered SKSs,' Jesse rubbed his chin.

'So?' Molly felt her face drop in anticipation of bad news.

'So, prior to the 1996 gun reforms, you could mail order an SKK, which is similar but not quite the same, from Queensland.'

'Oh, my God! So, there are potentially hundreds out there.'

'Possibly the SKK, but not the SKS.'

Molly thought that scenario sounded like a nightmare either way.

'Listen, I know the Senior Sergeant in Ceduna, Roger Parsons; he was an old mate of my dad's. What if I take a drive up and speak to him tomorrow. He knows most of the old families in the area going back to the eighties. He may have known the old bloke and his son too.' Jesse shrugged. 'You never know.'

'We have nothing to lose,' Molly muttered.

'Because we've got nothing else.'

'Dead right.'

Jesse appeared as glum as she felt, but Molly gave her best attempt at a smile.

'Sounds like a plan, Jesse. I'll stay in Henderson until you get back tomorrow. Oh, and let me know how Ravi gets on.'

'He won't have any test results straight away, but if there's any news I'll call.'

While Jesse packed a duffle bag, Molly looked around the station.

In the old lock-up, there was a camp bed and sleeping bag. So, Molly decided she would sleep here tonight and, if it was comfortable enough, the night after too.

It may have been her imagination or perhaps her guilty conscience, but the receptionist at the Henderson Motel seemed to give her a knowing look the last time she and Ben had stayed there. She was not in the mood to be the subject of innuendo. Too bad if the lady had guessed correctly.

At least, she thought, I don't have to lie to Ferdi tonight.

*

Roger Parsons was only two months away from retirement, so it didn't surprise Jesse that the man opted to eat at the pub rather than dining on a stale sandwich in the Ceduna police station lunchroom. What did surprise Jesse, however, was that Roger bought them both a beer.

'Hey, I have to drive,' Jesse said as he eyed off the pint glass.

Roger shrugged. 'Just have one then. You'll be fine by the time you leave.' He held his glass near Jesse's and said, "Cheers."

After ten minutes of catch-up banter, Roger reached for some paper files in his attaché case. 'I tracked down Lyall Cox; he's the son of Albert Cox, who owned the rifle you were asking about. The SKS.'

'Great stuff,' Jesse said. He didn't want to get his hopes up, but he felt that something had to give in this case.

'Lyall is one of the local chemists here. Nice bloke.'

'Did he know where the gun might have ended up?'

'Well, his dad had quite a few handguns and rifles. Lyall thinks Albert might have given them to the other members of his local gun club following his cancer diagnosis. It was a brain tumour, and apparently, he had to be rid of them once his eyesight was affected.'

'All? How many did he have?'

'According to Lyall, five handguns and maybe four rifles. All of them were registered back in the day.'

'But the SKS was a semi-automatic, so it had to be handed into the police, didn't it?'

'You would think so, but there is no record.'

'So, you think he gave it away? Who were the other club members?'

Roger stretched back in his chair and took a long drink of beer. 'There aren't any club records that go back that far. I have a list of people who had gun licenses in this area then, but you must remember that laws were pretty lax. I'm sure many people who weren't licensed used the club anyway.'

The bar attendant placed their T-bone steaks and salads on the table. Jesse didn't realise how ravenous he was until he took a bite. Their conversation was put on hold while they devoured their meals.

'Top food,' Jesse said as he wiped the grease from his lips.

'Yeah, they do a mean porterhouse too.' Roger delicately wiped each finger clean before rummaging through his briefcase once more. 'Lyall dropped this off at the station. He thought it might be helpful.' Roger placed the photo album on the table between them. 'These are old pictures of winners from shooting competitions held at the gun club.'

'Okay.' Jesse felt a frisson of tension mixed with excitement. He swallowed down the last of his beer.

Roger opened the book to the last page. 'This is the final year that Albert attended the club meetings, and these are the members, so any of these fellas could have inherited the rifle.' He poked a chubby finger individually at five men and two women. 'You can count these out because they've since passed away.'

'Do we have names for any of these people?'

'Some names have been jotted on the back, and Lyall was able to put a few names to faces too.'

'Okay, I guess that's helpful.' Again, Jesse felt an anxious quiver.

'What are you going to do next?' Roger asked.

Jesse thumbed through the album. 'I suppose I'll check to see if any of these people are still active gun club members and find out where they live.'

'You really don't have much evidence for this murder, do you?'

'Not yet, no.'

'The shooter's probably long gone by now.'

Jesse put his elbows on the table and rested his head in his hands. The excitement was gone; he now felt drained. 'Yup.'

'Are you sure the victim was the target?'

'No. I'm not sure about anything in this case.'

'Well, whether the target was the grandson or the grandmother, you should be looking at family. Most domestic assaults are perpetrated by a spouse, after that, family or someone known to the victim.'

'Well, I'm certain it wasn't Ravi's mum.' Jesse gave a humourless chuckle.

'His siblings? His father?'

'There's a sister, but she was in Fiji at the time. And the father is pretty sick.'

'You've seen him?'

Jesse frowned. 'No.' He'd taken Emily's word for it, which wasn't good policing. 'But I will.'

Roger drank down the last of his beer. 'Well, you better not have another drink; you've got to drive,' he said as he pointed to his glass. 'But I bloody well am!'

Jesse glanced at his watch. There was no way he was driving to Adelaide from here because the trip was eight hundred kilometres, just one way. From Henderson, it was around six hundred one way and probably a wild goose chase, but that niggling thought couldn't be ignored. Ravi's father may have had no reason to harm his son, but his mother-in-law, that might be another story.

'Well, Roger, it's been constructive, but I've got a long day tomorrow, so I'd better go.' Jesse picked up the photo album. 'Thanks a lot for this.'

'Let me know how you get on.' Roger smiled as the bar attendant placed a fresh beer before him. 'By the way, who have you got working with you from Major Crimes?'

'Molly Hunter and Ben Richards from Port Lincoln.'

'Ah, Molly. She's a nice girl, smart too. But that Richards bloke, he's an utter wanker.'

Jesse patted the older cop on the back and laughed, 'You got that right, mate.'

Chapter Twelve

When Jesse returned to Henderson and told Molly of his intention to drive to Adelaide the following day to speak to Ravi's father, she recommended he phone the care home first. And it turned out Molly was right. The nurse Jesse spoke with said a visit would not be possible as Randy Singh was extremely ill and had been admitted to hospital. Jesse was guilty of feeling some disappointment when he heard how frail the man was. Ravi had been right. If the man was so weak, he could not have killed Edith.

'This sickness could have caused a swift deterioration,' Molly had said as if reading his mind. 'He may have been much stronger at the start of December.'

Jesse shook his head with frustration, teeth grinding. 'I was so sure we were on to something this time.'

'I know. Listen Jesse, you have time off booked. Were you really going to work through it?'

'I had to Molly. What if we'd missed something so glaringly obvious?

'I get it, Jesse, I do, but Randy Singh isn't going anywhere, and you need a break.' Although Molly hovered near the kettle, it wasn't milk she took from the fridge; it was two beers. She handed him one. 'Cheers, Jesse, here's to your two-day break. Do you have some plans?'

'Yeah, it's Emily's birthday tomorrow.'

'Oh?'

Jesse chuckled and then looked her right in the eye. 'Apparently, everyone knows we're a couple, so don't pretend you didn't know.'

Molly held up her hands. 'I wasn't going to mention it if you didn't. But I admire your choice. She seems like a keeper.'

'Yeah.' Jesse took a long drink.

'Of course, it could be seen as a conflict of interest,' Molly pointed out.

'I know. That's why she has been staying down in Adelaide so much, plus it's hard for her to return to Edith's. She and her mum were really close.'

'It might be best to keep her at arm's length. Deny the relationship until this is all over.'

'You're not going to report it?'

'Report what?' Molly took a slug of beer.

Jesse grinned for a second. 'Okay.'

'Now, go on, off you go. Have a fantastic break. If there are any important updates, I'll message you.'

'Thanks, Molly.' Jesse aimed his empty bottle at the wastepaper basket over two metres away. It fell straight in, and he punched the air. 'Bye.'

'Boys!' He heard Molly mutter.

Emily arrived from Adelaide that night, just before midnight. She and Jesse talked for almost an hour before going to bed. Jesse didn't enjoy keeping things from her, especially when she was so open with him. But he didn't mention her ex-husband, his illness, or that Randy was a possible suspect. Jesse didn't want to ruin their time together.

The following morning, while they lay on the bed, Jesse brushed a curl of hair from her cheek. He kissed her soft skin as she dozed. Emily moaned, the corners of her lips twitching into a smile for only a second before sleep's sombre mask settled again. He pulled on his jeans and t-shirt and tip-toed from the room.

He blended a chunk of pineapple, banana and coconut milk into a smoothie in the kitchen. If it had been a working day, then only coffee would have hit the spot, but today was a holiday, a time to chill out. He was watering his two houseplants, which he often neglected, when he felt Emily's arms around his waist. He turned and kissed her for a long moment.

'You're up early,' he said, looking at his watch. 'I was going to let you keep sleeping.'

'I heard you out here.' She shrugged. 'And I'm awake now. So what's the plan for today?'

'I'm yours for two days.' Jesse grinned, but Emily was looking out the window, so he nudged her. 'I'm all yours, to do with as you please.' The innuendo was far from subtle.

She returned his smile and said, 'Maybe later, but first up, where are you taking me to lunch?'

'Where would you like to go? We have all day. We could drive to Port Lincoln and try that new seafood restaurant we read about.'

'Sure. That sounds great.'

But Jesse saw her frown.

'What?' he asked.

'I know that Ravi has been trying to keep me at a distance - and you too, because of the case…'

'For your own safety,' Jesse butted in.

'Yes, but what if we invite him to lunch too. He needs a break as much as I do.'

Jesse felt hot irritation wash over him, but he forced a smile. 'Really? I thought today would be about you and me, you know, a bit of romance.' He turned from her and mopped up the water spill from around his ferns.

Emily sighed. 'You're right. I'm sorry I wasn't thinking along those lines. Today should be about you and me.'

Her sweetness caused a pang of guilt. He put his arms around her and pulled her close. 'No honey, I'm sorry. Today's your day,' he said, 'we can do whatever you like. If you want Ravi to come too, then send him a text. Just make sure he's ready by about ten-thirty because it's a long drive.'

'No. Jesse, you're right. Let's have a romantic day. Just the two of us.'

He grinned again as an idea came to him. 'Why just the day? We could stay the night. Maybe get a room in that hotel by the marina. One with a big bed.'

'That sounds perfect. I'll pack my things,' she said with genuine enthusiasm.

When Emily appeared holding a small suitcase and duffle bag less than ten minutes later, Jesse was proofreading the file he'd written for Molly based on Roger Parsons's information. The photo album was opened to the group photograph of the gun club members, placed by his elbow.

'What's that?' Emily asked as she stepped closer.

'Historical pictures of past Ceduna gun club members.' He said without looking up from the computer screen.

'May I look?'

'Sure.'

'Do you have names for these people?'

Jesse nodded as he continued checking the document for errors. 'There are some names on the back, first names mostly, so I'm not sure how helpful it is.'

Emily picked up the group photo and turned it over. 'Ah, I thought so.' She put the picture on the table and tapped at it with her index finger. 'That's Donna Donovan's mother, Gwen Winters.'

'What?' Jesse took a closer look. 'Are you sure?'

'Well, yeah. I used to see her at school all the time when I was a kid. Donna used to talk about how her mum was a great shooter. Judging by the trophy she's holding, it was true.

'What about her husband, Maury? Is he in that photo?'

'Mo?' Emily squinted, looking hard. 'No. I can't see him in this one, but maybe he took it. I'm pretty sure they went to competitions together back in the day.'

'So, Maury Winters knew Albert Cox.' Jesse said more to himself than to Emily.

'Who is Albert Cox?'

'He was one of three registered gun owners of the same type of rifle we've been looking for.'

'The gun that killed my mother,' Emily whispered.

Jesse stood so quickly that his chair rocked and threatened to fall. He reached out and embraced Emily. 'Hey, I'm so sorry.' He looked into her misting eyes. 'I wasn't thinking. That was stupid of me. Listen, I'll pack up this stuff. I need to send Molly this email, and then we'll go.' He put a hand on the photo album. 'I must drop this to Molly at the station, but I'll be in and out.'

'It's okay, Jesse. You're just doing your job, and I'm glad you are doing this work because I know you care, and I know you'll find whoever did it.'

'No, Em, it really was thoughtless of me. You are doing such a brilliant job of staying upbeat despite everything, and I go and ruin it.' He kissed her quickly and said, 'It will do us both good to have a break from here. I promise we'll have fun.'

Emily smiled, but Jesse could see it was forced.

'Thank you, Jesse. It's hard being in Henderson just now. If it weren't for you and Ravi…'

'I know.' He held up two fingers. 'This many minutes,' he promised.

Jesse waited until she took her bags to the car before sending Molly the information about the Ceduna gun club link. Once done, he headed for the bedroom to collect his things. He berated himself for being so stupid and insensitive. He thanked the heavens that Emily was made of stronger stuff than her son.

*

Ravi was fetching his car keys and training manual from his depot locker when his phone sounded with a text message. His morning had been spent carrying out electrical fire drills, and he intended to go home and study for the remainder of the day. He read the message and smiled. Jesse Plackis would spoil his mum for her birthday by taking her away for the night. She certainly deserved a bit of pampering, and Ravi felt she was safer being far from him.

More than one month had passed since the shooting, and with each day, Ravi's confidence returned. Since hearing the news that his brain scans and other tests were clear, Ravi's spirits were buoyed. But in the back of his mind was always the thought that his grandma's killer could be biding their time, perhaps waiting to catch Ravi off guard and would then try again. Regardless, the passing weeks had begun to soothe his worries.

He sent a reply text, telling his mum he had a present for her, but it could wait until she returned. It was about time his mother started living again. His father's decline had been rapid and hopeless, but Emily had been supportive through the worst of the man's behaviour. But, at some point over the years, her love for him had finally waned, and with it, some of her misery too. The cop may not have been Ravi's partner of choice for her, but he would never tell his mum that.

Once back at the house, Ravi and Hank sat on the sunroom couch. Ravi studying, Hank snoring. The hours passed, and Ravi's gurgling stomach prompted him to take a break. But the doorbell rang just as he cut his ham and cheese sandwich in half.

Without waiting, Bailey burst through the door, pausing to lean against the wall and rubbing her right foot. She spilled cola from the can she was holding all over the floor, and her ill-timed entrance caused Hank to begin barking.

Ravi clutched the side of the bench as anger shot through his body. The sensation heated him, consumed him. Ravi saw his reflection in the stainless steel kettle; he looked like a madman. He had to get away from her.

'Hi Ravi, sorry to burst in, but I broke my sandal getting out of the car, and the path was red hot. Hey, where are you going?'

'Um, just to the bathroom.' Under his breath he silently cursed her and her stupid footwear.

Ravi closed and latched the door behind him. He could hear her speaking but couldn't make out the words over the cyclonic noise erupting in his throbbing head. He took deep breaths and walked to the hand basin, splashing cold water on his face and rubbing it vigorously with the hand towel.

'Keep calm, keep calm,' he muttered to his red-faced image above the sink. 'There's nothing wrong.' But did the doctors really know? 'This is not normal,' he hissed.

Fumbling, he searched the cabinet until he found the vial of tablets prescribed for his anxiety. He took two pills and swallowed them down with tap water. After a few minutes, his heart stopped galloping, and his palms went from wet to clammy. He stripped off his damp shirt and gave his armpits a squirt of deodorant. When he opened the door, Bailey was standing on the other side. Her face tight with concern.

'Is everything alright?' she asked. Her eyes were fearful.

He gave a smile that felt fake, and it seemed she wasn't buying it. She shook her head and asked, 'What is it, Ravi? You look dreadful.'

Ravi slumped back against the wall. 'It happened again. Just now, when you came in. I was so livid. It flooded over me, and I had no control. This feeling gets into my head – I can't describe it. It's like a burst of adrenaline, then this deafening noise, then pain, but - ' He held out his hand to her. 'I'm worried about what I could do in that state.'

'Oh, Ravi!' She pushed his hand away and hugged him tightly. 'Let's go and see the doctor right now. Maybe it's your blood pressure or low sugar.'

'I just had a whole bunch of scans and tests. They didn't find anything wrong with me. They said I'm suffering from anxiety, but that was all.'

'That may be how your angst manifests, perhaps stress sets it off.' Bailey didn't look convinced as she said it. 'Have you been taking your medication?'

'Yeah, just then. And I feel a bit better now, but – it was scary.'

She touched his cheek. 'Everything will be okay.'

Ravi swallowed hard as he followed her to the sunroom. He wasn't so sure. Worst of all, he was beginning to think he'd been angry enough to kill something or someone.

*

Ben arrived from Port Lincoln just before eight thirty that morning. Luckily he had walked down to the local service station to get coffee when Jesse Plackis came to see Molly. She was pleased her partner wasn't present because the hostility between the two men tested her patience. And it was no longer only Jesse that Ben seemed to resent; apparently, any human with testicles who glanced at Molly was seen to have unscrupulous intentions.

While she had enjoyed the softer, caring side of Ben's personality, this new jealous streak was growing more intense by the day. Each morning he would demand to know if she and Ferdi had slept together. Two days ago, it had been on the tip of her tongue to tell him that what she and her husband did was none of his business. And Ben had become intensely needy, light years away from his detached self of only a week or so ago. Molly wondered if this was her karma for cheating. If it was, then it was a fitting but severe punishment.

Mercifully, Jesse's visit was short; he seemed in a rush to leave, making for the door while Molly was still asking vital questions.

'It's all in the email. Just call if you need to know anything else,' he said as he exited the station.

She was pleased to avoid the clashing of horns, but not at the cost of sloppy information gathering. When Ben returned, she was reading through Jesse's notes.

'I just saw Plackis driving away. What did he want?' Ben asked.

Molly ignored his question and asked, 'I need to speak to Maury Winters. Do you mind setting up that interview with Ravi Sander's dad?'

'Why didn't Plackis do that himself?' Ben spat.

'The care home wouldn't allow him. Apparently, the man was unwell; he had liver issues and had to be hospitalised. The last we heard; he was being discharged back to the home sometime today. I need you there tomorrow.'

'Well, they better not dick us around.'

'You, Ben, they better not dick you around, not us. I can't afford for both of us to be gone away on a twelve-hour round trip. So, while you're at it, book yourself a hotel room so you can stay overnight.'

Molly kept her head down, studying the photograph album that Jesse had dropped off and waiting for Ben's protestations. She didn't have long to wait.

Ben stood behind her chair with his arms around her shoulders, his hot breath in her ear.

'Oh, come on, Molly. We could have an awesome time in the motel tonight and then go together to the city tomorrow.' He licked her earlobe. 'We could go out on the town.'

'No, I'm staying at the station while Jesse's away. The Inspector insisted on a video link for this interview with Randy Singh, but I told him the man is too unwell and unlikely to speak unless it's face to face.' Molly moved sideways in her chair, putting distance between them. 'Of course, if you don't, I'm sure Jesse will do it once he's back.'

'Of course, he will. He's so fucking perfect!'

Ben's disdain annoyed her, but was it directed at Jesse or *her*?

'You don't have to worry, Molly. I'll do it,' he said as he walked away.

Molly heard the squeak of his office chair as he sat and the terse conversation as he booked an interview time with the care home, but the rest of the morning consisted of stony silence.

By eleven o'clock, she was happy to leave the hostility behind.

*

Jesse had warned Molly that Maury Winters could be a prickly fellow, so she was prepared for the worst. She followed the directions on her GPS and reached the entrance gate of the sheep farm. The old sign identifying the property was battered and rusting. As she drove closer, she noticed that the farmhouse needed a coat of paint too, but beyond it, the golden paddocks rolled to the horizon, dotted with cream-coloured sheep; it looked like a scene from a postcard. A large dam lined with swaying gums was set in the middle of the small valley below. When she exited her car, a horse in a nearby yard neighed to her, ears pricked as it stomped at the ground. Molly smiled at the welcome.

But the face of the older man who appeared on the porch looked less than friendly.

'Good morning,' Molly said as she walked towards him.

'You can get off my property right now. Whatever you're selling, I'm not interested.' Maury tilted his chin and flicked his hand toward the gate. 'Go.'

Molly flashed her police ID badge and smiled. 'I'm not selling anything. I want to speak to you, Mister Winters. This is police business. May I please come in?'

The man didn't move immediately; he seemed to be considering his options, but finally, he relented. 'Follow me,' he growled.

There was no offer of coffee or a seat, but Molly sat anyway. The kitchen table was laden with cuts of fresh lamb meat.

'You do your own butchering?' she asked.

'Yeah, what of it? I don't sell it. It's for my own use.'

'It was just an observation, Mister Winters. I don't work for the Health Department.'

Molly placed the photo album open in front of him. Something about the pictures clearly drew his interest. He sat, staring at the book and flipping through the pages.

'Where did you get this?' he asked.

'Did you know Albert Cox?' Molly asked.

Maury's face blanched.

'Did you?' she repeated.

'Never heard of him.'

Molly reached over and found the photograph with Gwen Winters in it. 'You know this lady, don't you?'

'Well, yeah. Of course, it's Gwen, my wife. What's this all about?'

'I was wondering when you were going to ask that.' Molly gave a bland smile. 'It's usually the first thing most people want to know.'

'What's that supposed to mean?'

Molly shrugged. 'Hopefully, nothing. But it could mean you were expecting a visit from the police.'

'I already came into the station when Plackis asked me to.'

'Yes. He told me. Did you know that Albert Cox once owned the same type of rifle that killed Edith Sanders?'

'So what? I don't know who Albert Cox is.'

Molly pointed to the photo. 'He would be this man standing just to the left of your wife.'

'She went to lots of shooting competitions. She was damn good. But we didn't know every person that attended them.'

'And you went too?'

'Yeah, nearly all of them.'

'But not this one?'

'Oh God. I don't recall. That was taken bloody years ago. My memory's not that sharp anymore.'

Molly observed Maury's body language. He was a hard one to read. The scowl never slipped, and everything about him said defiance. But, if he was lying, it was undoubtedly masked with boldness.

'Albert Cox gave up shooting when he became sick,' Molly continued. 'According to his son Lyall, Albert either gave away or sold his guns around the time of the government buyback scheme in 1996 or seven. Does that sound familiar? Do you know anyone who acquired an SKS rifle back then?'

Without hesitation, Maury shook his head. 'No way. Those rifles were semi-automatic. No one around here uses a rifle like that to dispatch foxes or feral dogs. We're marksmen, not bloody mutilators.'

Molly raised her left eyebrow as she recalled the state of Edith Sanders' body. 'Interesting choice of words.' But before he could respond, she asked, 'So, if someone around here had an SKS, do you think you'd know about it?'

'Maybe. I'm pretty sure. Most gun owners like to talk about guns with like-minded people.'

'So, would you ask around your club for me?' Molly asked.

Maury gave a careless shrug and said, 'I suppose I could.'

Molly picked up the photo album and slid it into her briefcase. 'Well, I guess I can't ask for much more. Thanks for your time, Mister Winters.'

Maury's indifference didn't err, but as Molly turned the car towards the gate, she saw him in the rear-view mirror. He looked relieved and happy, and his smile was disturbing.

Chapter Thirteen

Ben was within two hundred kilometres of Adelaide when he got a call from the care home. Raymond Settler's voice was tremulous as he explained that the visit Ben had planned with Randy Singh had to be cancelled. Ben stared out the car window in disbelief. The monotonous landscape of stubbly paddocks flew by as the man offered his pathetic excuses.

Ben's disbelief turned to rage. 'You can't cancel me! I'm a police officer; I won't be cancelled.' There was no way he had travelled all these tedious hours just to be fobbed off by some bloke because it was inconvenient. 'I'll be there in just over two hours, and I *will* be seeing him.'

'I'm sorry, sir, but you don't seem to understand me. Unfortunately, there is no one to see. Mister Singh has passed away. He died at some time during the night. I'm so sorry you have made a wasted trip. My assistant tried calling you some time ago.'

Ben clutched the steering wheel. He had ignored his phone when it rang back on the Eyre Peninsula because he'd assumed it was Molly and was determined to give her the cold shoulder. Now it was almost midday, and he'd been driving since dawn. He was tired and hungry, a bad combination for his tolerance levels. 'Look, mate, I am coming there regardless. Even if it is just to see a corpse.' He hung up before the man could reply. 'Shit, shit, shit!' he cursed as he bashed the top of the dashboard.

It was almost one pm when Ben finally arrived at "Raymond's Shelter." By then, his disposition was moody, with a high chance of volatility. There was an unmarked police car parked by the front entrance and a funeral home van sporting a discreet logo.

Raymond met Ben at the door in a flurry of apologies and excuses.

'Where's the body?' Ben demanded to know.

'Come this way.' There was no argument from Raymond.

The corridor was blocked by a gurney and body bag. Two bored-looking, plain-clothed cops stood on either side of the doorway as Ben shoved past. An older man in a grey suit was filling out paperwork while another man, wearing the same attire, was attaching a bar-coded tag around the dead man's ankle. The deceased was tall with gangly limbs and tawny-grey skin. There was a strong resemblance to Ravi Sanders.

'What happened?' Ben asked. 'How did he die?'

'And you are?' The older man asked.

'Sergeant Ben Richards, Major Crimes, Port Lincoln,' Ben growled. 'How did he die?'

The man glanced from Ben to a plain-clothed police officer who was now pushing his way into the room.

'Senior Sergeant Jared Creighton,' the cop said as he displayed his ID. 'There was a doctor here earlier. There will be a post-mortem to ascertain the cause of death.'

'Why?' Ben blinked. 'I mean, I thought he was sick, like dying from a lifetime of booze and bad living?'

'The doctor had reason to suspect asphyxiation.'

'Wow! Really?' Ben's irritation was replaced with interest.

The cop read from the medical notes in his hand. 'The doctor noticed petechial haemorrhaging on the man's face, chest and eyes, not a normal sign given the man's co-morbidities. He says these can be common signs of straining from coughing or vomiting, but the deceased had none of those issues before death. Also there was cyanosis to the lips and fingertips.' Creighton shrugged. 'I don't know anything about medicine, and it could be nothing, but it sounds like the doctor wanted to cover his butt.'

'Who was the last person to see Randy Singh alive?' Ben asked.

Creighton stood taller and held the paperwork against his chest. 'This matter is already being investigated here in Adelaide. We don't require assistance from a Major Crimes officer assigned to cases on the Eyre Peninsula, but if you would like us to share information such as the post-mortem summary, I'm sure you know how to correctly request it, assuming it has some relevance.'

'Of course, it has relevance. I haven't driven all the way here just to peek at a dead body!'

'Calm down, sir,' Creighton said with a slight grin.

Ben clenched his teeth, his voice hissing through them. 'This bloke was the son-in-law of a murdered woman whose case I am investigating. He may have had something to do with her death or had information about it. That's what I came here to find out. So, if you can shed any light on what happened here, I would be extremely grateful.' Ben's face was neither reasonable nor appreciative. It took all his will not to shout.

There was an awkward silence in the room for almost a minute. Eventually, Creighton said, 'According to Mister Settler, the deceased was informed that he had an inoperable liver tumour during a recent hospital stay. His condition was considered terminal, with a maximum life expectancy of only a few months. According to the visitor's book, the deceased's friend, Brian Matheson, came to visit him last night. Matheson was the last person to see Mister Singh alive, so Matheson has been taken to the Adelaide station to help with our inquiries.'

'I see. Someone put a dying man out of his misery,' Ben said. He gave a deflated sigh.

'We can't say definitively.'

'No. Of course not.' Ben walked over to the deceased man, who looked much like his son and stared for a minute or two. 'Well, I'll leave you to it. Thank you for the information.'

He strode to the door and was gone before anyone bothered to acknowledge his departure.

*

Jesse and Emily were strolling along the beachside path after their evening meal. A light breeze had sprung up, bringing sea scent and chilly tingles to Emily's skin. She gave a slight shiver as Jesse put an arm around her shoulders. They stopped and kissed for a moment before walking on.

'Are you okay?' Jesse asked.

'Sure,' she replied.

She didn't want to talk about the feeling of foreboding that had darkened her mood over the past day. It was probably her concern for Ravi, which she didn't want to mention. She knew Jesse already thought her son was a milksop, and besides, she had to let Ravi deal with his own challenges. But as much as Emily tried to shrug off the ominous frame of mind, the leaden sensation in her stomach remained menacing. On the surface, she tried to appear light-hearted, knowing how much Jesse wanted her to enjoy their time together. He had been so thoughtful to organise this break for them, but it was hard to shrug off this gloom.

'How does a nightcap before bed sound?' Jesse asked.

Emily gazed out to the lights of a distant trawler. It was the only thing visible in the blackness. 'That would be wonderful.'

As they were returning to the hotel when Jesse's phone sounded. He mumbled something, turning away to glance at the screen. Emily felt his stare, but she gave a shrug and said, 'You need to answer it if it's work. I understand, Jesse.'

'It's Ben,' he said dismissively. 'He can call back if it's important.' Jesse pocketed the mobile, but only seconds later, it rang again.

'Take it,' Emily encouraged. She touched his arm and nodded despite the feeling of dread.

She walked ahead, savouring the thought of sleep, when something in Jesse's tone changed. His voice dropped, and when she turned to face him, his eyes were wide, head slowly shaking. Something was wrong. This thought was reinforced when Jesse's hand went to his brow, and he stood side-on to her.

Is he covering his face? Hiding his reaction to something?

Jesse said "yeah" several times before hanging up and then appeared unable to immediately look in her direction.

He's planning his words, breaking bad news. Somehow, she was positive. Was it Ravi? Her gut pitched again. She stopped dead with her hands on her hips and shouted, 'Out with it Jesse. Just tell me.'

Jesse took a step towards her, head bowed but nodding. 'It's your ex-husband. I'm afraid he's passed away.'

'Oh,' she whispered, suddenly unsure how to react and wondering if she should correct Jesse, as she and Randy were still technically married. 'How – how did he die?' The mellow timbre of her voice sounded alien, emotionless. Her calmness surprised her.

'That's not certain yet, but he died in the care home, so I'm sure we'll get the details soon.'

'Of course. I knew Randy wasn't well.' Suddenly the pleasant sea breeze smelled sickly, and the chill in the air made her shudder uncontrollably. 'I think I need to sit down.'

Jesse rushed to her side and supported her. It was impossible not to cling to him when her legs felt so unsteady.

'Sorry,' she muttered. 'I'm a bit lightheaded.'

'I've got you. I'll take you up to the room. I'm so sorry, Emily.'

'Does Ravi know?'

Jesse shook his head. 'No, but he will soon because he's next of kin. You know Ravi better than anyone, so Ben thought you would know – how best to break it to him, or maybe you want to be there with him? This will be a tough thing for Ravi.'

Emily took deep breaths, feeling her head clear and her stomach return to normal. Then, after a moment, she said, 'No Jesse. Ravi is a man, and he can deal with this himself. I won't always be around, so he must face this alone.'

'Really?'

Something about Jesse's astonishment irked her. 'Really,' she repeated more harshly than she intended. 'He'll have to cope with losing me one day. I won't always be there to hold his hand.'

Jesse touched his fingers to her cheek. His expression startled.

'Or do you think that's cruel?' she asked, her confidence momentarily rocked.

'No, Emily. I think you are totally right. And I know that isn't easy for a mum to do.' He leant closer and kissed her brow. 'I'm proud of you.'

'I hope he can do it,' she said more to herself than to Jesse as they crossed the foyer to the elevator.

'Me too.' And then, as what seemed an afterthought, Jesse added. 'I'm sure he'll be fine.'

'I think bed sounds good,' she said.

When they reached the elevator, Emily tried out a smile, and it didn't feel forced, but it wasn't heartfelt either. When Jesse helped her out of her dress a few minutes later, she tried to push her dead husband and needy son from her mind but knew it was impossible. As Jesse peeled off his shirt, forgetting them got easier. His body was warm and comforting and helped to keep the ghosts at bay.

*

Ben had been brusque on the phone, and Molly knew he was still pissed off at her. He told her about Randy Singh's death and that she would need to deliver the news to Ravi. When she quizzed him regarding the circumstance, Ben said the post-mortem was pending. When she asked if there was any suspicion about the cause of death, Ben said, 'I don't fucking know!' And hung up.

It made her furious that her partner could not act professionally and leave their personal relationship out of it. He had taken the fling between them too seriously. He had not seen it for what it was – lust. Molly was not proud that she had given in to her primal desires, but it was done now and she had to move on. Ben had been a poor choice of lover, not that it had been her intention to seek out a paramour, it just happened.

And while the sex had been more than satisfying, especially with the added thrills; the danger of being caught the main one, Molly had known from the onset that it wouldn't last.

There was more to her relationship with Ferdi than just companionship. Over the years, they had both participated in sexual dalliances with other partners, but rather than test their love, these short-lived affairs added spice to their connection. It may not work for some couples, but for Molly and Ferdi, it was solidifying. They always came home to the other one.

The evening was warm, and Molly drove to Ravi's house with the window down. There were no streetlights at his end of the beach, and the blackness appeared solid. As she pulled up alongside the home, there was a clear view of the moon peeking over the dark water. The sand glowed white while silhouettes of saltbush swayed in the light breeze. Somewhere in the scrub past the dunes, she heard the shriek of a barn owl, or at least, Molly hoped that was what it was. This place was beautiful and a bit frightening at night.

Molly rapped on the front door twice before it was answered. The porch light came on at the same second.

She heard footfalls approach from inside. Ravi's clothes were dishevelled, and his hair was messy. He pulled the door wide, began to smile, and then frowned instead.

'It's late. Is something wrong?' he asked.

Molly pushed against the door and said, 'I'm afraid so.'

The kitchen table was crowded with textbooks and notepads. 'Studying?' Molly asked.

'Yeah. Firefighting safety procedures. I have an assessment next weekend.'

'Good for you Ravi. Can we sit somewhere?'

She heard Ravi sigh before he pointed to the sunroom. They sat in the dimly lit space, Molly deep in the recliner while Ravi sat on the edge of the leather couch. He looked ready to get up and run, staring at her expectantly until she spoke.

'I'm sorry, Ravi, but there is no easy way to tell you this; your father has passed away.'

'What? No.' He sat silently for a minute, hands covering his face with splayed fingers as though they could filter out the bad news.

'I'm afraid I don't have details at this stage.'

'Was he – alone?'

'I'm not sure. Why do you ask?'

'Because the last time I spoke to him, he feared dying alone. I asked if he wanted to be moved up here, where I could visit him, but he said "no," Raymond's Shelter was his home.'

'Well, he was at the care facility when he passed, so I'm sure someone else was with him.'

'I hope so.'

'When did you last see him, Ravi?'

'About two weeks ago.'

'So, you weren't estranged?'

'I hadn't seen him for a long time before that. Maybe five years.' Ravi dropped his head for a moment. 'My grandma left me a message. I guess she didn't think I'd read it until…'

Molly sat upright in the recliner. 'Until her death?'

'Well, yeah. That's what it seemed like. I mean, why else would I be going through Grandma's things?'

'What did the message say?'

'It was personal. It was an explanation for my father's absence in my life. Grandma put it inside an old Babushka doll I had loved as a child. She would have known I couldn't resist looking at it. The note was hidden inside.'

'Can I read the note, Ravi?' Molly was sure he would decline.

After a few seconds Ravi stood and walked to his pile of notebooks. He picked up a black vinyl folder and unzipped it. He said nothing as he handed her the letter and immediately returned to the kitchen.

While the familiar sound of a kettle came to the boil in the background, Molly read the note three times. She jotted down some questions that needed answers.

But as Ravi shuffled back into the room with two mugs of coffee, Molly knew this was not the time to ask them. She shoved her notebook into her vest pocket and took the cup.

'Thanks, Ravi.'

To her surprise, Ravi must have been considering the same questions.

'After I read that letter,' he said. 'I wondered if my dad might have been involved in Grandma's death. After all, Grandma told my mum what happened to me back when I was a kid, which pretty much ended his marriage and broke up his family. So, I guess he had a reason to hate Grandma, a motive.'

Molly started at the word but said nothing.

'I drove down to Adelaide to see him.' Ravi gave a bitter laugh as he shook his head. 'He couldn't even stand unaided. I knew he could never have driven all this way and then shoot at the house using a semi-automatic rifle. The idea was ludicrous.'

'Did you tell him what happened to your grandma?'

'No. I didn't want Dad to think that was why I visited. Given how sick and old he looked, I wondered then if it might be the last time I would ever see him, so I didn't mention it.'

'You see Ravi, if your father's death wasn't natural, then it could be seen as an admission of guilt.'

'My dad's death is suspicious?' In this light, Ravi's eyes looked black and as hard as stones. 'What do you mean? Are you talking suicide - or murder?'

Molly shook her head and shrugged, not sure how much to divulge, but certain this was not the time or the place. She gave a weak smile. 'No, Ravi. We don't know any details yet, but hypothetically, you can see how it might look, but of course, there is no point speculating until we know for sure.'

'I guess,' Ravi agreed. 'But in my mind, I'm certain he wasn't involved. He mentioned Grandma in passing, not in the past tense and not with animosity.

'Thanks for being so open with me, Ravi. It's been helpful, and I'm sorry to have to ask these things, especially under such painful circumstances.'

'To be honest, it's not that harrowing.' Ravi put down his mug and stared towards the blank TV screen. 'I guess that sounds bad, but I hardly remember my dad being in my life. There was no bond between us. I know I look like him, but I wasn't overcome with affection when I visited him. On the contrary, I felt sorry for the poor old bloke, who wasn't even that old. He'd messed himself up with booze. It was pitiful to see someone ruin their life like that. He was more like a stranger, a dying stranger.'

Molly smiled and placed her half-empty cup on the coffee table. From beside it, she collected her phone and keys. She felt instinctively confident that Ravi wasn't covering for his father. 'I'm sorry that you're grieving again. You've been through a lot in such a short amount of time. It's cruel.'

Ravi stared at her; his dark eyes hard and – menacing? She shifted in her chair as a chill ran up her spine. She stood slowly, wondering if she'd made a mistake to come here alone and unarmed. But then Ravi shook his head and rubbed his eyes.

'Sorry,' he said. 'I just realised that my immediate family are dropping like flies.'

Molly's hand began to tremble, rattling her keys. She thrust them into her vest pocket. 'You've been through a lot, Ravi. Do you want me to call someone?'

'No. It's okay. I'll get my shit together and ask Bailey to come over.'

'Sure. That sounds like a good idea. Well, I'll leave you to it. Thanks again, Ravi.'

But before she reached the door, he said, 'My Grandma meant so much to me. I would never cover for my dad if I thought he was involved. I want whoever killed her to rot in hell. No matter who it was.'

'I understand. Take it easy Ravi.'

Molly was glad to be away from the house where Edith Sanders was gunned down. Perhaps because the place itself and its horrific crime scene were indelibly etched in her mind, or maybe she thought she saw a glimpse of what Ravi Sanders had the potential to become when provoked. Either way, future visits here wouldn't be solo, and hopefully, they would take place in the light of day. She glanced up at the black sky as she opened her car door, wishing she didn't have to sleep alone tonight.

*

Ravi watched as Molly's taillights were swallowed by darkness. He knew he should call Bailey, but he didn't want her sympathy right now. He wanted to avoid hearing her sensible words or suggestions on how to look after himself. And he didn't want to call his mother either. She would be worried about him, fawn over him and treat him like a child.

He glimpsed himself in the large gilt mirror hanging above the chiffonier in the dining room. From this distance, he looked his age, not his CAS accelerated years. Nevertheless, the image drew him closer. He hit the light switch as he strolled through the archway and stood a metre from his reflection. He moved the tall art deco statue of a dancing woman to the edge of the chiffonier to give himself a better view and unbuttoned his shirt. Despite his regular gym workouts, he had the beginnings of man boobs. There was a lack of elasticity to his skin, and his once taut abdominal muscles were softening to flab.

Would he get his years back again? Did the reversal treatment work, as well as the ageing process?

'It was an accident,' Ravi said fervently to his reflection. 'I didn't mean to hurt her. I'm not some arsehole who would assault another person.'

But the face he was not yet accustomed to, began to crumble. 'Are you going to cry?' he asked his image. 'You're a pathetic worm!' he sobbed.

The storm was beginning to brew in his head again, and with it came the accompanying anger. Ravi knew he should take his medication, especially considering this tragic news he'd just received; after all, the drugs were prescribed for his anxiety, and surely losing a parent was stressful. But he found himself unable to move, rooted to the spot, growing increasingly enraged as the maelstrom made off with his sensibility.

Ravi had some sense that Hank was tugging at the hem of his track pants, but he couldn't respond. The cyclone roared in his ears, and his vision dimmed to shadows. And then suddenly, he felt nothing; his perception failed. He wasn't even sure if he was standing up or lying down. Hank's frantic barking was a faint echo, and the shards of flying glass a mere ripple in a pond.

The slant of bright sunlight hit Ravi's eyes just before seven am. The rattle of the passing garbage truck indicating that it was Wednesday morning. He rolled onto his back, hearing the crunch before a piece of mirror bit into his skin. He sat up suddenly, his mouth dry and head pounding. Had he been drinking? The dizzy feeling overwhelmed him as he tried to get to his feet. The carved oak chair creaked under his weight as he strained and tottered, but finally, he stood.

The dining room floor was strewn with fragments of the mirror. All that was left of the dancing woman was her head and left shoulder. Her remaining arm pointing to the roof with a fingerless hand. Her destruction had not removed the smug expression from her perfect porcelain face; somehow, that sent a flicker of anger coursing through Ravi's body. Hank was nowhere to be seen, but a puddle of urine gave away his trauma of the previous evening.

When Ravi glanced upwards, only one section of the mirror remained intact. The face looking back at him was gaunt, defeated, and much like his father's. When Ravi began to cry this time, there was no outrage, only misery - and a thirst. He shuffled to his grandma's drinks cabinet and selected a bottle of rum, pouring three fingers into a crystal tumbler. It smelled pungent and tasted intense. He found ice cubes in the bar freezer, so he loaded the glass, swirling the drink and knocking it back in three gulps. The first drink burned all the way to the pit of his stomach. The second went down equally fast, but he felt his mood improve as he finished it. The third and fourth were imbibed much slower; they were savoured. By the fifth, he was giggling as he lurched dangerously across the floor.

He made it to the armchair in the sunroom, and Hank came to sit by his feet.

*

When Ravi woke hours later, Jesse Plackis stood over him, his mother working busily with a broom and dustpan in the dining room. The cop was speaking, but Ravi's head was awash with the sound of the storm. He tried to tell Jesse to shut up because he was provoking the rage, but his words failed him. Instead, the turmoil in his brain made him nauseous, and he belched a rum-scented cloud, retching once and then spewing brownish bile onto the floor rug.

Jesse stepped back, shaking his head, Ravi's mother suddenly at his side.

'Please go,' Ravi said between gasping breaths. 'Leave me alone.'

They stood staring at him for what seemed like a century, both working themselves into a frenzy. Jesse scolded Ravi for his lack of maturity, while his mother blamed herself between bouts of tears. But Ravi refused to be moved, either emotionally or physically, and at some stage of their ranting, they gave up, leaving in a flurry of promises, threats and exasperation. Ravi didn't care.

His eyes wandered to the drink cabinet. He knew how to take the pain and anger away.

Chapter Fourteen

Tash's death profoundly affected Carl. He hadn't slept for over a week; images of her last seconds and his desperate attempt to save her ruined his slumber. He woke in a cold sweat, night after night. The ambulance physician had given him two weeks of sick leave and a script for sleeping tablets. One of those weeks had passed, but things weren't getting any easier.

He usually wouldn't have had time to bemoan the tininess of his apartment, but days without the distraction of work had transformed his home into a cloying prison. So he escaped on his Kawasaki Ninja to the Adelaide Hills on the eighth day, finding the space he badly craved. While he navigated the corners and cambers of wind-swept roads, thoughts of Tash vanished, but once he arrived on the open freeway, there was nothing else to occupy his mind.

Carl wasn't in a relationship, and most of his friends were mere work colleagues. Tash had been a real mate. Even Angela, who Tash loved dearly, confessed a level of jealousy at the ease of communication between the two ambos. They had shared the same love of work and sense of humour. Angela had messaged him the previous night. She was going to stay with her mother in Sydney until the funeral. It seemed her house was too empty without Tash.

Carl knew he needed someone to talk to, but his options were limited. His family weren't close. His mother had remarried a retired politician and lived in

Broome. His sister was a bitch, and his brother was dim. That left his dad. Carl groaned at the thought of speaking with his overachieving, perfectionist old man. Bob Carruthers never failed to voice his disappointment regarding Carl's choice to become a paramedic instead of a doctor. But at least his dad cared.

Carl moved into the right-hand lane, pulling an illegal U-turn in front of the advancing traffic. As the bike screamed up to one hundred kilometres per hour, he hit a swarm of bees. He swore at his shit luck as they splatted against his visor and muddied his vision. His glove smeared most of the goo into a film, but he could see well enough. He kept his bike at the speed limit and went down the hills and into the city.

His father's office was in the biological studies section of Adelaide University. Carl had only been there a handful of times. Yet, as he parked the bike and gazed at the beautiful Georgian-style building, he had a vivid memory of the last time he visited, sitting in the fusty man's cramped space that smelled of old books and the horse liniment that seemed to address his every ache and pain, waiting tedious minutes for the old fart to hurry up and finish writing.

'Oh Christ, what am I doing here,' Carl muttered as he crossed the road.

He went through the labyrinth corridors and knocked on his dad's door. Instead of a reply, his father appeared at the door a moment later. He peered at his son over the top of his reading glasses, his expression curious but not displeased.

'Hi, Dad,' Carl said as the door opened.

'This is a pleasant surprise.' His father pointed to the helmet in Carl's hand. 'Still flirting with death, I see.'

'Don't, Dad,' Carl said wearily.

'What's wrong?' His father said as he cleared books from a chair leaning against the wall. 'Have a seat.'

'One of my work friends has died.'

'Oh, dear. Not the attack last week?'

'Yes.'

'Were you there?' His father's soft and compassionate voice brought unwanted tears to Carl's eyes. 'I'm so sorry, son. Have you – asked for some help?'

Carl nodded. 'I'm on leave. I've talked to a doctor.'

'How can I help?'

'I don't really know. I guess I need to talk.'

Carl watched his father's brow rearrange, furrows deepening, while long grey eyebrows knitted and crossed. 'Tell me what happened.'

The unwanted tears stung twice more during the ten minutes it took to tell the horrid story, and at the end of it, Carl felt drained.

'It's a nasty process they're using on those prisoners,' his father said. 'I've read a little about it and discussed it with Dorian. Do you remember Dorian Lindquist? He is, among other things, a microbiologist and gerontologist. He came to my sixtieth birthday party. A tall fellow with a bad comb-over.'

'Um – I think I remember him.'

'He has a particular interest in the effects of ageing on a cellular level. He was part of a panel selected by the federal government in the nascent stages of the CAS drug research. As I have been led to believe, this drug that the prison system uses changes different parts of individual cells. It works by creating dysfunction in the cell structures directly related to replication and division, it causes oxidisation in Mitochondrial DNA, stem cell exhaustion, and other insidious damage. It really is a terrible drug. I can't understand how it was ever approved.'

'Can it make people go crazy?' Carl asked.

Again, the eyebrows crossed and uncrossed. 'As far as I know, it accelerates the hallmarks of ageing. The government are making out that this is a medication with a half-life, but that seems impossible. One injection causes massive cellular changes, unlike medications that are given at an effective dose and then maintained. And the other aspect to consider is that this process would have a psychological bearing on the recipient. To become suddenly older is not normal, so what impact can that have on a person's psyche, say to age by ten years or more? And, of course, the influence would vary from person to person. So to answer your question – certain people may become overwhelmed and react - insanely.'

'Could it speed up diseases like dementia?'

'Well, yes. Theoretically, chromosomal aberrations could be exacerbated by this drug, but unlike the normal ageing process, the changes would progress swiftly. I'm sure these people would be overwhelmed by the sudden onset of symptoms.'

'There are thousands of genetically related diseases,' Carl added, 'that could be kicked off prematurely by the treatment, and the thousands of prisoners who probably have no idea of their genetic background. They have become ticking time bombs.'

'Yes. That's right because many of those diseases don't affect people until their advanced years.'

Carl rubbed his temple, which was beginning to throb. 'So, in effect, if the recipient has a dose that will cut their life short by a long span, plus an underlying genetic disease, it's pretty much a death sentence.'

'Yes. Prisoners are potentially receiving a much harsher penalty than the court stipulated.'

'But the government's response in the media didn't say that. Instead, they said the CAS drug was metered out in accordance with the punishment decided by a judge. They also said that there is a reversal treatment available. Is that a lie?'

Carl's father shrugged. 'I don't know. Dorian distanced himself from the studies on moral grounds a couple of years back. He was disturbed by the shortened trial period of the drug, so I don't know whether he is still abreast with the drug's development or not. I'm sure he still has colleagues who are involved.' Carl's father regarded him with an intense stare. 'You need to take great care with any patients you suspect have had this treatment. To use your own analogy, I would regard them as ticking bombs.'

'I think I'm going to do more than that, Dad.' Carl stood and put a hand on his father's shoulder. An idea that he'd pondered now flourished into a plan. 'I've already witnessed three people whose lives have been ruined by this drug, four if you count Tash. I'm going to the media with her story. I'll tell them what we saw and how she died. People in the community need to be aware for their own safety.'

The older man nodded. There was no surprise in his calm expression. 'I can speak to Dorian if you like and find out if the pharmaceutical scientists did indeed meter the efficacy and if they manufactured a reversal.'

'Thanks, Dad, but even if the manufacturers swear it's foolproof, we must put some doubt out there. There is no way this drug was scrutinised in proper clinicals trial before they used it on prisoners.'

'No, it doesn't seem that way. I hope what you are going to do works, son, but be aware that there are many horrible people out there. So please think about it long and hard before you say anything you can't take back. You can put the truth in front of their faces, but the ignorant, narrow-minded, and easily swayed will always believe what suits them, not what is correct.'

Carl suspected that his father was including his mother in this mini rant. Although seemingly innocuous to Carl, this woman who embraced spiritualism over science and homeopathy over medicine terrified his dad and broke his heart more profoundly than any infidelity ever could.

'I get it Dad. You can't reach everyone.'

Carl hugged his father before he departed.

*

The police station office was quiet and cool at seven in the morning. Molly had gone to the roadhouse two blocks away to get her first coffee of the working day. She didn't communicate well pre-caffeine hit, so Jesse encouraged her to get them both a beverage.

Earlier, Jesse had left Emily in bed, asleep. He was glad to be away before the reality of her son's emotional breakdown ruined her normally cheery manner. He guessed it was a bit cowardly, but Ravi and his dramas tended to overshadow the case, which was no closer to completion. Emily could deal with her son alone today. Jesse needed to work.

He opened his SAPOL intranet email folder and read his mail. The fourth communication he opened made him frown. It was from the Department of Correctional Services concerning an inquiry Jesse had made immediately following Edith Sanders' death, regarding information about Amos Khalil. It was a list of Khalil's visitors for the previous two months. Jesse was about to delete the document, as they had pretty much ruled out any link between Khalil to the shooting when a name jumped out at him. Piper Summerton.

'Bloody hell!' he muttered. 'She was Ravi's old girlfriend.'

Jesse jotted down the visit date and time while waiting impatiently for Ravi to answer his phone. Unfortunately, the state Ravi had been in the previous night did not bode well for a response so early this morning, so Jesse cancelled the call instead, picked up his car keys and drove there.

Hank greeted Jesse at the gate with a single bark and laps around the garden, churning up the lawn. Instead of waiting for Ravi to answer the door, the cop went to the rear entrance. He knew the back screen door would be open for the dog to come and go.

'Ravi! Ravi!' Jesse yelled as he walked from the back lobby to the sunroom.

Ravi hadn't moved from the armchair where his mother had covered him before leaving the previous night. The sunroom was filled with the fug of booze and smelly socks. Jesse pulled open the curtains and then the window, making a din while letting in bright sunlight and chilly morning air. Ravi uttered a few grunts of protest, which Jesse ignored. Instead, he dragged a chair across the room and sat facing Ravi.

'Wake up!' Jesse shouted only centimetres from the sleeping man's face.

The cold and brightness took more than ten minutes to coax Ravi awake. Finally, he sat up, scratching his stomach and dragging fingers through his messy hair. He gazed at Jesse through bloodshot eyes.

'What?' Ravi asked.

'Sit up Ravi. I have some questions for you, and I want clear answers.' When Ravi's eyes began to close again, Jesse grasped his t-shirt collar and shook him so hard that Hank started to bark. 'Sit down Hank!' Jesse growled.

Ravi struggled upright, licking his gummy lips. 'What?' he asked again.

'I need you to tell me what happened the day you tried to steal Maryjo Katz's car.'

'What? Why?'

'Just tell me!'

'Can I – can I get a drink?'

'Sure,' Jesse said through gritted teeth. He stomped to the kitchen and back again. 'Here,' he said, shoving a glass of water under Ravi's nose.

If Ravi was disappointed it wasn't alcohol, he didn't remark on it. Instead, he drank the water down in long chugs.

'Right. Now start. How did the idea of stealing the car come up?'

Ravi shook his head. 'Stealing a car was never the plan.' He rubbed his forehead and winced. 'I was told the car had been sold and paid for, but the woman selling it changed her mind at the last moment. She was being difficult even though the transaction had gone through. All I had to do was pick the car up and take it to the new rightful owner. I was doing the job as a favour to my girlfriend. She stood to make a few bucks once the new owner had the car, but she had no choice about doing the job.'

'Who was the new owner?'

'I dunno.'

'Your girlfriend gave you the car keys?'

'Yeah. I mean. I guess they were the car keys. I never got to use them because Maryjo caught me just after I sat in the car – and then everything turned to shit. I tried to run, but we collided. She was screaming and bleeding. Someone must have called the cops coz they got there fast. I couldn't see Piper anywhere. I guess she was scared and drove off.' Ravi shrugged. 'And, you know the rest.'

'What happened to the keys?'

'I still have them.'

'What?'

'Yeah. The cops took my phone and the keys when they arrested me.'

'Did they know they were Maryjo's keys?'

Ravi shrugged. 'I guess they assumed they were mine. They gave them back to me when I was released.'

'Did you tell your lawyer you had the car keys, that it wasn't a robbery?'

'No.' Ravi hung his head.

'Because you suspected Piper had lied to you?'

'I guess.'

'Did you know Amos Khalil?'

'No. Of course not. I heard that he had killed someone. I guess it was on the news, or I read it somewhere.'

'Did Piper know him?'

Ravi shook his head; his expression was dubious. 'No way.'

Jesse pulled the email printout from his top pocket and shook it in Ravi's face. 'Read this!'

Ravi squinted, his mouth working while he read the words. 'Piper?' he whispered before staring up at Jesse. 'Piper visited Khalil in prison. She knew him?'

'It certainly seems that way. Did Piper ever explain why she made you pick up the car? She could have got it herself.'

'She was scared. I said I'd help. I offered.'

'Did she know you would offer?'

Ravi hung his head, managing to appear even more morose. 'I guess. She knew she only had to ask. I was such a fool.'

'When was the last time you heard from her?'

'She disappeared that day. I haven't seen her since. I didn't mention her to the police when I was arrested. I tried to contact her, but her phone was disconnected, and she disappeared from social media. I guess she was afraid I was going to blame her. I asked my mum to try to get in touch with her, but all she managed to find out was that Piper had gone to Thailand.' Ravi shrugged. 'I didn't know she had enough money to go there. She was always broke, always in need of cash.'

'You got played, Ravi.' Jesse took no enjoyment out of stating this fact. And Ravi obviously got no joy from hearing it.

'Does this mean that Khalil *did* shoot my grandma, and the bullets were meant for me?'

Jesse shook his head and sighed. 'I don't know what it means, Ravi. I've asked the city guys to track down Maryjo. I'm expecting a video link with her sometime today so she may give us some answers. Are you sure there isn't anything Piper may have said or done that was out of the ordinary?'

'I dunno,' Ravi said. 'I think everything Piper ever did was out of the ordinary. I guess that's what I liked about her.'

'Well, you can't sit here feeling sorry for yourself.' Jesse stood and pointed to the bathroom. 'Shower, now! And while you're in there, I'm confiscating all the booze from this house.' He pointed his finger at Ravi. 'If Bailey had come over here last night and saw you in such a mess, she would have walked out on you, and you would have deserved it. Now get up and get your shit together. You are not sabotaging your life. I know you've lost your dad, and I'm sorry, but I'm pretty sure the last thing your old man would have wanted was for you to follow in his piss-head footsteps. Agree?'

Ravi mumbled something, but it wasn't good enough for Jesse.

'Agree?' he growled.

'Agree,' Ravi said.

'Right. Bathroom, and don't come out until you smell like a God-damn flower!'

*

Bailey unsaddled her horse and tried to hose her down, but the mare kept turning to rub her face against Bailey's chest. Stinging flies drove the horse to distraction during their ride that morning, and now her eyes were inflamed and weeping. Bailey let the mare rub against her shoulder for a minute or two.

'It's okay girl.' She said as she gently shooed away the persistent insects. 'I'll get you a fly veil.'

The mare stamped her feet and then rubbed her face downwards along her foreleg as Bailey walked to the tack room. Bailey searched the cupboard, open shelves and even an old tea chest but failed to find a veil or mesh protector. Grandpa was fixing a fence in the top paddock with his farmhand, and she knew he never carried his mobile phone with him, so she searched the homestead laundry. It was doubtful Grandpa would have known where much of the horse gear was anyway, so Bailey tried her mother but gave up after the second unanswered call.

In the lobby cupboard, she discovered a medical kit filled with human and animal treatments but no other equine paraphernalia. Then, just as she closed the door, her phone rang.

'Hi, Mum. I'm at Grandpa's. I took Belle for a ride to the beach, but the sand flies have been driving her nuts. Where might I find some insect spray or a fly veil? I've looked in the tack room and the laundry.'

There was a moment's pause before her mother answered. 'I don't think your Grandpa would like you nosing around his place. Just leave it.'

'But mum, her eyes are running and swollen. She needs some protection so they don't get worse.'

After a sharp intake of air, Donna said. 'If you can't find one, then there isn't one. Don't go snooping around someone else's home. It's not polite.'

'But I know I've seen one. I know she had one on last summer.'

'Then maybe she wrecked it or lost it out in the paddock. I have to go to Port Lincoln on Thursday. I'll stop in at the Saddler's.'

Bailey shook her head but said, 'Okay.'

'Alright, now get out of there before he returns, or you won't be popular.'

'Sure. Thanks Mum.'

When Bailey walked back towards Belle's yard, the horse bent her head to the ground and was violently rubbing her eye against her leg. The eyelid had swollen to double the size.

'Oh, bugger this!' Bailey said.

She saturated an old handtowel, using it as a cold compress until the mare stopped fidgeting. But more flies were buzzing around the horse's other eye, and again Bailey cursed. She knew there was a fly veil was somewhere, so she searched the stables and shearing shed but came up empty. The back room of the shearer's space was locked, which seemed unusual because the only things in there were a table and some chairs; it was where the shearers relaxed and ate meals during shearing season.

Bailey strode back to the house and took the big bunch of keys from the hook inside the bread hatch. Grandpa had kept them there since time immemorial. Bailey thumbed through them until she found a few that resembled padlock keys. The first two didn't work, but the third did.

The room smelled faintly of bleach and damp wood. Along the side wall was a shelf of crockery and a tall cupboard. The cupboard door opened with a squeal. Bailey pulled out a broom and mop, leaning against a pile of blankets. She pulled back a sheet, and a rifle clattered to the floor.

Bailey frowned. Grandpa was strict with his firearms. All weapons and ammunition were locked in the gun safe. How could he be so careless? But then she took a closer look at the rifle. She was no expert but knew what a military-style weapon looked like. This gun was not for culling the odd fox or rabbit. This was a gun for war, a people killer.

'Oh shit!' Bailey said as she backed away from it. 'What the hell?'

It was impossible to conceive that her grandfather was involved in Edith Sanders' murder, but this rifle said otherwise. Or perhaps the real killer had hidden it here. But why? Bailey's mind was overloaded with questions without answers. She bit down on her index finger to help herself concentrate.

'Okay, what's the right thing to do?'

Calling the police was the obvious answer, but what would that mean for Grandpa? Even if it wasn't his weapon, he would be a suspect. And what if they found him guilty and sent him to prison? What about his farmhand? Could he have put it here? The lad was still at school part-time. Surely he wasn't a murderer?

Bailey glanced around the room that wouldn't be used again in June, maybe May at the earliest. Did whoever put this gun here know that? Was the real killer going to come back for it before then? Did that mean that Grandpa was in danger? Yes, calling Jesse was the right course of action, but still, she hesitated. Bailey had an impetuous streak; everyone who knew her said that.

'Take a breath. Think about this carefully,' she muttered to herself.

But her hands shook so badly that she dropped the keys on the floor. Her heart thumped furiously as she picked them up.

'Calm, keep calm.'

Whoever put the rifle here knew they had time up their sleeve, so maybe Bailey had some time too; time to examine all possible consequences before she made a potentially life-changing decision. 'Yes,' she mumbled. Waiting made sense. Acting like a bull at a gate did not.

She gingerly picked up the edges of the sheet and threw it over the gun, and then lifting it slowly and steadily, she placed it back where she found it. Once it was safely back in the cupboard, Bailey took a deep breath. She grabbed a washcloth from the shelf and wiped down the door handle. Then she backed out of the room, flicking the cloth to muddle her footprints on the dusty floor. It didn't look convincing, but it would have to do.

'Maybe Grandpa will hand the gun in,' she muttered, although it didn't seem likely.

With no other option, Bailey took a can of insect spray and doused the wet hand towel with the contents. Belle was eating from her hay net, but flies still buzzed around her. The mare backed away, snorting as Bailey dabbed her face with the strange-smelling insecticide, but after a moment, the horse was munching again, and the flies had mostly disappeared.

The distant sound of a vehicle bumping down the dirt track got Bailey moving. An altercation with her grandfather was the last thing she needed. This dilemma with the automatic rifle was better considered in quiet contemplation. She ran back to the house and returned the keys, letting the back door slam as she exited.

Bailey could hear the car engine idle as the gate between the sheep paddocks and homestead was opened, and then a farewell call from the farmhand as he walked towards the hayshed. This pause gave Bailey a head start, and she took off running to her car. She quickly drove to the other side of the tractor shed before Grandpa's utility came into view.

There was a nervous wait until she heard the engine cut out and the back door squeal open. But once she heard the muffled sound of the news radio station streaming from the kitchen window, she knew she'd been unseen. Bailey was still trembling as she departed the property. It wasn't until she reached the highway exit that she felt composed. She wound down her window and let the warm air blow through the car.

'No spur-of-the-moment decisions, Bailey,' she said to the breeze. She nodded. Her mum had uttered those words to her many times, and they felt right. The pang of guilt, that was only her impetuousness protesting, nothing more.

Just now, waiting was best. She needed time to come to the right decision.

*

Molly sat beside Jesse as they waited for Maryjo's video call. The visual feed came in before the audio. The woman on the screen appeared annoyed, so Jesse started the conversation by apologising for requesting another interview, and then asked Maryjo to recall the day Ravi tried to steal her car. Maryjo protested at first, having told the story many times before, but finally conceded. Her recollection was the same as her statements.

'Maryjo,' Jesse said, taking the car keys from his pocket. 'Do you recognise these?'

'Hold them closer to the webcam. Oh wow! They're my keys. Where did you get them?'

But Jesse ignored her question and instead asked, 'When did you last have these in your possession?'

'Um, I lost them going to the gym about a week before the carjacking. We looked everywhere for them, but they must have fallen out of my bag as I came from the car. I had to use my spare set after that.'

'Which gym was that?'

'Up-tight, on Pitt Street in the city. Only a few blocks from my apartment.' Maryjo's eyes narrowed. 'Why?'

Again, Jesse ignored her question. 'Do you know Piper Summerton?'

Maryjo began to smile, but it froze on her face. 'Yeah.'

Molly nudged Jesse with her elbow but said nothing.

'Tell me about her,' Jesse prompted.

'We were gym buddies. I didn't know much about her, but we hung out together. You know, coffee or a cold drink after sessions. If it was a special day, like someone in the class's birthday, we'd go for a few drinks.'

'Did she mention her boyfriend?'

'Piper said she was in a relationship, but it wasn't going anywhere. We rarely talked about it. I think it made her feel uncomfortable. She was often flirting with Andreas, a guy who worked at the gym. He was cute, and I think all the girls liked him, but he liked Piper.'

'Piper was at the gym the day these keys went missing?'

Maryjo frowned. 'What are you saying?'

'When was the last time you saw Piper?'

'Not for ages. She moved to Thailand.' Maryjo chewed her thumbnail for a moment. 'Are you saying Piper stole my car keys?'

'I think so. I think she may have given them to her boyfriend, *Ravi Sanders*, and told him to take your car.'

'Oh, my God! Ravi was her boyfriend?'

'Yes. And as far as he was aware at the time, someone else had legally purchased the car. He was asked to go and pick it up.'

Maryjo stared blindly for a second while her mouth fell open. 'Bloody hell! That bloke has the crappiest luck.'

Jesse gave a humourless laugh. 'You're dead right there.'

'So, you never suspected Piper of taking your car keys?' Molly interjected.

'No, never. I really liked Piper. We had fun together.' Maryjo shook her head. 'I thought we were friends. I was going to invite her to my place for Christmas lunch, but I never saw her again.'

'I'm sorry Maryjo. Would you like us to post the keys back to you?' Jesse asked.

'No. Don't bother. I traded the car in, and I no longer live in that apartment. Just chuck them in the bin.'

'Sure.'

'What about Ravi?' Maryjo asked. 'He had that treatment, didn't he? That ageing thing that makes people go crazy.'

'So far, he seems okay. He was hoping to have the reversal treatment.' Jesse shrugged. 'But now, in light of the complications with the initial drug, well, they are putting a hold on that until they do more testing.'

'Poor Ravi. He didn't deserve what happened. And his grandmother? Have you found out who shot her?'

'The investigation is ongoing,' Molly said. 'Thank you for your co-operation, Maryjo. We may be in touch again.' She ended the communication and turned to face Jesse. 'That woman really knows how to pick her friends.'

'Mmm. And Ravi isn't much better. Piper - what a piece of work.'

'So, Ravi's medical test results returned fine, but how do the doctors account for his volatile reactions to certain things? I heard about him damaging stuff in his house and shouting at Bailey.'

Jesse didn't ask where the gossip came from but suspected Andy Ruther's. After a minute Jesse said: 'The psychologist I spoke to this morning thinks Ravi is reacting to his situation rather than the drug. He has been through an awful lot. I guess some shock reaction is to be expected.' Jesse felt a twinge of guilt as he spoke. He had been one of Ravi's detractors, and he still thought the bloke was acting like a spoilt brat.

'Well, keep a close eye on him. The news from the Health Department this morning was optimistic about reversing the effects of the CAS drug, but they've been wrong before. Or they may be trying to convince the public that this isn't a clusterfuck, which it is.' Molly gave a weary sigh and stretched in her chair. 'Ravi may never get the reversal treatment.' She yawned.

'Not sleeping?' Jesse had seen the rumpled stretcher bed in the cell room.

'Something like that.'

'Do you want to talk about it?'

Molly's grin seemed controlled. 'Not really. It's personal stuff that will sort itself out.'

'I'm not an ogre, you know.'

Now her smile was genuine. 'I know Jesse. I wish there were more men like you in the world. I'll sort this thing out. If there's one thing I am good at, it's organisation.'

'Sure,' Jesse said as he stood up. 'Just don't be too hard on yourself. We all make mistakes.'

Molly nodded and looked away. She made no attempt to argue with him.

*

Chapter Fifteen

Ravi touched Bailey's hair while she slept. The short spiky haircut suited her elfin face, enhancing her childlike features. In this early morning light, it resembled blonde fluff. This was the fourth night she had stayed with him in two weeks. He'd given her half of his hanging space in the wardrobe. Ravi smiled, wondering if it was possible to stay happy. Sometimes it seemed simple, but it was fleeting, a con, he knew, lulling him until the inevitable blackness returned. He slipped silently from the bed.

Last night he sat staring at the drink cabinet. Although it was empty, Ravi was practically salivating. His skin felt like bugs lived beneath it, and he fidgeted like a junkie. The sensation calmed after an hour or so, and once Bailey arrived, the feeling was long gone, but it had taken an age to fall asleep, and now he was awake again. It was only six-thirty.

The cyclone in his head was starting again. He guessed that was what woke him, so he slipped on his shoes and ran to the beach before the intensity grew. As he pounded beside the surf, he screamed at the sky until he felt lightheaded. Activity seemed to lessen the effects of whatever it was going on in his brain, so he ran and ran, covering three bays, before finally turning for home.

When he returned home, over an hour later, he was sweating and his muscles ached, but his head had cleared. It seemed he had outrun the storm in his head. Bailey was waiting on his back porch, wrapped in a thin blanket. She was sitting very still and quiet for once, and looked so vulnerable that he swept her up. She felt fragile as he carried her in his arms to his bed.

Their lovemaking was different this time, not vocal and physical, but mellow, perhaps a little sombre but beautiful. Maybe she knew he was hiding something from her, but he had no choice because he was still trying to figure himself out. He couldn't share this problem that he could not yet identify. At some stage of his contemplations, her eyes had opened. She stared up at him with a misty gaze.

'Are you okay?' he asked.

She wiped her eyes and stretched her arms. 'Sure,' she replied. 'Why were you awake so early?'

'I'm helping at the depot at eight. I must get up.'

'Well, I don't.' She pulled up the sheet and rolled over.

'Bailey?' He saw her clutch the bedding. 'Thank you for sticking with me. I know I've been hard work.'

'Sure. Now, let me sleep.'

Ravi slid from the bed once more and showered. The cold needles stung his skin and eyes. Outside, the temperature was rising. There was still another month and a half of summer, but bushfire season wouldn't finish until April. The thought that he was needed energised him more than the chilly shower. He dressed in his uniform and slid his phone into his pocket.

'Ravi?' Bailey clung to the doorway, wearing only a t-shirt.

'Yeah?' he said. I'm making coffee. Do you want one?'

She came closer and rested her head against his chest. He held her momentarily before saying, 'I'm leaving for the depot soon.'

'Oh. Do you have a job?'

'No, not yet. I'm helping with the vehicle check, and then I need to talk to Andy.'

'What about?'

Ravi took a deep breath, still indecisive despite the adamant words he was about to utter. 'I'm going to join AA.'

'Why? You hardly drink at all. You're the epitome of a two-pot screamer.' Her laugh was a little cruel.

'Bailey, it's genetic. I believe it's my future if I don't get it under control.'

'Where is this coming from? Your mum? Jesse?'

'My alcoholic dad just drank himself to death – or, close enough. I think that's what this rage I feel is, and it's getting worse.'

Her mouth opened, and she frowned, but a second later, she nodded. 'Yes, Ravi, that makes sense.'

'Do you think?' He was aware of the uncertainty in his voice. He had doubted his own theory.

'Of course. And even if you're wrong, it can't hurt to bolster your self-control or connect with others. You have a higher power within you. I know you do.'

Only a moment ago, he had felt like a man who had made a life-changing decision, but now her words moved him to tears. Like a child, he thought, like a frigging baby. 'Aren't I ever going to grow up!' he blubbered.

'Ravi, I am really proud of you.' She spoke as though he hadn't heard him. 'You just decided something that millions of people fail at daily.' She smiled and touched his nose. 'You've got this, Ravi,' Bailey whispered. 'You are really strong.'

He wished he could share her confidence, but he nodded despite his doubts.

*

Tash's funeral should have been a small gathering of family, friends and colleagues, but, Carl suspected the recent media attention had much to do with the groups of onlookers outside the chapel. Some held placards voicing rants at the government, police and the criminal justice system, but the truth was Tash had made a bad call in a bad situation. It should never have happened.

Carl slipped into one of the back pews, but after a minute or two, a chapel attendant beckoned him to the aisleway.

'Ms Streeter would like you to sit with her.' The man pointed to Angela in the front row.

Carl cleared his throat before sitting beside her, but she touched his hand when he opened his mouth to speak.

'It's fine Carl. Don't say anything, or I won't be able to keep my shit together. Okay?'

He nodded, and she went back to shredding tissues in her lap. After an hour of predictable words, anecdotes, photographs and music, they finally departed. Carl held Angela's hand as they stepped out onto the sunny street.

'I've got a three-thirty flight back to Sydney,' she explained. 'I can't put on a brave face while a bunch of drunk people tell me what a great woman she was.'

'I know,' Carl agreed. 'I can't handle it either.'

Most of the protesting crowd had dwindled in the hot sun by then, but the die-hards had prevailed in their quest to be photographed or filmed for various forms of media. As Carl watched Angela's taxi pull away, he had a microphone shoved in his face.

'Hi Mr Carruthers, is it true that Natasha Pawlowski was murdered while four SAPOL officers looked on?'

'What? No. Get away from me!'

'Ms Pawlowski's killer was not fired upon by police while her throat was slashed, is that correct?' The reporter asked as his camerawoman edged closer.

Carl ran, but the two reporters followed him for almost a block before giving up. He continued jogging an extra hundred metres before returning to where he'd parked his bike. Just as he was about to hit the ignition switch, his phone vibrated inside his jacket pocket. He pulled his helmet off and glanced at the phone screen. It was his father, messaging to give his condolences. Carl frowned for a moment and then called his dad.

'Are you okay, son?'

'Yeah Dad. I was wondering if you had spoken to your friend Dorian yet?'

'I'm with him right now as it happens. We just finished nine holes of golf, but we've called it a day. It's too hot.'

'Sure. Are you at the Grange Club?'

'Yes. Would you like to come down for a chat?'

A group of people carrying placards were moving along the footpath towards him. They were still rowdy and angry. At the next change of the traffic lights, they might see him, and if they recognised him as the tv bloke had, perhaps they might harass him.

'Sure, Dad. See you soon.'

Carl took a deep breath before putting his helmet back on. Then, as the lights changed, he zoomed through the intersection.

The golf club was crowded with people. The bar staff were dashing about, carrying trays laden with food and drinks. Carl had hoped for a more subdued atmosphere, so he was pleased to see his father sitting on the outer area of the clubroom patio. Beside him was a tall man wearing baggy grey trousers and a short-sleeved business shirt.

'Hi,' Carl said as he shook the man's hand. 'Dorian?'

'Yes, Carl. Your dad's told me a lot about you. Salt of the earth, you hardworking ambos.'

Carl coughed out a laugh. 'I don't know about that. I suppose we try.'

'Now, self-deprecation will get you nowhere, so take the kudos while you can.'

'Drink, son?' his father asked.

'No. Thanks dad. I'm riding.'

'Unfortunate business about your friend, Carl. I'm sorry for your loss,' Dorian said.

'Yeah. It shouldn't have happened.'

'Bob tells me you want to talk to the media.'

The red-faced journo who accosted him following the funeral service, flashed through Carl's mind. That wasn't the kind of media attention he'd had in mind.

'I'm still thinking about it.'

'Well,' Dorian said. 'I can tell you that the CAS is being pulled. It should never have been given the go-ahead. It was modelled on a foreign system that's still in use.'

'Really? Whereabouts?'

Dorian gave a condescending smile. 'Sorry, Carl, that information is not for the public.'

'Some place where human rights abuse is the norm?' Carl guessed.

'Let's just say they're red to their gills.'

'Fair enough.'

'The system seems to work for them, but then again, if it was a failure, would they ever tell us?'

'So why would Australia choose such a dodgy model?'

'In principle, it had promise. The government spends over five billion dollars annually on our correctional facilities. Just think of the improvements that money could make to the health budget. Hospital beds, better mental health facilities, less ambulance ramping.'

'But the drug they used failed.'

'No. The drug worked as it should, but the authorities didn't prepare for the psychological harm rapid ageing might cause, or, in the case of the man who killed your friend, the type of diseases it could precipitate with catastrophic outcomes.

'You see, the median age of prisoners in Australia is around thirty-five, so adding twenty to twenty-five years propels them into an older age bracket and, of course, exposes them to all the diseases associated with that age group.'

'But the government believed that they would be rehabilitated by ageing them. Didn't they?'

'No. The prisoners would have served their sentence – that's all. The ones selected for the program were not serial offenders or hardened criminals; those types were purposely not chosen for the CAS. But, of course, they weren't harmless either; some had raped or killed. But prison isn't just about depriving people of years of freedom. It is about the journey too.

'Think about life in prison over multiple years. Who are your peers? Who are your heroes going to be? Outside life is cut off for you, so your influencers will come from within those walls. A wealth of knowledge can be gained if crime is your thing. We want to think that every second inmate is studying law, but that isn't true. If you were locked up for ten years with a bunch of doctors, I believe you would learn a lot about medicine, but the reality of prison is that you are locked up with a bunch of criminals – so you learn a lot about crime.'

'The CAS recipients miss out on those interactions,' Carl said. 'So that's a good thing.'

'That's right. The CAS meant convicted people would not spend time with criminal influences in their lives,' Dorian said.

'No wonder the government saw it as a magic bullet.' Carl looked from his father to Dorian. 'On paper, it sounds like the perfect answer to an expensive problem.'

'Also, Carl,' Dorian continued. 'Some people will slide back into recidivism. Although our state has the best statistical outcomes for criminals not reoffending, about a third will end up back in prison within two years. That leaves two-thirds with the possibility of a new crime-free life. Not bad odds compared to the rest of the country.'

'But the statistical outcome was likely to be even better under the CAS, wasn't it?' Carl asked.

Dorian nodded. 'The government saw it as a good reason to fast-track the program.'

'But not enough time to realise the problems.' Carl said. 'Like the man who killed Tash and others who were sent crazy.'

'Yes. Conditions like rapid onset dementia, whether Alzheimer's or Prion-based aetiology, progress anywhere between weeks to a few years. There may be roughly thirty thousand people suffering from these diseases in Australia right now. Still, by 2060 it's likely to be half a million, so when we press fast forward on someone's life….'

'We are increasing the risk exponentially,' Carl said.

Dorian shrugged. 'Yes. Turning maniacs out into the public.'

'What about the reversal? Is there such a thing?'

Dorian gazed at his empty glass. 'Again, this is not something I can speak about.'

So,' Carl said. 'Until every person who has been a recipient of the CAS drug either dies or is institutionalised, we will see more violence.'

'If it's any consolation, son,' Bob said. 'The statistical model shows those potentially aggressive dementias would affect only a tiny percentage of the prison population, and those similar diseases with a much slower onset may be managed.'

'Yes, that's right,' Dorian agreed. 'You have been unlucky, Carl. The odds have not been in your favour to have encountered more than one of those patients.'

'But the nasty cases will come on suddenly and violently until they're all gone.'

The two older men stared at Carl. It seemed there was nothing left for them to say except, "Be careful."

*

Ravi's t-shirt collar felt too tight, but whether it had shrunk in the wash or was his imagination, the perplexing stares from Molly and Jesse added to his discomfort.

'Thank you for coming in, Ravi,' Molly said. But her tone sounded far from pleased.

Ravi glanced from one to the other. 'What's this all about? Do you have news about Grandma's death?'

'Unfortunately, not,' Jesse said. 'But we have some questions regarding Piper Summerton.'

'Piper? Why?'

'Because Piper may have committed a crime.'

'What sort of crime?'

'Please, Ravi, just answer the questions.' Molly cleared her throat and leaned across the desk towards him. Her eyes were fixed on his, and her gaze seemed calculating. 'Tell us about Piper. I want to know how you met her, what you did together, people you knew, anything of any significance.' Molly shrugged. 'Even things that aren't important, just tell us as much as you can.'

'Okay. I met Piper just after finishing my second stint at uni. We both worked in a bar on Hindley Street in Adelaide. I had applied for positions as a data analyst with some big companies but had no luck, so the pub job kept the wolves from the door. Piper was trying to get into modelling. She had a small portfolio, mostly fashion shoots for online department stores, but it hadn't become a career. Eventually, she worked on editing for a small newspaper. I had a small flat just north of the city centre, and she was sharing a house with some people at Seaford.'

'Before you go today, Ravi,' Jesse interrupted. 'Please write down names and addresses, as much as you can remember, for anyone Piper had contact with.' Jesse pushed a pad and biro across the desk.

'Okay,' Ravi said.

'Please go on,' Molly said.

'Sure. So, Piper and I went to a concert together about five years ago. The Black Keys. It was great. After the concert, we went out for a few drinks. It all started from there.'

'Who were her friends?' Jesse asked.

'She lived with Ella, Amy and Milo, but I don't think they were good mates. Sometimes I'd stay at her place, but that was before she moved in with me, and they weren't friendly towards either of us. One day, when I got there, it was obvious Piper had been arguing with Amy. They were huffy towards each other, and Amy kept swearing under her breath. It wasn't long after that that Piper asked if she could move in.' Ravi paused and then began recounting things they did together. 'Um, we went to Melbourne a couple of times a year and a few times to Sydney to visit her grandparents…'

'Again, Ravi,' Jesse said as he pointed to the notepad. 'I want all these people's details.'

'Um, sure. Anyway, I guess we were just like any couple.' He shrugged. 'Sometimes we went to restaurants, movies, concerts, fringe events. Piper liked watching men's basketball, but it didn't appeal to me; sometimes, I went with her. Sometimes she jogged with me, but mostly, she preferred the gym. I liked doing weights but not the classes that she liked.'

'What about her friends?'

'I guess her closest friend was her sister, Chelsea. When we first got together, she and Chelsea were inseparable, but something happened about six months before she left me. Piper wouldn't say, but afterwards, she didn't hear from her sister. I asked, but Piper said it was nothing.'

Jessie and Molly exchanged a glance.

'Ravi,' Molly asked. 'Did you know Andreas from the gym that Piper frequented?'

Ravi felt another wave of heat rise up his neck. He took a sip of water and wrenched at his shirt collar. 'Yeah. I knew who Andreas was.'

'You know that Piper was friendly with him?'

Ravi nodded. 'One of the other women who worked the day shift at the bar told me. At first, I thought the woman was spreading a nasty rumour, but the more

I thought about it, the more I guessed there was some truth. Piper had been shutting me out. She'd stay up late every night and then sleep on the couch. Sometimes she'd go out and come back wearing different clothes, and a couple of nights, she didn't come home at all. In the end, I just knew.'

'Did you confront her about it?' Molly asked.

'Eventually, I did. It was strange because she denied that anything was going on, and for a few weeks, she was back to her old self, except she was still sleeping on the couch. But she was nice to me, sweet even, and then she asked me to pick up that car.'

Jesse was shaking his head. 'Why that car?' He turned to Molly. 'Was Maryjo's car impounded following the attempted theft?'

'Not that I recall.'

'Maybe it wasn't the car that Piper was after.'

'Perhaps there was something of Khalil's inside the car.' Molly stood and picked up her phone. 'I'll call Adelaide and find out if it was impounded.'

As Molly walked towards the station's reception area, Jesse watched Ravi.

'What?' Ravi said.

'Nothing.' To Ravi's surprise, the cop broke into a smile. 'But we may be getting somewhere.

Ravi wasn't so sure. He knew from experience that anything to do with Piper spelled trouble.

*

There was no chance that Maury could arrive home and surprise Bailey at the farm today because she had just dropped him off in town for a tooth extraction. The dentist's receptionist told Bailey the procedure would take at least an hour and a half because the doctor was running late. Bailey glanced at the two women sitting on the other side of the waiting room. Their faces were stony as her grandpa, grumbling under his breath, sat between them. Bailey suppressed a chuckle as she departed.

Once back at the farm, and without the pressure of nerves, Bailey unlocked the shearer's lunchroom. The cupboard sprang open, and she pulled back the sheet. The rifle was still there. She wondered what she would have done if it had been gone. 'All the more reason to report it now,' she whispered.

Bailey hadn't decided lightly; the arguments for and against had disturbed her sleep for two nights now. She wished she could have talked it over with Ravi, but he was fragile. And Bailey hadn't spoken to her mother about it, in case she knew about the gun. After all, it had been Donna who told her not to snoop around Grandpa's property.

Of course, Grandpa would be pissed, royally pissed, when he found out, whether he knew about it or not, but Bailey could hardly let that stop her. She had discovered a weapon that was likely used to murder someone. In the end, this was the only decision she could live with.

After placing the rifle in the boot of her car, she phoned Jesse.

*

Molly flew alone from Port Lincoln to Adelaide. The day was windless, and the trip was surprisingly restful. Not having Ben around, with his needy gazes and obsequious compliments, made the journey even more pleasant. When they touched down, Molly knew she was already running late.

The interview with Chelsea Summerton was taking place in a small room at the Adelaide Central Police Station. The woman was waiting when Molly arrived, harried and red-faced from her taxi drop off, over two hundred metres from the police complex.

'I'm so sorry to keep you waiting, Chelsea. Thank you for meeting with me,' Molly said breathlessly.

'That's okay.'

Chelsea looked nothing like her sister. In her photos, Piper was a raven-haired beauty with piercing dark eyes; Chelsea was beyond plain. Her face appeared flattened, sloe eyes that were widely spaced, and judging from images on social media, without the spark or seductiveness of her sibling.

'I wanted to ask you some questions about your sister, Piper.'

Chelsea gave a mirthless laugh. 'That figures.'

'Why would you say that?' Molly asked.

'The world revolves around Piper.'

'Oh. Okay. So, would you say you two are close?'

Chelsea's expression was wistful. 'I always thought so, but she changed in the last year or so.'

'How so?'

'When she was first with Ravi, she seemed so happy. She enjoyed being part of a couple, playing house, that sort of thing. Then she got a job as a sub-editor for a community newspaper. She loved the work, but the workplace sounded toxic. Piper always tried to find easier ways to make a living.'

'She didn't just change jobs?'

'That would have been admitting defeat. Piper liked to win or to appear to conquer.'

'Okay, so what sort of money-making projects did she try?'

'She started gambling.'

'Oh. Did Ravi know?'

'He did when the landlord threatened to evict him. He'd given Piper the rent money, and she blew it.' Chelsea gave a smile that transformed her face. Her grin was engaging. 'She came to me, and I helped her. She told Ravi she'd misplaced the money and then found it.'

'But you gave it to her.'

'Yes, with the promise that she would never do it again.'

'And did she?'

'Probably, but whatever she did, she kept hidden from me. That was the turning point in our relationship, and I'm not sure why. We still met up pretty often, but she was distant. I would never have mentioned the money again, but her pride wouldn't allow me to hold the moral high ground, not that I would have. Our relationship was more important to me than money or pride.'

'Did she ever mention Amos Khalil to you?'

'No. But I saw him once. He dropped Piper off in front of my place. He was riding a Harley. You could hear the thing coming from blocks away.'

'You recognised him?'

'Well, not at the time, but just a week later, he was arrested for murder. His face was all over the media, and it was a face that was hard to forget.' Chelsea gestured to her own neck and throat area. 'I asked Piper about him, and she said he was cool. So I asked her to be careful, and she laughed.'

'You tried to be a good sister,' Molly observed.

'I did try. I never wanted to compete with her. We were never competitive as kids, and I couldn't understand why she became like that.'

'Are you still in contact with her?' Molly asked.

'No, but recently she contacted Mum from Thailand.'

'Will your mother give you the contact details?'

Chelsea grinned again. 'No, but eventually, she will. Mum always folds under pressure. When she does, I plan to go over and see Piper. I need her to know that I'm on her side.'

'Did Piper ever mention Maryjo Katz to you?'

'Yeah. A few times. She said she was a dumb bimbo. A stripper, I think. She was Amos' girlfriend. I got the feeling that Piper was a bit envious of her.'

'Did you know Piper went to the same gym with her?'

'Yeah. They were friendly at first. Then Piper met Amos, and that's when the jealousy started. I don't think Piper fancied Amos as much as she wanted a powerful man to look after her.'

'Ravi wasn't that man?'

'No. Ravi was great but soft. Piper was always going to break his heart.'

'So, you liked Ravi?'

'Yeah. You couldn't help but like Ravi. He didn't have a nasty bone, but not much backbone either.'

'You never saw Ravi violent?'

Chelsea shook her head. 'Never.'

'What do you know about Ravi stealing Maryjo's car?'

'Only what I saw on the media, and the allegation of assault, that was pure bullshit. Piper never spoke about it, but after it happened, she told Mum some story that made it seem like they had broken up before the event. I knew that wasn't true.'

'How?'

'I know my sister. Ravi had outlived his usefulness. I think he was set up.'

Molly nodded. 'I do too. Tell you what, Chelsea, if you see your sister, find out if she set him up. She may not ever pay for what she's done, but it may help Ravi to hear about it.'

Chelsea gave a beaming smile, and this time she was beautiful. 'I sure will! Ravi was too good for my sister.'

Molly handed Chelsea her SAPOL card as she stood to leave. 'Good luck Chelsea.'

Despite nights of rough sleeping, Molly didn't doze on the plane trip home. The prospect of her own bed and the coming weekend should have elicited some joy, but Molly's mind was consumed with Edith Sander's case. So many stories had come to light during this investigation, and finding the truth was likely to be disappointing rather than enlightening, so it was with an uncharacteristic pessimism that she departed the plane.

The cool air in the terminal engulfed her, and Molly took a deep breath. She saw Ferdi, tall and slim, leaning against a pillar, reading something on his phone. He glanced over and gave a smile, irreverent and seductive. The gesture lit something inside her, and she grinned back.

'Welcome home, babe,' he said before leading her away.

*

Chapter Sixteen

Now that Ravi was physically fit and had passed his basic training and First Aid certificate, he was offered the chance to train as a paid firefighter. The course, which took between thirteen to twenty-one weeks, could be done, in part, externally. There would be study blocks he needed to attend elsewhere, but his hours of experience on the truck could be signed off by Andy. With two paid firies planning to retire during the year, Ravi was sure to be advanced to full-time work.

'Edith would have been so proud, Ravi,' Andy said just after he delivered the offer. 'She dedicated a big part of her life to the CFS. She'd be so chuffed to know you're following in her footsteps.'

'What if I get a job and I'm scared?' Ravi asked.

'You won't, mate. The more you learn about fire hazard analysis and accident scenes, the more confidence you'll have in a building fire or traffic accident. Staying safe will become second nature; you'll be able to read fires and have the tools to halt them. Being afraid will be the last thing on your mind.'

'I dunno. I'm not much of a hero.'

'Good. Anyone trying to be a hero doesn't last long in this job. You need to use your head. And I wouldn't have put you forward for this if I didn't think you'd make it.'

'Not just because of my grandma?' Ravi asked.

Andy rubbed his chin, holding Ravi's gaze. 'Maybe initially there was some nepotism, but not now. You've done good work on the truck, especially when you've had so much going on.' He frowned at Ravi. 'You want this, don't you?'

'Absolutely. I'm going to try my hardest.'

Andy broke into a gap-toothed smile and slapped him on the back quite forcefully. Ravi had to fight down the urge to whimper.

'How's that girlfriend of yours going?' Andy asked. 'Is she moving in with you anytime soon?'

'Um, yeah, she's good.' Ravi changed the subject back to firefighting. 'Are you sure I'm ready? I don't want to let the team down.'

'You'll be fine mate.' Andy's index finger pointed upwards. 'Ah, you just reminded me we must audit our road crash rescue equipment by Friday. Go see what Jacko's doing and ask him to help you, but before you leave, come and see me so you can sign your online application. The sooner I get it sent, the sooner you'll start your intense training.'

Ravi thought about sending his mum a text, telling her the news. He shook his head, knowing the moment he did, she'd call him, wanting to know all the details. He didn't have time to chat just now. Maybe he'd phone her tonight while having a beer. No. He shook his head, not that. Although he wasn't convinced that he'd become a full-blown alcoholic, he wasn't prepared to take that risk. Perhaps Bailey would come around and take his mind off drinking. And if she didn't, it didn't matter.

'I've got this!' he hissed.

But despite his verbal bravado, Ravi was worried. Lately, something horrible seemed to happen every time things began to look up for him. The latest being his father's death. The new year had not got off to a positive start.

His dad's funeral was being held that Friday in the same church he had married Emily in, all those years ago. It would be strange and sad to say goodbye to a man he hardly knew. With luck, Bailey would be able to accompany him. His mother was great, but she would have her own sadness to confront. Bailey would have all the logical answers and refuse to indulge his self-pity. He needed her clarity.

'No, I don't,' he mumbled. But despite the mantra, he knew he was lying to himself once more, and that thought opened the floodgates for his self-doubt. He picked up the audit checklist, hoping work would distract him, and after a while it did.

*

Molly's weekend at home was a disaster. After too many nights of sleeping in the Henderson station on the torturous stretcher bed, returning to her comfortable home sounded like bliss, but the reality was dismal. Perhaps the cool change that came with lashing winds and constant rain didn't help. The weather left Molly housebound and antsy, and to make things worse, Ferdi's cantankerous sister, Eva, had come to stay with them. Eva interrupted every conversation with her savage opinions. She seemed to have a second sense whenever

Molly and Ferdi got within two metres of each other. The woman would appear from nowhere with some ghastly plan for a group activity. Molly found herself wishing that Monday would come sooner.

Ben seemed to take Molly's enthusiasm, as she bundled herself into the car when he picked her up that morning, as a sure sign of her affection towards him. He had thoughtfully bought her a takeaway coffee from her favourite vendor and drawn a love heart on the lid. It was a small gesture that she found endearing.

After the long drive to work, their day in Henderson was mundane, apart from a video meeting with their superior. The woman wanted a progress report on the murder case, making it clear that their resources were needed elsewhere if no new leads had emerged by the week's end. The new year, the woman said, meant new cases. Once the communication finished, Molly spun her chair around and leapt to her feet.

'That's all we need,' she said to Ben, who was chewing his fingernails. 'I mean, if Jesse has to continue alone, this case will never be solved.'

'Why, because he's stupid?'

'No! Because there is still so much legwork that needs to be done. Where are we with approval to tele-interview Khalil from prison? Where is the post-mortem report on Randy Singh? And how about feedback from the Thai police regarding the whereabouts of Piper Summerton? Come to think about it, where are the extradition details I enquired about last week from Adelaide?'

'Okay, Molly, don't have a meltdown. We can only do so much. If they pull us out of here, and I hope to hell they do, it's not our problem anymore.'

'That's just the point! Surely Jesse can't be expected to do everything alone. I mean, do they want us to catch this killer or not? Unfortunately, since almost two months have gone by, the media have lost interest, and so have the hierarchy.'

'No Molly. It just means that we have other work too. And yeah, Jesse has a lot of things to chase up, and progress may be slower, but this case will only be cracked by perseverance. Our time is better spent somewhere else.'

'Yes, you'd like that wouldn't you?'

'That we get out of this shitty little backwater? Yes. Yes, I would like to go home to decent coffee, a five-minute drive to work, decent motel rooms…' He gave her a lascivious glance, poking his tongue between his lips.

'Oh, stop it. What are you? A goddamned teenager?' Molly's neck prickled with heated outrage.

She sensed, rather than saw, Ben moving up behind her. She was propped, ready to unleash her anger if he touched her, when Jesse barged through the station's front door. Protruding from the bundle in his arms was a long barrel.

'I think we have the murder weapon!' He said excitedly as he placed the rifle on the desk in front of Molly.

'That's great stuff!' Molly said in amazement. 'Where was it?'

'At Maury Winter's farm. It was concealed in his shearing shed. Bailey Donaldson found it and brought it to me.'

'His granddaughter?' Ben asked.

'Yes. But she's also Ravi's girlfriend.' Molly tapped her index finger against her top lip.

'Let's hope this gun has got some prints on it. You need to get forensics here,' Ben said to Jesse.

'Already done. Someone is coming and should be here within the next two hours.'

'What about the place where the gun was hidden? Is that forensically compromised?' Molly asked.

Jesse nodded. 'Bailey touched the doors to the room and the cupboard. Apparently, she was looking for something for her horse, so she's coming to the station this morning to have her fingerprints taken and make a statement. But any other prints found could be gold for us.'

Molly rubbed her hands together. 'Oh God, I hope so.'

Ben checked his watch and glanced at Molly. 'Well, if we wrap this up, we can return to Port Lincoln at a decent hour. With luck, this may be one of the last times we have to come to this shithole.'

'Ben!' Molly warned as she paced the floor.

Jesse grinned and said, 'goes both ways, mate. I can't wait to see the arse-end of you.'

'Enough! Come on, you two. We are so close now.' She spun around to glare at Ben. 'I am staying here this week. We have a lot of ground to cover, and I'm giving it my all. If you want to leave, go, but I'm staying.'

'Aw, Molly!' Ben whined.

But Molly ignored him, striding over to face Jesse. 'Our biggest problem, in this case, has been not knowing who the intended victim was. Without knowing that, we haven't got a motive.' She pointed to the rifle. 'If this gun was found on Maury's property and wasn't planted there, then…'

'That would mean that Maury was the shooter,' Jesse said.

'Yes, so what possible motive could he have?' Molly finished.

Ben put his index finger in the air. 'If it was Maury, then the target must have been Ravi and not Edith because Edith saved his kids in that fire years ago.'

'But what was his motive for trying to kill Ravi?' Molly asked.

'Perhaps he didn't like Ravi sleazing around his granddaughter?'

'No,' Jesse said, shaking his head. 'I'm sure Ravi didn't meet Bailey until after Edith was shot.'

'Maybe Maury didn't want a criminal living in the same town,' Ben said lamely.

'Edith didn't save all of his kids,' Jesse muttered.

'What? What did you say?' Molly asked.

'The kids. Edith saved Gwen and Maury's two daughters but not his son.' Jesse stared from Molly to Ben. 'What if they didn't matter to him as much. What if losing his son was unbearable, and now that Gwen has passed away…'

'The time frame fits,' Molly said. 'But – I'm not sure.' She walked to the kettle and flicked the switch. 'I need coffee.'

'What if the gun was placed there, but it wasn't Maury who did the shooting?' Ben asked.

'Bailey may have wanted to frame Maury because she was bound to get an inheritance. A chunk of the farm may yield a good deal of money,' Molly offered.

'Only if he dies. He could survive in prison for years.' Jesse pursed his lips. 'Nah, and land around here is cheap. I don't buy that theory.'

'You're too involved with the locals. You don't think objectively,' Ben said.

Jesse shrugged. 'Maybe, but Maury wouldn't have much to leave. Sure, there are a few thriving properties around here, but Maury's isn't one of them. Only a year or two ago, he had to sell off acreage on the other side of the highway to pay his council rates.'

Molly stamped her foot and gave a growl. 'Shit!' she hissed.

'Okay,' Jesse said. 'If the target is Ravi. Who do we have as a suspect?'

'Well, Maury, obviously, but without a motive so far. Khalil perhaps, but he had a rock-solid alibi…'

Molly interrupted Ben. 'Khalil could have organised someone to carry out the shooting. I mean, organised crime, that's what he does, right?'

'Someone who would drive here and shoot up a house,' Jesse said. 'That's not everyday stuff. So, it was likely to be one of Khalil's criminal friends.'

'We've been down this path before with Wainwright,' Molly reminded him. 'I bet there are dozens of crims out there who Khalil knows.'

'We also have no real motive. Maryjo said that Khalil didn't care about her, so why would he bother?'

The three of them stood staring at the gun. Molly knew that Jesse wanted this crime solved for Edith, Edith's family, and his town. Ben just wanted to move on to something else. Molly's incentive fell somewhere between duty and ego. She guessed that made her a bad person, but she didn't care. Of the three, she felt she had the best chance of unravelling this case.

*

Carl's first day back on shift was thankfully easy. The first case of the day was a woman experiencing diabetic hypoglycaemia. It was textbook stuff. The second was a schoolboy who fell and fractured his clavicle, also a standard treatment. The third case of the morning was a man with atrial fibrillation. The bloke had

responded well to treatment before arriving at the ED.
Carl breathed a sigh of relief.

Following that, Carl had a lunchtime meeting with
his psychologist for trauma counselling. He was replaced
by another paramedic until two o'clock in the afternoon.
While Carl knew he had dodged a bullet that morning, his
replacement wasn't so lucky; when Carl re-joined the
ambulance, it was caught in a hospital ramping queue
until six that afternoon. Being ramped was the next worst
nightmare besides having a violent CAS recipient patient.

Carl tried to relax during the long wait. Luckily
their patient was not seriously ill and didn't deteriorate.
The hours dragged, and their pagers activated only
minutes after they finally cleared from the hospital. Carl
gave a start when he read the details on the mobile data
terminal – Lavender Court. He uttered more than one
expletive while his gut churned. The case was a man with
abdominal pain, but Carl was wary. This patient was a
flagged CAS recipient.

Just turning into the small enclave caused Carl's
pulse rate to rise. He tasted blood from biting the inside
of his lip, which he hadn't been aware of chewing, and by
the time he reached the patient's front door he was
sweating. Only three houses up the road was the scene of
Tash's horrific demise. Now Carl wrestled against the
past images crowding into his mind.

The door was opened by a young cop who
seemed to smile apologetically. 'Hi mate,' the woman said.
'I know these properties are in the warning zone for now,
but this guy won't trouble you. He seems like a lovely old
bloke.'

The man didn't look much older than his mid-forties. Not even ten years older than me, Carl thought. And the news that the man was non-violent went a long way to calming Carl's jangled nerves.

As he moved closer, he saw two young police officers standing back from the patient, who was sitting cross-legged on the lounge room floor.

'What seems to be the problem?' Carl asked as he drew closer.

The coffee table was littered with takeaway food containers, and the area smelled of chicken fat and vomit.

'I've got this pain that seems to come and go, but when it comes, it's awful.'

The man pointed to an area of his tattooed abdomen and described the sensation while Carl drew up a nasal application of Fentanyl. But before Carl could administer the synthetic opioid, the man's pain returned. He began to groan and writhe on the floor. Carl held the man's head still and encouraged him to inhale deeply, breathing in the drug. Afterwards, the man lay on his side, occasionally grinding his teeth. Carl monitored his vital signs as the medication took effect. In a few minutes, the discomfort seemed to have abated. The man sat upright with his back to the settee, taking long noisy breaths.

'Feeling better?' Carl asked.

'Much. That shit packs a punch, but I think the spasm, or whatever it was, has stopped too.'

'Yeah. I think you may have a gallstone or pancreatitis. They'll run some tests at the hospital.'

The man gave a groan of protest. 'Do I have to go?'

'Absolutely. That pain is acute, it could be any number of things, and some can kill you without treatment.' Carl called to his crewmate. 'Bring the stretcher in, please, Cheryl.'

The patient held out his hand. 'Paul,' he said by way of introduction.

Carl shook the man's hand, trying to hide his trepidation. 'Have you ever had an episode like this before?'

'No.' Paul frowned and then shook his head. 'But I had something, a kind of turn, but not like this, only a little while ago.'

'Can you describe what happened?'

He glanced at the cop to his right. 'I – um, no, not really.'

'You can talk to me, mate.' Carl offered. 'I've seen and heard just about everything.'

'Yeah, I suppose you have; it's just...' Paul glanced around as Carl's partner wheeled the stretcher through the front door and shook his head. Despite a verbal prodding from Carl, Paul remained silent for most of the journey to the hospital, but with only a few blocks to go, he asked, 'Do you know how to tell if a person is going crazy?'

Carl had to clear his throat because it was suddenly hard to swallow or speak. 'What do you mean?'

Paul glanced unseeingly towards the curtained window. 'I had this thing I was supposed to do, a job.' He gazed at Carl, clearly edgy.

'Oh. I get it. It might not have been legal, hey?'

Paul nodded. 'Something like that. It was all pretty straightforward, you know, drop in on someone. Put the frighteners on them and leave very fast.'

'It went wrong?' Carl prompted.

'Maybe.' Paul gave a shrug. 'I dunno. That's the thing. Next thing I was home. My mind had just taken a walk somewhere without me.'

Carl nodded as the back doors of the ambulance were opened. 'Make sure you tell the doctor what happened.'

But during the ensuing handover, Paul stayed silent about his memory loss. Carl could hardly blame the man because the doctor didn't listen. Instead, the clinician waved Carl away with a disinterested stare once he received the paperwork.

As Carl prepared to depart the emergency department, he went to Paul's bedside, 'You need to talk to someone, Paul. Lapses in your memory are dangerous. You need to stay safe.'

Paul gave a small smile which became a wince as his pain kicked in again. Then, between breaths, he said, 'Thanks, mate.'

Carl checked his watch as he reached the door. His shift was over, but instead of feeling relief, he was now concerned about the next stint in twelve hours time.

He was anxious about seeing more patients at Lavender Court, and he fretted over what Paul might be capable of doing the next time his mind stepped away.

*

'How could you do that to your own family? Your own grandfather?' Maury's face was blood red.

'But grandpa, that gun was probably used to murder Edith Sanders. What did you expect me to do?' Bailey had never seen her grandpa so angry. His eyebrows looked bright white against his florid face, and spittle flew from his lips as he mumbled curses. 'Please, Grandpa, I didn't do it to hurt you. I did it to keep you out of trouble.'

'What trouble could I have got into? It's not my gun, and I didn't bring it here.'

'But the police need that weapon. It can help them find out who killed Edith. Don't you see I had no choice? If you didn't know about it, then you aren't guilty.'

'Oh, I know what the cops are like. They'll come up with some story that fits. They get desperate when they can't catch killers, and then they make shit up. Why do you think I hid the bastard thing in the first place?'

'Then whose was it, Grandpa?'

'I don't friggin' know. I don't have any answers, not for you and not for the police. Now get out of here, Bailey, and don't bother coming to visit me in jail!'

'But, Grandpa, you won't go to jail if you haven't done anything!'

'You're an ignorant little brat.'

'Grandpa, I did it because I care.'

'Go! Get off this property, and don't come back!'

Bailey knew there was no point in staying. The police would arrive at any moment now, and the scene would get uglier. Her need to give her grandpa the heads-up seemed sensible until now. He was the most stubborn person she knew, and his anger would burn fierce and long. The only logical thing to do was give him time, but what if he was right about the police needing a culprit at any cost? Surely Jesse wouldn't let that happen. And what would Ravi think about this direct connection between her family and the murder of his grandmother?

Bailey knew this was the best course of action, so why did she feel so bad? Why did her once happy life seem to be fraying at the edges? A cloud of gloom settled over her as she drove away from the old man and farm she loved.

*

Ben and Jesse had departed to bring Maury Winters in for questioning just as a video call came through from the Goulburn Correctional Centre in New South Wales. The SAPOL request to interview Amos Khalil had been either delayed or ignored until Molly phoned the centre that morning. She used strong words and implied that the institution was impeding a homicide investigation. However, she stopped short of threatening a probe into the centre's management because they had suddenly agreed to set up communication with the prisoner.

One of the reasons the CAS had not been utilised for lifers was that it was considered a death sentence to take twenty-five or more years from a person. So, Goulburn was filled with the worst criminals in the country while lower security prisons were empty. But they would fill again now that a Royal Commission was underway. All CAS treatments had been halted nationally, pending the commission's outcome.

Molly had never liked the idea of prematurely ageing people, but she disliked prisons too. Although for offenders such as Khalil, a nasty thug who had lived a life of crime and violence, there seemed no other option to keep the public safe.

When Khalil's face first appeared on the screen, Molly felt she recognised him. Or perhaps she just knew his type. His smug face tilted high. Was it to show off his neck tattoos and scars, or because the only way to happily observe her was for him to be looking downwards? His black hair was slick with oil or gel. His mouth was a sullen line, and his nostrils widened with disdain. He was the epitome of hate.

Molly gave him her best smile and said, 'Thanks for speaking with me, Mr Khalil,' in the most pleasant voice she could muster.

His eyes bulged instantly. Her politeness had needled him as she hoped it would. He grunted a reply and looked away.

'I'd like you to tell me about Piper Summerton.'

'Who's he?'

'He is a she.' Molly held up Piper's photo. 'Recognise her?'

Khalil shrugged and said, 'I probably fucked her.' He began to laugh until someone in the room with him growled a warning.

Molly gave an internal groan at the man's predictable misogynistic remark but retained her affable expression. 'So, do you know her?'

'Nup.'

Molly had been prepared for these negative responses. When the director of Goulburn had finally acquiesced to this enterview, she asked for some background into Khalil. Molly was determined to find a sweetener. Among other things, the prisoner had quite the penchant for single-malt whiskey. Molly saw this detail as a bargaining chip.

'Amos, I have a bottle of Aberlour sixteen-year-old whiskey with your name on it. If you help me, it's yours as soon as we're done.'

Khalil sneered while raising one eyebrow.

'Tell him.' Molly's request was aimed at the security officer in the prison interview room. She heard the muttered confirmation from a man out of camera view.

Khalil shrugged and then gave a nod. When he faced the webcam again, he had a satisfied smirk on his face. 'Yeah, I know her.'

'Is she a friend?'

'Maybe.'

'How did you meet her?'

His face screwed up in apparent concentration. 'I was at Maryjo's place fixing her front door. It sustained some damage.' Khalil gave a cocky laugh. 'Someone's fist had gone through it. Anyway, I decided to do the nice thing and repair it. Piper came to see Maryjo.'

'Maryjo wasn't there?'

'Nah, she was workin'.' Piper had heard of me.' Khalil gave a smarmy grin as he mimed a slam dunk. 'What can I say? I'm well known. Anyway, after we talked for a while, it seemed like she was looking for a way to make some extra cash, but not the usual way.'

'Sex?'

'Yeah. She said she didn't fuck for money. So, I kept her in mind for something easy.'

'Like stealing Maryjo's car?'

He shrugged. 'Bitch asked for it.'

'Because she was going to dump you?' It was out before Molly knew it.

The smile was gone, and the black eyes were threatening. 'No one dumps me,' he said in a surprisingly gentle voice. 'I decided to part ways. Which I did,' he gestured to his surroundings.

'Sure.' Molly cleared her throat. 'So, Piper got her boyfriend to do the stealing, and he got caught.'

'Yeah. She wanted him out of the picture.'

'She intended for Ravi to be caught?' Molly wondered if he'd picked up the astonishment in her tone.

'Yeah. So, you know. The job was killin' two birds with one stone.'

'Why did Piper want Ravi to be in trouble?'

'She had someone new. She wanted a new life and the old boyfriend gone. But then he didn't get punished the way she thought. Piper wanted him put away. He should have been doing a brick for hitting Maryjo, but instead, he got that new shit that messes with people's heads. The CAS.'

Molly thought for a moment; doing a brick meant ten years. That was far longer than stealing a car would have reaped. So, had Piper foreseen the physical confrontation between Maryjo and Ravi, knowing such an outcome would incur a lengthy sentence? The timing for such an altercation had to be spot on. Maryjo was extremely fit, so catching Ravi in the act, well, Molly could imagine her defending her property with force.

'How did Piper react when Ravi didn't get put away?' Molly asked.

'She came and saw me. Asked me to send him a message.'

'To kill him?'

'Nah, nah, nah. Nothin' like that. Just a scare. I think she felt ripped off, so when he didn't get thrown in the can like she planned, she wanted to see him shit his frillies.'

'You organised it?'

'Me? Nah. How could I? Unless you hadn't noticed, I'm in the boot. And besides, that would be illegal.' Khalil laughed, mouth open to display missing teeth and his bifurcated tongue tip.

'If you had to guess who carried out this "scare", who would that be?'

'I have no idea.'

'When did you last see Piper?'

'Just before she took off to Thailand. She came to see me in this glorious establishment.'

'Did you help fund her trip?'

'Me? No. It was a business trip, I think.' Again, the unctuous smile.

'Like transportation of goods?'

'I dunno. How would I know?'

'Is she coming back?'

'I dunno? Maybe one day.'

'Do you know how to contact her?'

'Wouldn't have a clue. I don't speak gook.'

Molly ignored his racist comment and asked, 'I guess you have quite a few scary friends?'

'I've got heaps.'

'I've met Mr Wainwright. Is he a scary man?'

'Nah. He's just a dude that likes young girls. He's not hard enough to scare anyone.'

'Okay, just suppose I got you two bottles of Aberlour. Would that help to jog your memory? Would you give me a scary man's name?'

Khalil leaned closer to the screen. His fists were bunched on the desk in front of him. 'I'm no dog, lady. I won't rat on no one.'

'You told me about Piper.'

'I didn't tell you anything that isn't common knowledge. She didn't do anything wrong anyway.'

Molly doubted that. 'You've been very accommodating, Mr Khalil. Thank you very much.'

'How about that second bottle then?'

Molly shook her head and ended the call, pressing the disconnect with a flourish. 'What a creep!' she whispered.

For the next thirty minutes, she made follow-up phone enquiries about the extradition process for a suspected criminal residing in Thailand. But because Piper had not been convicted of a crime, the results weren't encouraging.

Chapter Seventeen

Ravi suspected that Bailey was avoiding his phone calls, but finally, that morning, she had sent him a text message. She said she needed to talk. Ravi groaned; he'd heard that before. He had a horrible feeling it meant the relationship was over. He knew it was coming, and he wasn't surprised. What self-respecting woman wanted to be with a nutcase. With his head in his hands, he glanced down at the books on the coffee table. Had all his studies had been a waste of time? Where the best things in his life going to fail anyway? Ravi's despondency grew and soon his stare was diverted to his grandma's cocktail cabinet – his cocktail cabinet. It was empty, but it could be refilled.

'Why the hell not?' he muttered.

But instead of driving to the pub, he sent a reply to Bailey, telling her he would be somewhere on the beach. Before she could reply he pulled on his runners and called out to Hank.

'Come on, boy. Let's go for a run. What do you say?'

Hank gave one short bark and ran to the hook by the back door, staring at his lead. Ravi smiled. The dog's leash was superfluous, but he took it anyway. You never knew if some intrepid tourist might venture this far; if they did, they might have a little fluffy dog in tow. Hank loved nothing better than to make fluffy things squeak;

he didn't bite them, but he did like to step on them. Tourists took a dim view of that.

Ravi sprinted for about two hundred metres and settled into a slow jog. Hank kept pace easily. The morning was cool; come midday, it would be sweltering again, but for now, it was wonderful and Ravi's mood began to lift. The morning tide had brought in a variety of creatures, and Hank slowed to pick up the occasional small crab. A couple of crunches, and then he would discard them. When they reached the bay's end, Ravi's phone pinged with a message. Bailey was here.

'Come on, mate,' Ravi called. 'Showtime.'

But instead of jogging back, Ravi took off his runners, and they strolled in the shallows. Hank tried to bite the foamy wave-tops and run after gulls. It made Ravi smile.

I should take anything good while I have it, he thought, because things are going to get bad again.

And he was right, but he was wrong. Bailey was still ten metres away when she blurted out her apology. At first, Ravi had a hard time making sense of her words, wondering why her grandfather had anything to do with their breakup, but finally, he understood. This wasn't the finish of their relationship in the traditional sense.

Bailey's grandfather had been found with the rifle that had killed his grandma.

'When did you know?' he asked. Surprised by the harshness in his own voice.

She whined her answer, and Ravi felt his face crumple in disbelief. She had kept it from him for more than two days! How could she? There could only be one reason for her lack of contact: guilt. Ravi wandered back into the waves, trying to block out her pleas. Thankfully, Hank began barking at gulls again, dimming her pitiful cries and explanations.

Ravi felt adrift.

Bailey had held him together after his grandma died, but now this betrayal. He felt her hand as she tried to grip his, and he turned to stare at her. Tears streaked her face, and snot bubbled as she repeated her apologies. She was red-faced, like a chastised child, and as she stood hunched over, she seemed smaller, vulnerable, he gazed down and wondered what kind of man could allow her suffering to continue?

'Go away,' he hissed.

He may as well have struck her. She wilted to her knees, hands covering her face. The waves lapped up to her chin while she begged incoherently. Then, something snapped inside him. His chest began to heave, and he thought he heard his grandma's voice chastising his behaviour.

Suddenly Ravi realised how his father had lived the way he did. Using his own mistakes and ill luck as an excuse to hide in the solace of a bottle of booze. Ravi's grandma had always known his weakness. Was that why she and his mother protected him from harm? Did they see the potential alcoholic searching for reasons to fulfil destiny?

Ravi stopped walking and turned. Hank and Bailey trailed a few metres behind. Hank was shaking the water from his coat, Bailey, miserable in her heartbreak, head down, shuffling and defeated. He waited for them to catch up and took Bailey by the hand.

'It's okay Bailey. I'm sorry,' he was about to say more, but she crushed herself against him.

In that one small act, he knew he could be stronger than he thought.

*

Maury sat, stony-faced and silent, not responding to questions or accusations. Sitting beside Jesse, Ben had a hard time keeping still. His fists twitched and ramming them into his trouser pockets apparently didn't help his impatience. Ben's whispered curses could be heard during any pause in Molly's interrogation of the old farmer. She had been at it for over half an hour, and it was clear that the mulish bloke would not speak. Jesse had tried contacting Bailey in the hope that Maury would respond to them in her presence, but she wasn't answering.

Finally, Molly turned to Ben. 'Put him in a cell.' She crushed her takeaway coffee cup and flung it into a nearby bin.

Maury appeared smug as Ben marched him away. Jesse was impressed that Molly had maintained her temper considering how flushed and tired she looked. Jesse believed himself unflappable, but Maury was testing everyone's patience. Perhaps letting Ben loose on the old boy would get him talking but Jesse shook his head with the insanity of the idea.

As if knowing his thoughts, Ben returned to the room, cracking his knuckles and said, 'Let me try.'

Molly shook her head and doodled on a pad. 'He needs some time to think.'

'We don't have much time,' Jesse reminded her.

She rubbed her nose. Her ponytail had fallen loose, and her dishevelled hair looked at odds with her crisp white shirt and black vest. She drew a long breath before saying, 'I think we need to appeal to the public for help.'

'Go to the media?' Jesse asked. 'But what's the point? Most people haven't even heard of Henderson.'

'He's right about that,' Ben agreed.

'Maybe that could work in our favour,' Molly said. 'If anyone has mentioned this town by name, well, then that could be memorable because, as you say, this is such an obscure place.'

'That's a pretty slim chance,' Ben said.

Without looking up, Molly scratched her brow and said, 'Well, short of ripping out my hair, I don't have any better ideas.'

The sound of an arriving email pinged on all three computers at once.

'Oh, please, God, give us some good news,' Jesse said.

Ben reached for his laptop first. 'Forensics. It's the fingerprint results. Nothing on the rifle. It's clean. The only prints on the cabinet are Bailey's and Maury's.

'Shit!' Molly's cheeks glowed red, and her eyes were bright with anger. 'Right. We do a press release. I'll talk to the Media and Communications Adviser now. Ben, contact the coroner's department and find out what the is holdup with Randy Singh's autopsy results. Yell at them, scream at them if you must, just get it! Jesse, check for any way to contact Piper Summerton. Look at every form of social media, Instagram, YouTube, Snapchat - just all of them. Bum's down and heads up. Let's go!'

*

It seemed that time, after all, did help Carl come to terms with his trauma. Perhaps he was just lucky, but he encountered grateful patients with positive outcomes in the few days he'd been back working. By the time his working week was over Carl felt relaxed and positive. It was during this optimistic frame of mind that he answered his phone. It was his father.

'Hello, son, how are you?

'Not too bad, Dad. How are you?'

'Good. Have you heard about the Royal Commission?

'Yes, I have. Tash's case is to be highlighted.'

'Are you attending?'

'Yes. I'll have to, but it's months away.'

'It will be your opportunity to speak about your colleague's death. Your turn to converse on her behalf.'

'I guess. I'm not looking forward to it.'

'No, son, I don't blame you, but it is a good result, making them accountable. Hopefully, it will ensure the end of the CAS permanently.'

'Yeah, sure, Dad. The problem is there are still so many affected people out there. Which means the potential for more harm.'

'You sound scared. Why don't you take some more time off?'

'I must work. I need to keep busy.'

'Ah, just like your mother. She could never stay still, never take it easy.'

Carl grimaced. Any talk of his mother invariably led to bitter recriminations and insults against her that he was not in the mood to hear. 'Anyway, Dad. I am doing better, so stop worrying.'

'Sure, son. I still have the beach shack, you know, if you want to get away.'

'That's a good thought. Maybe I'll take you up on it, but I'll keep working for now. And, thanks dad.'

'Take it easy, son.'

Carl ended the call. He stretched and stood. The only other person in the depot was his partner for the shift. She was dozing in an armchair while the television played an old black-and-white movie. Carl screwed up his face and changed the station. But after at least twenty selections, he gave up and turned off the set. He walked to his locker and took out his iPad. Back in the rec. room, he sat in a recliner, three seats across from his snoring crew mate, and connected to the internet.

Carl read the Facebook post from SAPOL three times before fully understanding the relevance of the request. It was a call to anyone who could shed light on a drive-by murder in the sticks somewhere far away. The police had few leads and no apparent motive. They presumed whoever was involved had a background in guns – specifically semi-automatic weapons- possibly a person with biker affiliations.

Immediately Carl thought of Paul. The man with biker tattoos. Yes, it could have been Paul – the bloke that stepped away from his mind. A CAS recipient who had clearly been out of control. Carl had seen first-hand what those people were capable of. Could it be Paul? He seemed like such a nice bloke, but he was an ex-crim.

It was a long shot; after all, the shooting had taken place at least six hours from Adelaide. Perhaps the cops would laugh at him if he suggested Paul as a suspect, but that feeling of humiliation was not enough to quiet the gnawing idea. Somehow, he felt sure he was right. Without the distraction of any callouts, Carl had two more hours to ponder his theory. By six o'clock, when his shift finished, he was positive. At two minutes past, and he slipped out of the depot. He was so inspired he jogged to his bike.

Carl was determined to make someone listen.

After forty-eight hours of waiting for a return phone call from SAPOL, Carl was convinced that his theory had been ignored. When he had initially phoned the police hotline, the woman he spoke to had not seemed terribly interested, but she assured Carl that all enquiries would promptly be followed up by one of the team members. Two days and no word, Carl shook his head; that meant the cops were ignoring his conjecture.

So, despite the voice of reason in his subconscious, which sounded very much like his father, Carl decided to visit Paul. The man was almost certainly still in hospital, which, Carl argued, was a perfectly safe place to approach him. This fact seemed to quiet the more vocal protests in his mind. But he couldn't totally deny there was a potential danger.

Carl's shift that day was busy but not so challenging that it distracted him from his intention. He didn't go home to change his clothes, knowing that his uniform would open more doors, doors that may otherwise be closed. And so, with the knowledge of Paul's identity and address still fresh in his memory, Carl faced the hospital reception desk.

'He's in room three-eighteen, third floor,' the young man behind the desk said cheerily.

So far so good. But when he arrived there, Carl was hesitant about entering the room. He stood hovering in the hallway. When a gurney flanked by two doctors turned into the corridor and was soon baring down on him, it spurred Carl to move. He ducked inside before the doctors could ask any questions. Carl glanced around the room. The bed was rumpled but empty. He heard the toilet flush only a few seconds later, and Paul stepped towards his bed.

'How are you going, Paul?' Carl asked.

The man stopped mid-step, blinking to clear his vision and wiping sweat from his lower lip.

'I've been better. Hey, I know you. You brought me here, didn't you?'

'Yeah. I was just in the area and thought I'd see how you were. Still in a lot of pain?'

Paul nodded as his face grew paler.

Carl reached forward and grasped Paul's elbow, steering him to the bed. 'Come and lie down.'

'They're opening me up tomorrow morning.' Paul gave a protracted groan as he positioned himself. 'Cutting a hole in me and shoving some camera inside.'

'What do they think is the problem?'

'Gall stones. As you said. They gave me an ultrasound. Apparently, they're big bastards.'

'Well, that's good,' Carl sounded upbeat. 'By tomorrow, you'll be a new man.'

'Good. I bloody well hope so. Since they gave me that God-awful CAS bullshit, I feel like I'm a hundred years old.'

'How long was your sentence?'

'Fifteen years.'

'Wow, what did you do, kill a politician?' Carl smiled.

'Nah. A kilo of horse.'

'Heroin? Well, it's not like you killed someone,' Carl said dryly.

'I was set up.'

'You didn't really have the drugs?'

'Nah, I mean yeah. I did have the drugs, but the drug bust was a set-up. Some bastard dobbed me in.'

'Shit. That's no good.' Carl tried not to seem too curious, but he needed to ask. 'So, you trusted the wrong people?'

'Sort of. The wrong people wanted revenge for some other business. Anyway, it's done now.' He gave a dull grin. 'It's nice of you to come and see me, man, seriously. I don't suppose you got any of that good stuff on you? That stuff you gave me the other day was awesome.'

'No. I'm off duty now, but I can speak to the nurses on the desk. They might see their way clear to give you something better.'

'Would you man?'

'Sure. You shouldn't have to be in pain.'

'Oh, that's great.'

'You wait right here. I'll go see them now.'

A young nurse was speaking on the phone at the nurse's desk. His scrub top was covered in cartoon ponies. He glanced up and smiled before pointing to the phone and then held a finger gun to his head, pulling a dead face. Carl laughed.

'Sorry about that,' the nurse said once he had hung up. 'Some people!'

'You got that right,' Carl agreed.

'So, what can I help you with?'

'I was visiting my mate, Paul, in room three-eighteen.'

'Oh, yeah.'

'Cholelithiasis with acute pain.' Carl glanced skyward. 'I know how he looks, a biker, and he has had a hard life, but his condition is real, and the pain is getting to him. He won't complain, but he was a mess when I arrived. He was crying.' Carl stared directly at the man.

'Oh, gee, that's not good.'

'He's holding himself together, but it's an act. I think he needs stronger analgesia. I'm not telling you your job, but - .' Carl shrugged.

'No. That's good. Thanks for letting me know.' The nurse scanned Paul's notes and nodded. 'He's been prescribed up to double the dose we've given him.' He gave an apologetic smile. 'I guess when they look like that…'

Carl spread his hands in a gesture of openness. 'I hear you mate. It's the same for us too. We're all guilty of judging books by their covers, but I know he's genuine.'

'I'll send someone down right away.'

'Thanks, mate, appreciate it.'

When Carl re-entered the room, Paul clutched the bed clothes and ground his teeth. He glanced at Carl and shook his head.

'Take it easy Paul. They're coming to give you a shot.'

Paul didn't reply but grunted throughout the painful spasms. Only moments later, a greying nurse with a stooped spine appeared. He mumbled as he injected into the intravenous line, and only seconds later, Paul's face relaxed. Before he left, the man gently placed a damp flannel on Paul's brow. He nodded to Carl as he left the room.

'Thank you,' Carl said. He sat in a chair by the bed and waited.

The television flashed colour and light as a game show played. The volume was turned down, so Carl could only guess what they said. Ten minutes into watching it, he felt a tap on his sleeve. Paul nodded slowly as he struggled to keep his eyes open.

'Thanks man.'

'That's okay. Hey, you know how you were worried about losing your mind?'

Paul blinked a couple of times and then nodded.

'Did it ever come back to you? You know that time you thought you lost?'

Paul squinted with concentration. 'It was at the beach,' he mumbled. 'I remember the beach. Out in butt-fuck nowhere.'

Carl's fingernails bit into the arms of his chair, but Paul didn't seem to notice. 'Was it a place called Henderson?'

Paul blinked again, and his eyes seemed clearer. 'Yeah. Yeah, it was.'

'And the job?'

'The job. Oh yeah, the job was easy.' He mimed shooting a rifle.

'What did you do?' Carl held his breath.

'Scared someone. Easy peasy.' Paul's eyes closed and he smiled.

'In Henderson?' Carl struggled to keep the desperation out of his voice.

'Easy peasy – in Henderson.' Paul's mouth fell slack. A moment later, he began to snore.

*

'Hi Donna,' Jesse said from the doorstep of the neat transportable home. It was almost dark, and the evening air was cooling. 'I've come to talk with Bailey. Her car's out the back, but she's not there.'

'Oh, Hi Jesse. She rode her bicycle over to Ravi's.' Donna shrugged and swatted away, circling moths from the porch light. 'She does that sometimes.'

'Sure. I'll find her.'

Jesse turned to leave but then heard Donna smother a sob. When he looked back, he saw that she had covered her mouth with the sleeve of her dressing gown.

'I'm sorry Jesse, but I heard you've taken Dad into custody.'

Jesse nodded. 'We wanted to ask Maury some questions. All he had to do was answer them, and this would be over, but he's so damn stubborn.'

'Questions about what?'

Jesse held his breath momentarily, unsure how much to divulge, but then he pictured Maury's pig-headed expression. It could hardly do any harm. 'Donna, the rifle used to kill Edith Sanders was hidden in Maury's shearing shed.'

Donna now covered her mouth with both sleeves. Her eyes were huge. 'No!' she whispered.

Jesse looked up and down the street. 'Listen, can I come in and talk?'

It seemed she didn't trust her voice, so she puffed out her cheeks and nodded. Jesse followed her to the kitchen and sat in the chair closest to the door.

'Maury won't tell us how he came to have the firearm in his possession. We can't let him go until we know. I don't suppose you can tell me anything about it?'

'A rifle, no. Dad has the old shotgun and keeps fox-shot, but every farmer around here has that.'

'This weapon was an SKS assault rifle. They're old-style military semi-automatics. There aren't many of them around in Australia, but the few that have come to police attention have been used by biker gangs. There was a shoot-out in Sydney a few months ago, and one was confiscated, but apart from that, they are rarely seen.'

'Why would Dad have a weapon like that?'

'That's what we want to know. He must talk to us. Do you think you could persuade him?'

Donna stared at her slipper-clad feet for a moment; when she glanced up, her eyes were brimming. 'Dad's not really speaking to me right now.'

'I'm sorry Donna.'

She gave a vigorous shake of her head. 'He's been such an old fool lately. I know he's not well; I guess it's old age. I think he's being ornery just for the sake of it.'

'Do you know where he'd get a gun like that?'

'No.' She shrugged and thought a moment. 'No. I don't, but then again, he's not himself. He does odd things. Since Mum died, sometimes he seems like another person. He's so angry all the time. Like he's hurting, so he must hit back at us.'

'Do you think he's angry enough to shoot someone?'

'I wouldn't have thought so, but these days he has a lot of hate. He constantly talks about the past, regrets, and Colin…'

'Your brother.'

'Mmm, yeah. He told me he saw him a few weeks ago.'

'Saw him?'

Donna shook her head. 'Of course, he didn't really. He'd been out at the old family plot, down near the coast, looking at the monument they erected for Colin. He said Colin was sitting there. I asked if he'd been drinking, and he went quiet. Silly old fool.'

'Donna, do you think your father blamed Edith for not saving Colin?'

She chewed at a loose thread on her sleeve and nodded. 'Yes. He always has. Mum told me, but he was never allowed to mention it while she was alive. Mum would rip strips off him.' She shrugged. 'And besides, it hurt Michelle and me. Poor Edith couldn't save all of us. So, what does he really think? Does he think she should have left one of us behind instead?'

Donna covered her mouth once more, biting down on fresh tears. Jesse heard footfalls in the hallway. Donna's husband was a massive brick of a man with shoulders like a Brahman bull. He glanced from his wife to Jesse without speaking, his frown and shadow darkening the doorway.

'Hi, Jerry.' Jesse said. 'I'm sorry; I brought up some painful issues. I'll get out of your hair.'

As Jesse reached the doorway, Jerry stood aside, and Donna sniffed. 'I'll come by the station after lunch tomorrow,' she said. 'I'll try to talk sense into the silly old bugger.'

'Thanks, Donna. Thanks a lot.'

*

Chapter Eighteen

'It's a motive, of sorts,' Molly said before taking a bite of her tuna and lettuce sandwich.

'We must charge him with something or let him go,' Ben reminded her.

Jesse stared from one to the other. The smell of Ben's Risotto was foul. He seemed oblivious to the stench as he ploughed his fork into it. Molly, too, seemed more distracted by her lunch than the conversation. It appeared neither cop was very interested in what Jesse was telling them.

'We might have our murderer.' Jesse pointed towards the back room. 'Already in a cell!'

Molly pushed her sandwich crusts to the side of her plate and wiped her mouth. 'Listen, Jesse, I know what the old fella said about blaming Edith for his son's death. It sounds incriminating, but we have no prints on the gun and…'

'We have him in possession of the murder weapon!'

'I took the liberty of having the local GP give him a physical examination,' Molly said.

'When?' Jesse asked. 'And why?' He paced to the window to dispel some of his building annoyance. They were not listening.

'The doctor came just this morning. Look, I know everything seems to point to Maury Winters, but something about it felt wrong.' Molly stared at Jesse for a moment and then bit her top lip. 'I went to give him his breakfast yesterday, and he dropped the tray.'

'So!' Jesse stopped walking and faced her.

'So, I picked it up for him and took it away. Ben went over to the bakery and bought another croissant. This time I handed it to Maury without letting go of the tray. He couldn't hold it. He swore at me and told me to set it down on the bed. I watched him, Jesse; he had a tremor and very little strength in his hands. I had the doctor examine him. He says that Maury was diagnosed with Parkinson's disease twelve months ago. As far as I know, it's public knowledge. Bailey signed him up to a Parkinson's support group, but I don't think he's attended yet.'

'Shit!' Jesse wondered if Donna knew. Maybe not, because she didn't mention it the previous evening.

'He couldn't have done it, Jesse. I asked the doctor if he thought Maury could fire a semi-automatic shotgun. The bloke laughed at me. He thought I was nuts.' Molly shrugged. 'I'm sorry, Jesse, but it will never stand up in court.'

'But he still manages his farm,' Jesse mumbled. 'And he's been using the firing range.'

'According to his doctor, that's part of a balance and coordination exercise program worked out by his physio. Maury shoots a Sig Sauer air pistol. It weighs less than nine hundred grams. He can't hold anything heavier, and those things have no kick. The GP said that Maury's driver's license was revoked because of his ill health.

Maury drives around his property but has a farmhand to do most of the work hard. He does some things around his farm, sure, but Bailey takes him to his doctor and dental appointments.' Molly shrugged. 'We're talking pounds of recoil from that SKS rifle. A tricky enough feat for a strong bloke, let alone a weakened older man. Maury couldn't fire that weapon.'

'So, you got the wrong guy,' Ben said with a smile.

Jesse let the comment slide. He was too disappointed to allow the obnoxious cop to rile him.

'But good work Jesse. Ruling out Maury ticks one more box.' Molly stood and brushed the crumbs from the front of her black trousers. 'One less suspect means we work even harder.' She turned to Ben and asked, 'Where are we with Randy Singh's autopsy results? I thought you told me they were coming through today?'

Ben scraped the last of the rice from his plate. He gave Molly a strange glance, part disdain, part nonchalance. Jesse noticed Molly stiffen, her left hand throttling the pen she was holding. Their body language towards each other had changed of late. Jesse had initially thought the two were an item, but this past week Molly appeared standoffish, and Ben seemed sulkier than usual.

'I think the report just came through,' Ben said finally.

'Well?' Molly glared at him.

'I thought I'd eat first. I was feeling a bit lightheaded.' Ben grinned.

'Just open the God damn email and read it out!'

Jesse covered his smirk by coughing into his hand while Ben frantically used his mouse.

'I got it,' Ben said. 'Let's see. Cause of death — asphyxiation.'

Molly opened her mouth, but before she could speak, her phone rang. She held up her index finger for silence and answered the call. Jesse watched her face. She was doing more listening than speaking, nodding occasionally while her expression grew glum, then a sigh of resignation. 'Okay, thank you.' She finished the call.

'Bad news?' Jesse asked.

'That was Sergeant Jared Creighton in Adelaide. It seems that one of Randy Singh's old drinking buddies has confessed to smothering Randy in his bed.' Molly gave a shrug. 'According to the friend, the two had made a pact that he'd help Randy on his way when he got too sick.'

'Jesus!' Jesse said.

'Apparently, this mate had been drinking that evening. When he called into the care home, Randy was in a distressed state and begged the man to help him end it all. The friend said it only took a minute.'

'So he says,' Ben scoffed.

Molly spun and pointed her finger at Ben. 'You need to grow up. That bloke will be charged with manslaughter for ending his friend's pain. He risks a lengthy prison sentence because he put his friend's suffering above his own well-being. That takes a lot of guts and selflessness.'

'He broke the law!' Now Ben was on his feet.

'Whoa, whoa, you two.' Jesse walked between them but faced Molly. 'As you said, Molly, we just ticked one more suspect off our list. Like it or not, we are gradually getting answers.'

Molly hung her head. 'You're right Jesse. Sorry, Ben.' But her tone was far from remorseful. 'We need to crack on.' She was already striding towards her desk and stabbing at her phone. 'I need to speak to Piper Summerton. Jesse, please take Maury back to his home.'

Jesse stood and glanced at Ben, who was smacking his mouse against the desk. His face was livid. Molly had tasked him with trawling through many hours of CCTV footage from the day of the murder, taken from the two nearest petrol stations to Henderson. It seemed she didn't believe he'd done a thorough examination of the material initially. It was a mind-numbing process and likely to be futile. So perhaps the mundane job had been given to Ben as punishment for something. Jesse wondered what that was but didn't dare ask.

When Ben peered over his computer to glare at Jesse, Jesse gave him a grin and a thumbs-up and then made a hasty exit to the cells.

*

When Ravi's pager sounded, he didn't read the message. He already knew about the fire his crew were being called to; in fact, as they rounded the corner, he could see the billowing smoke. A concerned citizen had driven directly to the CFS depot to alert the team five minutes ago. Ray's Automotive Repairs was reportedly gutted by flames.

They parked the truck at an angle to the fire hydrant on the road, and the doors opened.

Andy barked orders to the firies as they piled out. Mason and Christa ran for the hose and extensions while Jasmine and Eli attached the reticulation hose to the mains water.

'Ravi, check the building.' Andy pointed to a man standing past the workshop doors. 'That's Ray; make sure no one else is inside and get him another hundred metres back! There could be fuel, and God knows what else in that shed.'

Ravi shrugged on his breathing apparatus unit, tightening belts and charging his oxygen cylinder. With swift movements Ravi pulled his respirator over his face, donning his hood and helmet, before nodding to Andy. He took off at an awkward run towards the man. The heat was extreme, and the air smelled of burning grass. As he passed the signage for the business Ravi read that the place doubled as a fodder supply store. He swore. No wonder the site was burning so intensely.

'Come away from there, mate!' Ravi shouted to the man.

But instead of moving back, Ray advanced towards the open double doorway. 'I left Harry in there!' he shrieked.

'What? Who's Harry?'

But Ray was running closer to the inferno. He made it another ten metres before the heat affected him; he stumbled and fell. The firies were positioned to Ravi's left, water cannoning towards the flames. Christa swivelled to glance at Ray, the nozzle and flow of pressurised water diverting a metre or so with the movement. Supporting the hose from behind her, Mason looked across too and then waved them away. Ravi caught Ray around the waist and half carried him back in the direction of the fire truck. He covered around forty metres when the bloke deliberately elbowed him in the chin. Ravi grasped at his dislodged mask, which dripped blood from his bitten tongue.

'Shit!' he cursed as Ray ran back towards the burning shed. His sudden anger seemed to flip a switch in his mind. Both the noise from the flames and the horrid vortex erupted in Ravi's head simultaneously. 'No!' he screamed as the familiar sensation engulfed him. Suddenly his veins were running with heated rage. 'Not now!' He stood bent over with his hands on his knees for support while his brain reeled. 'No, no, no!'

Ray had once more been dashed to the ground by the heat of the flames, so Ravi focussed all his attention on the fallen man. He roared as he ran, venting his ire and ignoring all other senses. Again, he sprinted despite the weight of his equipment. This time he picked Ray up off the ground and over his shoulder, hearing a clang as Ray's head met with the oxygen bottle on his back.

'Too bad,' Ravi growled as he ran to the truck, delivering Ray in front of Andy, who paused from yelling into his phone.

'Talk to this guy,' Ravi shouted through his mask. 'He keeps trying to get back in there.'

Andy stared at Ray, who was whining.

'It's Harry! I didn't get him out! I must get him!' Ray yelled.

Andy grasped Ray by the shoulders and shook him hard. 'I'm sorry, Ray, but you can't go in there. Harry is gone by now. I'm sorry, but it's too late.'

Ray fell against the side of the truck and howled.

Ravi pulled off his respirator mask, ignoring the steady drips of blood. The storm in his head had receded, his anger ebbing away. 'Who is Harry?' he asked between breaths.

Andy gestured with his head to step away from Ray. Once they were out of earshot, Andy said, 'his budgie. It was his wife's. The little fella meant a lot to him.'

A chuckle caused Ravi's shoulders to hitch, so he rammed his mask back on. He was sad that the man had lost his bird, but Ravi was relieved it wasn't a human casualty.

'Ravi, you go take over from Christa; she can swap with Mason.' Andy said, 'I've requested backup. We've got a water tanker coming, so tell Mason to direct it over the other side of the shed. The wind's dying, and most of the fodder fuel has burnt but the vehicles in the service bay could still cause issues. And Ravi, what happened to your face?'

Ravi glanced at Ray, who had slumped to a sitting position, staring sadly at his ruined business and shedding tears for his dead bird.

'It's okay; it was just a bump.'

'Alright, get going!' Andy said as he watched the billowing flames.

＊

The Wi-Fi connectivity in Bailey's flat was unreliable, so she studied in her mother's dining room. Most of her textbooks and notepads were left there permanently during the week. Bailey still wore her uniform bearing the nursing home logo; for once her morning shift had been spent assisting the Occupational Therapist, so her clothes were spared their usual soiling. Outside the air was still heavy with smoke from the now contained fire only a few blocks away. Ravi had messaged with news of the inferno, and to say he was safe.

Bailey's mum was bottling preserved fruit when they both heard a car squeal to a halt outside the house.

'What was that?' Bailey called.

There was no reply from the kitchen, only the sound of the front door opening. Bailey thought nothing of it until she heard her grandpa shouting and her mother's quieter but shrill responses. Bailey ran to the entranceway. Grandpa was pushing Donna with his elbows; she was up against the wall, eyes wide with fear.

'Grandpa, stop that right now! Don't you dare treat my mum like that; get away!' Bailey managed to squeeze between the two, facing her grandfather as he raised his trembling fist. 'Don't you bloody dare!'

The old man's rage appeared to diminish when he saw Bailey's outrage. His head and hands dropped in unison. After such an uproar, the silence felt fragile. Grandpa hobbled into the lounge room, shoulders slumped, and collapsed onto the sofa. A moment later, he began to sob. Bailey wrapped her arms around her mother and held her until she stopped shaking. 'It's okay,' Bailey crooned. She kissed her mum on the cheek and then stormed to the lounge.

'Is this outburst because the police wanted to ask you a few questions?' Bailey asked her grandpa.

He glared at her. The fire suddenly back in his eyes. 'No, it's because my family turned on me! You wanted to see me in prison.'

'Oh, rubbish Grandpa. For some reason, you had the rifle used to murder Edith Sanders hidden in the shearer's mess. Why? That's a question that needed answering.' Bailey towered over him, pointing her finger in angry jabs. 'All you had to do was help the police. If you had no idea how the gun got there, then that should have been your answer, but oh no, you had to come across like the hard man. "I'm not going to help the police!" Well, all you did was make a fool of yourself. You stewed away in that jail cell, getting angrier and angrier at everyone but the person you should have been angry at.' Bailey poked her finger at his chest and lowered her voice. 'And if you ever talk to my mum like that again, you'll find yourself in the lock-down section of a care home somewhere, and it won't be anywhere near us! Because we will ever come and visit you.'

'You would lock me away?' he whimpered.

Bailey's eyes stung, and she looked away. Near the fireplace, her mother was shaking her head slowly. Suddenly aware that words couldn't be taken back, Bailey exhaled a huge breath. She knelt and hugged him. 'Of course, I wouldn't. But you must promise not to act that way again. If anyone wants to speak to you, police or anyone else, you must ensure I'm with you, okay?'

Grandpa's lips trembled, and he nodded.

'And you can't be driving. They took your license from you for a reason, Grandpa. For your safety and everyone else's. You must stop being reckless.'

Donna sat on a settee on the other side of the room. Then, for more than five minutes, there was an uneasy hush. Finally, Grandpa spoke. His voice was tremulous, and he didn't take his eyes off his knees.

'I know you don't understand, but it didn't seem fair when Colin died. Gwen still had two daughters who adored her, and I had no one. I hadn't spent much time with you girls,' he stared at Donna. 'Back then, men had their sons and did manly things, hunting, fishing, camping. I didn't know how to be a father to girls. You always seemed a bit – foreign to me. Like another species. And you didn't seem to need me, only your mum. But it didn't mean I didn't love you both. You were so much like your mum, little versions of her, and she was always a bit of a mystery to me. I suppose I felt outnumbered, and that made me miss my boy even more. I was bitter. Still am, and I can't help it.' After a moment, he said. 'But I'm sorry for that.'

Donna nodded slowly. 'At least you never had a problem with Bailey. I was always grateful for that.'

'No.' He shook his head. 'Never. She wasn't like a girl or a boy. She just did things, had a go at anything.'

When he smiled at Bailey, his face brightened. She knew she had always been his favourite, but she kept silent as Grandpa cleared his throat before continuing.

'I suppose, Donna, she was the kid I'd always dreamed of having. She always had to be on the back of the tractor, or a motorbike, or a horse. Didn't matter if it wasn't clean or she tore her clothes doing stuff.' He gave a cackle and grinned at Bailey. 'Grandma called you a tom-boy, but you weren't you were just you, filling a hole in my life.' He clasped his hands before him, nodding as though trying to find the right words. 'Something changed when Grandma died. I was alone, and I started to feel resentful again for having lost Colin all those years ago. Bailey, you were always too busy, and I knew your study and work would probably take you away. It seemed to me that if I'd had a son, he'd be here for me.'

'You can't know that Dad!' Donna shouted. 'For all you know, he might have hated farming and moved to the city just like every other boy in this town with half a brain!'

Grandpa sucked in a breath. He looked truly flummoxed. He shook his head with uncertainty.

'Mum's right, Grandpa. Mum's the one who's always been here for you. Aunty Michele moved away, but Mum insisted that we stay here, even when Dad wanted to move to Port Lincoln so I could attend a better school. And after that, Dad had to turn down the job with the AG tech company because that meant moving away. He hates working at the farm supply shop but has no choice. They stay here because of you. We all stay here because of you.'

'What?' Grandpa pushed his hand over his mouth. His eyes bright with tears. 'I didn't know that.'

'You could fill a book with the things you don't know, you old fool!' Donna's words were harsh, but her eyes crinkled with the beginnings of a smile. 'And Bailey's right. From now on, you're going to do what she tells you. God knows you never listen to me!'

'I'm going to try. I really am.' Grandpa's voice was little more than a squeak.

Bailey had never heard her grandpa sound so needy or contrite. The disease, so the doctor had warned her, may possibly make him more obstinate, so maybe this was a good starting point for a change in his attitude.

But she wasn't kidding herself. Things were going to get a lot tougher.

*

It had been a long time since Carl had ridden his motorbike any great distance. When he was in his twenties, it had all seemed so effortless, but today, covering only half the almost seven hundred kilometres, he felt stiff and out of practice. It didn't help that his bike was not a tourer. The Kawasaki was great for zipping around the hills, but the open road was taxing. When Carl got off the bike to fuel up in Whyalla, his legs felt like they would buckle beneath him, and his shoulders were burning.

He opened his wallet with fingers that were tingling from the endless vibrations through the handlebars. The lady in the servo shook her head when she saw him eyeing off the pie in the warming oven.

Then, while she processed his petrol payment, she said, 'You look a bit knackered, love. Has it been a long trip?'

'Yeah,' Carl admitted. 'From a town on the other side of Adelaide, and I'm out of practice.'

'Where are you headed?'

'Henderson.'

'Yeah, why?'

'I got some business there.'

'You've still got a long way to go then.'

Carl exhaled loudly. 'Tell me about it.'

'You know, my uncle's got a nice little cafe near the caravan park, just here in town. Food's heaps better than here, and there's a lovely shady garden where you can sit to eat. I reckon you could do with a proper rest before you get riding again.'

Carl took his receipt and thanked the woman.

He took her advice, and she was right. Her uncle's food was delicious, and sitting back with his boots off felt wonderful. Moreover, it revitalised him for the next four hundred kilometres.

He arrived in Henderson, hot and dusty, just before eight pm that night. The local pub was bland, and his room was basic, but the bed, with its firm mattress and clean sheets, felt palatial. He slept like the dead.

*

The next morning Carl pulled up across the street from the local police station a little after nine. It was a tiny building, so he was surprised to see three cops standing out the front, holding an animated conversation. Only one was uniformed but all of them wore cop lanyards and ID. It seemed like overkill the have three staff in a struggling town, but he guessed it was because of the murder investigation. The cops watched him as he crossed the road. The hard-faced woman narrowed her eyes and asked him what his business was as he drew nearer.

'I want to speak to someone about the shooting that happened here. I think I have some information that may be helpful. I did call and speak to someone on that hotline the police set up, but I have yet to hear back from anyone. That was a few days ago, so I thought I'd come here in person.'

The only cop wearing a uniform stepped forward. He offered his hand and introduced himself as Jesse Plackis. He was a bit worn-looking. A man who was handsome in youth and now had an interesting appearance, maybe from a life lived outdoors or filled with more stress than a person should endure. Jesse gestured to the two plain-clothed officers, Ben and Molly, but Carl didn't get their last names.

Ben looked uptight; Molly looked underfed and hungry.

'Please,' Jesse said. 'Come on inside. Where are you from?'

'Tailem Bend.'

'Wow. That's quite a hike.'

'You're telling me. My arse is blistered.'

Ben and Molly followed behind, and once inside, they stood leaning against the office wall, allowing Jesse to ask the questions. Jesse pointed to a chair positioned on the other side of his desk. Carl slung his leather jacket onto the back of the seat and sat down gingerly.

'What's this information you have for us, Carl?' Jesse asked.

'Okay. You see, I'm a paramedic from Tailem Bend. A couple of weeks ago, my partner, Tash, was attacked and killed by a patient we'd been sent to treat.'

'The stabbing? The CAS recipient?' Molly asked.

'Yeah.'

'Jeez, I'm sorry, mate,' Jesse said.

'Yeah, me too. Anyway, our ambulance depot isn't far from Mobilong Prison, and a housing development set up for ex-offenders. It's called Lavender Court. That's where Tash was killed.'

Carl paused, looking from face to face. Jesse hung off his words. Molly appeared moved, her face softer in empathy. Ben examined his fingernails.

'Please, go on,' Jesse urged.

'There are quite a few CAS recipients residing there. For obvious reasons, we approach them with caution…'

'But your friend didn't.' Ben butted in. 'Or she'd still be alive.'

'You weren't there, so you have no bloody idea!' Carl was halfway out of his chair, propelled by anger. Just as suddenly, he stopped, aware that his behaviour could be perceived as threatening. He sat down. Losing his temper would not help. This is for Tash, he reminded himself.

'It's okay, Carl.' Jesse assured him.

Molly whispered something to her colleague, and he stalked from the room, slamming a door as he went. Then she walked to a bench by the wall and switched on the kettle. 'I'm sorry,' she said. 'Ben has problems with his manners sometimes.'

'And being part of the human race,' Jesse spat.

Carl wiped his brow and sniffed. 'Anyway, I treated a patient this week from Lavender Court. I think he knows something about the shooting here in Henderson.'

Molly almost dropped the coffee container she was holding. 'What?'

Carl told them about the circumstances of Paul requiring medical attention, Paul's admission of memory lapse and Carl's subsequent visit to see him in the hospital. Once he was done, Jesse jotted down notes while Molly sat in quiet contemplation. The room was so silent that Carl could hear his own breathing.

Molly was the first to speak. 'So, according to your recollection, you mentioned the town's name first?'

'Um, yeah. I guess. I'd just read about it.'

'So, could it be that this man merely agreed with what you said?' But before Carl could answer, Molly continued, 'I mean, a beach town in the middle of nowhere could be one of millions of places in Australia. You don't suppose you gave him a name to hang his story on?'

Molly sounded sceptical, but Jesse appeared excited.

'No, you were right to report this,' Jesse said. 'Carl. This man, Paul, you said he's an ex-biker? He admitted to being involved in illegal activity and that his actions may have escalated beyond his control.'

'But,' Molly interrupted again. 'He never mentioned a gun, did he? I mean, he said something about "putting on the frighteners" but not using a weapon. He could have been talking about a beating.'

'No, he didn't say the "gun" word, but tell me, was it a semi-automatic rifle?' Carl asked.

Molly and Jesse exchanged glances, but neither spoke.

'I know the media reports said the lady was gunned down by a rifle, but they didn't specify what type.' Carl asked again, 'So, was it a semi-automatic rifle?'

'Yes, it was, but we didn't want to panic the public. We kept that detail to ourselves,' Jesse said. 'Why?'

'Because a normal rifle fire wouldn't look like this.' Carl copied Paul's miming of the incident; one arm extended, gripping the barrel, the other hand holding the stock, and then the judder of multiple bullets firing into the air. When he finished, Carl dropped his arms and stared at the two cops. 'Because that was Paul's description of what he did.'

The room went dead quiet.

'Jesus!' Molly whispered. Her lips were pursed.

For a long while, she and Jesse just stared at each other.

Chapter Nineteen

'Some bastard in Adelaide is going to take all the credit for the work that we've done on this case!'

Ben's expression was petulant, and while it irked Molly, she had to agree with his sentiment. It wasn't fair, after all the time and effort they had put in, for someone else to arrest their suspect and take the glory.

'Let's talk to him,' she suggested.

'The nut case?'

Molly ignored Ben's remark. 'His name is Paul de Sousa.'

'Spanish?' Jesse asked.

'Portuguese father, but Paul was born in Sydney. According to Carl, he's still in hospital and, by all accounts – vulnerable.' Molly liked the sound of the word.

'What are you thinking?' Jesse asked.

'I want to talk to him.'

'You mean to question him,' Ben said.

'I want to find out as much as I can.'

'No, Molly. If you talk to him, you could jeopardise this entire case,' Jesse warned.

'Then what do you suggest?' Molly pushed her hair back from her sticky brow and fanned her face with an old road safety pamphlet.

'I suggest doing things by the book.'

Molly flinched at Jesse's pious tone and fanned even faster. She glared at Ben. 'Haven't you found the remote control for the air con yet?'

'No. You were the last person to use it, Molly. So why don't you find it?'

She crushed the pamphlet into a ball and lobbed it into the wastepaper basket. 'What exactly should we do, Jesse?' she snapped.

Jesse glanced at Ben. Something passed between the two and Molly suspected they had colluded behind her back.

'What?' she repeated. 'Are you two mates all of a sudden?' Jesse gave an exasperated sigh which caused Molly to thump her fist on the desk. 'Don't keep me in the dark. What have you two been discussing?' Her voice felt brittle with irritation.

'Carl should go back and talk to De Sousa. He has developed a rapport with the bloke. If we try speaking to him, he'll clam up. He's a bike gang member and ex-crim; why would he talk to cops?'

'Jesse's right,' Ben added.

At any other time, Molly would have been pleased that her colleagues were behaving civilly to each other, but in this baking office, nothing was satisfying to her. Ben had done nothing but sulk since she'd ended their fling, and Jesse was coming across as downright preacherly.

Christ, she thought, I feel like I'm back living with my cry-baby little brother and my overbearing father.

'If Carl can get De Sousa to tell him where he stashed the murder weapon, then we have a solid case.' Jesse glanced from Molly to Ben. 'But of course, if the city cops had this information, they would be searching De Sousa's house right now, and who knows what they might find.'

'No.' Molly pulled the hair tie from her ponytail, shook her head and re-fastened it while she considered her next words. 'They probably wouldn't act on it because all we have is an ex-criminal who may be spinning a story for shits and giggles. Additionally, the man is suffering from both a physical problem and mental condition. His violent outburst and amnesia may well have been exacerbated by the CAS.

'So down the track, the blame for his actions may fall on the law itself and, inevitably, us, as law enforcement. I think there is a need to tread carefully. You're right Jesse. I think Carl should speak to De Sousa again. We need real evidence before we ask Adelaide to proceed with searches or an arrest.' She held out her hands, palms up. 'Do we agree?'

The unanimous agreement alleviated some of her anxiety, but nothing could be done about the cloying heat in the room.

'Before Carl leaves town, I want to speak to him.' Molly stood and stretched. 'Right. I'm going to the cafe to cool down.' She reached the door and added, 'You know where to find me.'

*

Ravi frowned at the desiccated shrub that was his grandma's prized hydrangea bush. It grew in the roadside garden his grandma had established decades before. Ravi had neglected that section of shrubbery during the heat of summer and now he was regretting it. The hose wouldn't reached that far, and bucketing water in the oppressive sunshine wasn't appealing. Now most of the hydrangea leaves had burned. He remembered the plant being covered in shade cloth when he'd come here during the Christmas holidays years before; in hindsight, that had doubtless been for its protection against the elements. Ravi plucked off the crunchy leaves and threw them into his bucket. He thrust his finger into the soil. It was bone dry.

In the garden shed, he found some secateurs and a bag of pea-straw mulch. He didn't have much faith in his ability to resurrect the bush but felt he owed it to his grandma to give it a go.

Ravi found gardening cathartic, but his grandma's greening of the street and her own garden seemed over the top. After ten minutes, he paused and rolled his shoulders, stretching his neck. The tension he'd felt following the fire at Ray's was lifting, and Bailey was coming over tonight. His mood lifted in anticipation.

Once the pruning was done, he opened the pea straw. As he spread the mulch around the base of the plants, his nail connected with something hard. He heard a metallic click. Ravi used his fingertips to loosen the soil. The copper casing shone brightly in the morning sun. When he realised what it was, he flinched.

'What the ...' he muttered.

It was a bullet casing. A large one. Maybe the one from the fatal shot.

Five minutes after Ravi phoned and reported the find to Jesse, the cop's four-wheel drive was parked on the roadside.

'You didn't touch it, did you?' Jesse asked before he had closed his car door.

'No. I didn't.'

Jesse picked up the casing with a pair of forceps and placed it into an evidence bag. He held the bag at face height, and they gazed at it.

'They were big bullets,' Ravi said in little more than a whisper.

'Yeah.' Jesse put an arm across his shoulders. 'I'm so sorry, son.'

They stood for a moment, mesmerised by the ordnance. Then, finally, it was Jesse who broke the spell.

'Good job finding it, Ravi. And I heard you did great work yesterday at Ray's. That can't have been easy.'

'Thanks. I didn't save Ray's budgie, though.'

'Crikey! Was that old bird still alive?' Jesse asked.

'Apparently.'

'Wow. Aggie died ten years ago or more. So, that was one geriatric bird.'

'Ray took it hard. That rocked him more than losing the workshop.'

'Well, Ravi, you prevented him from being injured, and the fire was put out before it spread. If it had jumped the fence, most of the town could have gone up.'

'I guess.' Ravi gave a shrug and half a smile.

'You know, you need to give yourself a little more credit. Your grandma would be proud, and I know your mum is. She phoned this morning and went on about the fire for over an hour.'

Ravi felt his face heat, and he looked away. Jesse slapped his back so hard he stumbled forward. When he turned, the cop was smiling at him.

'I get it, Ravi. You don't like blowing your own trumpet, and I can relate to that.' Jesse held up the evidence bag. 'But regardless, this is good work.' He turned to walk back to the car.

'I hope you find who did it, Jesse.'

'Me too Ravi, me too.'

*

The ride home was no less harrowing than the journey to Henderson, but it gave Carl time to think without distractions. The cop, Molly, had given Carl plenty of suggestions on how to get Paul talking without using leading questions. Carl memorised all he needed to ask. But, of course, much would hinge on Paul's state of mind.

So far, Carl had only seen the bloke friendly and receptive, but Carl knew all too well about what some CAS recipients were capable of.

Molly had also spoken to the doctor in charge of Paul's case at the hospital. There had been some delays with the surgery schedules because of staff shortages. But the doctor confirmed that Paul was booked for a cholecystectomy at two o'clock that afternoon. He would stay in the hospital for at least two days post-operatively, longer if there were complications. This allowed Carl some time to go home, sleep – hopefully – and feel refreshed. He needed to be mentally primed to get some answers.

Once Carl had passed Whyalla, he found himself plagued with memories of Tash. Not the happy recollections of their fun times together but of the day she was murdered. It should never have happened, of course, but the man who killed her was not truly to blame. If Dorian Lindquist was correct, then the Criminal Ageing System was flawed from the outset. The government had been determined to implement the scheme and went ahead despite inadequate trials. Now it had been scrapped, but people were still being attacked. All the while, the recipients themselves were going through mental hell. Someone had to be held to account.

Didn't they?

The rude cop, Ben, had implied that Tash was at fault, and in a way, she was, but she had followed her compassion, the very thing that made her who she was. She had taken care but not seen the trap. Tash hadn't looked past a man suffering a medical emergency because deceit was alien to her. No. The cop was wrong, and Carl would make sure Tash's death was not in vain. Once Paul was arrested, Carl would tell her story. His father would probably disapprove, but if an educated public took more care when interacting with CAS recipients, Carl might find the peace lacking since her death. The thought bolstered him, and surprisingly the kilometres flashed by so much faster.

He arrived home just after six pm.

*

Molly was extremely grateful that Chelsea Summerton had agreed to a video link interview. This time it was Chelsea who was running late. And as luck would have it, Molly was about to go and pee out the three cups of coffee she had rapidly swigged that morning when the live feed came through. Chelsea beamed at the camera while an IT tech adjusted the monitor for picture quality. Molly hoped the smile was a positive sign.

'Thanks for agreeing to attend the station Chelsea,' Molly began.

Chelsea nodded. 'I phoned the number you gave me after I spoke to Piper.' Chelsea gestured to her surroundings. 'The communications man organised this.'

'That's great. So, how did you contact Piper?'

'I sent a message via Mum's Facebook messenger account. It was luck that Piper answered right away.'

'Was she surprised it was you and not her mother?'

'No. I told her it was me, and she switched to Facetime. I was pleased because I could always tell by looking at her if she was telling the truth.

'Great stuff,' Molly said. She had momentarily forgotten her over-full bladder because this was better news than she had expected. 'What did Piper have to say?'

'I asked her about Ravi. Whether she had set him up to steal the car. She had the decency to look embarrassed, but then she said she was merely paying him back for making her life miserable.' Chelsea shrugged. 'Pretty standard "Piper" defence – always blame someone else. So, I asked her what happened. She said that Amos Khalil suggested that Ravi wouldn't be such a problem if he was in jail. Then Piper would be free to live however she wanted, in his apartment, with the use of his car and everything else. Andreas was going to move in with her.'

'So, Piper didn't plan the car theft?'

'I think she did. Piper has this way of pursing her lips when she's lying. She's done it all her life. She was doing it when she told me it was Khalil's idea.'

'Okay. Did she tell you any details?'

'Not really. She said Ravi was a fool and dicked around too long. She said he was caught because he was an idiot. Piper said Maryjo's driver's seat was difficult to adjust. That's what held him up.'

'That information about the seat must have come from Khalil,' Molly said. 'He would have been aware of a detail like that. He had probably driven the car himself.'

'Maybe, Piper didn't say. But she said she realised it would stall Ravi because he was much taller than Maryjo. So he couldn't have driven without adjusting the seat.'

'Did Piper say where she was at the time of the incident?'

'Yes. She said she was watching from the window in the laundromat across the road. She also said she called the police. That's why they got there so fast. Ravi was supposed to be caught in the act.'

'She really is a piece of work,' Molly muttered.

'I know. I hate that she's my sister sometimes.'

'Chelsea, what did Piper say when Ravi was given the CAS sentence instead of incarceration?'

'Well, Piper said her blood was boiling. She couldn't stand the thought that he would still be in her life *and* be ten years older. So, Khalil suggested scaring Ravi off.'

'Scaring him?' Molly frowned. 'Not killing him?'

'No. And she didn't seem to be lying to me. Piper was distraught when I mentioned Ravi's grandmother and what had happened to her. The shots were meant to be fired over the house. Piper said that shooting at the house was not what had been organised. '

'Organised by Khalil?'

'She didn't mention him by name.' Chelsea shrugged. 'I believe her. I really do.'

'Do you think she'll return from Thailand?'

'I don't know. She's scared that she will be implicated in the murder. She might have come home if it wasn't for that, but I can't be sure.'

'Would she tell you?' Molly asked.

'Yeah. I think she would.' Chelsea gave a sigh. 'She seemed different when I spoke to her. I think the fear of prison has drained her of some of her sass. It might have been a good thing for her.'

'Maybe.' Molly doubted it. 'Would you contact me if she planned on returning?'

Chelsea chewed her bottom lip before replying. 'Not if it meant her being arrested.'

'Fair enough, but if we find out she planned the shooting, she would be arrested the second she returned anyway.'

'Then you wouldn't need to hear it from me.' There was an edge to Chelsea's tone.

'I understand your loyalty, misguided as it is. She is your sister. Thank you for being so helpful, Chelsea. I really appreciate it.'

Molly ended the call and sat back in her chair. Piper may not have set up a murder, but she was far from innocent. Of course, Chelsea may have been lying to cover for her. It took another five minutes of mental toing and froing before Molly was prompted by her dangerously full bladder.

Her pace to the toilet was swift.

*

Paul was in such a deep sleep, that with his head lolled to one side, face slack, and eyes slightly open, Carl felt momentary panic. The man looked dead, and in the murky light it was impossible to see the steady rise and fall of his chest. Carl hit the light switch above Paul's bed, and the illumination painted a healthier picture.

'What – what?' Paul mumbled as he covered his eyes.

'Hi, mate. Sorry. I didn't realise you were asleep.' Carl slid the visitor's armchair from beneath the window to the side of the hospital bed.

'Oh. It's okay mate. I was just a bit sleepy.' Then, as if to prove his point, Paul yawned.

'You look pretty good, all things considered.' Carl observed. 'How are you feeling?'

Paul grunted as he struggled to sit up. His white linen gown looked incongruous against his tattooed, weathered skin and gnarly hands.

'Here, let me help you.' Carl picked up the hand control and adjusted the backrest on the bed. Once Paul was almost upright, Carl hung the device on the side rail.

'What time is it?' Paul asked.

'Ten thirty. Can I get you something? I checked with the nurse. You can have tea or coffee if you want.'

'I could murder a coffee.'

Carl flinched at the hyperbole and then got to his feet. 'I'll be back in a minute.' He was gripped by a sudden bout of nerves. At the coffee machine, Carl caught sight of his reflection in the stainless steel. He looked drawn with worry. On the way back to the room, he breathed steadily, stopping before the doorway for two deep inhalations. He couldn't blow this opportunity. He had to remain calm.

Paul kept yawning while he drank his beverage. Finally, when he was done, he gave a belch and handed the cup to Carl. 'Oh man, that really hit the spot.'

'So, when do they think you can leave?'

'Probably tomorrow.' He pointed to a yellow-topped pathology pot sitting on his bedside drawer. 'That's the little sucker that caused me all that bloody pain.'

Carl turned the jar over in his hand. The dark green cholelithiasis rolled around the bottom. It was almost two centimetres in radius. 'No wonder you were in agony. That's a big stone.'

'I really owe you, man. You helped me through a rough time.'

'You're welcome – I um…' Carl faltered for a moment. He'd practised asking these questions in the mirror before leaving home, but now he felt tongue-tied and desperately afraid of stuffing everything up.

'Are you okay, man?' Paul frowned. All signs of grogginess were gone.

'I just wondered about the other problem you had. You know, with your memory.'

Paul stared towards the curtained window. He gave a brief nod. 'Yeah, that's all good, I think.'

'Because there was that lapse, you know, when you said your mind was somewhere else.' Carl held his breath, terrified he'd overstepped.

'Oh yeah. That job out in the country.'

'Yeah, what was the name of that place?'

Paul frowned. 'I remember.' He nodded. 'Probably shouldn't tell you about it, though.'

'No?'

'Nah. Coz then I'd have to kill you!' Paul gave a raucous laugh.

Carl forced a smile. This wasn't going to work. How naïve of him to think it would be so easy. He squirmed in his chair, glancing at the doorway.

'Hey man, don't go yet! I was only kidding about the killing bit.'

'Oh, sure. I can stay a bit longer.'

'Good. Yeah, I was in Henderson the day I lost that chunk of time.

Carl froze. After a second, he nodded.

'It's a little town on the west coast. Blink, and you miss it. Not that most people go through it coz it's too far off the highway. Nothing much there. Just a beach, and there are plenty of other beach towns with good shops and stuff.'

'Sounds nice.' Carl clasped the arms of the chair. 'I like quiet towns.'

'Yeah. Anyway, I had this job to do. But I don't remember it.'

'What, none of it?'

'I remember driving there. Finding the house – next thing I was driving along the beach. It was so fucking weird.'

'So, what happened then?'

Paul looked towards the end of the bed. Eyes narrowed. 'It was hot. I had to dump the car, so I drove along this deserted beach until I found a track in the dunes. I rolled the car to the bottom of a ditch and covered it with seaweed and branches. Then I walked along in the water for a while to cool down. My guitar case was making my back sweat.'

'Guitar case?'

Paul grinned. 'Handy for carrying things. Then I got to a fence and went west, back towards the main highway. I had to ring a mate to come and get me, but that would take some time. He was waiting in some nearby town.' Paul chewed on his thumbnail, squinting, and then said, 'I stopped at a water trough, hoping to get phone reception. There was a bunch of sheep there, and further down the road was an old family graveyard. Most of the headstones were crumbling.' Paul's eyes closed as though picturing it. 'Early settlers, I guess. Up by the gate was a memorial, new looking, in brown marble. I sat against the shady side and took a break. Not long after, this old farmer drives up in a white ute. Stares at me, stares at the headstone. He looks a bit confused.' Paul tapped the side of his head. 'Like he's not all there, you know? Trembly hands, strange way of walking.'

Carl nodded.

'So, he says to me, "Colin? Is that you Colin?" So, I play along and say, "Yeah, I'm Colin." Colin must have been his dead kid because the next thing he's talking about is all these things we used to do, rounding up sheep, rodeos, all that kind of shit. I keep agreeing with him and take a drive to his house. It's pretty run down. Probably nice back in the day, but this old bugger is past it. So, we have a few drinks, he tells me some story about his house burning down – shows me scars on his arms, says he tried to save me, and he cries a bit, well, a lot, actually. He reminisces a bit more, drinks a bit more, and then flakes out on the rug. I'm pretty sure he pissed his pants.'

'What did you do?'

'Nothin'. My mate picked me up about an hour later and drove me back home.'

'To Lavender Court.'

'Yeah.'

'But the job you were there to do. You don't remember that part?'

'Nah. I was having this strange head thing. It felt like someone put an air hose in my ear and turned it on full blast. Never felt anything like it. I didn't know up from down. Everything was a blur.'

'So, you don't know if you even finished what you were supposed to do?'

Paul winced, but it seemed from embarrassment rather than pain. 'I heard down the track that I might have gone a bit overboard. In fact. I think I fucked it up.'

'Oh?'

'Yeah. Best you don't know about that.'

'Sure. But still, you need to worry about that episode. Memory lapses can be a sign of a serious condition.'

'Yeah, I guess.'

'Really. It would be best if you were careful. I saw on your file that you were a CAS recipient. Other people have suffered effects from that treatment; believe me, mate, I've seen them. I'm going to let your doctor know and recommend scans.'

Paul reached out and touched Carl's elbow. 'You are a good bloke.'

'Thanks,' Carl mumbled. 'Oh wow, look at the time. I need to be somewhere.'

'Sure.'

'I'm glad you are looking so much better.'

'Thanks. Hey, don't be a stranger?'

'I'll call by.' Carl gave Paul the thumbs up, scooped his helmet from beside his chair, and strode to the door.

'Oi!' Paul yelled.

Carl froze with one hand on the door frame.

'What do you ride?'

'Um, a Ninja 1000SX.'

Paul chuckled. 'Get a decent bike! You big girl!'

Carl copied the laugh and waved once more.

But halfway down the hallway, he felt like puking.

Chapter Twenty

Ravi and Bailey had spent the previous evening together. Today they were both subdued and reflective, knowing their lives would soon change. This afternoon Bailey was travelling to Adelaide to begin her studies. Although she promised to return most weekends, they both knew that was impractical and costly with so many kilometres to cover.

The sun shone as they walked to the seashore. The nights were now cold, and the autumn warmth seemed like summer's last hurrah. Ravi tried to hide his bleak mood.

'Let's jog,' he suggested.

Hank ran in front. Chasing gulls, weaving from the sand to the surf. The bay was empty of people. There would be no more visitors here until the October long weekend, and even then, there would only be a scattering. It took just under forty minutes to cover the distance to the end of the bay and back. By the time they returned, they were sweating.

'Swim?' Bailey suggested. 'The water will be cold.'

'Sure.'

Ravi guessed he was overheated from the run; after all, it was hotter than he anticipated, but his head felt odd as they neared the water. He dreaded this feeling of strangeness, which he knew could be the precursor to an attack, so he dived into the waves, hoping to shake the sensation. Under the water, the sound was dim, but as he surfaced, the cyclone was upon him. He thrashed about in panic, dragging in huge breaths as the din muddled his thoughts. His arms flailed, and the world became murky green. He swallowed water when he battled the waves in his disoriented state, the heat in his throat kicking off the boiling sensation in his veins. And then, the anger was upon him.

Did he roar, or was it the storm in his head?

Ravi's hands slapped the water blindly, hunting for something to grasp, tear, and sate the rage. As he found his footing this time, he heard the roar as it tore from his throat. Then suddenly, the waves felt shallower, pushing against the backs of his calves, urging him towards the shore. He whipped his arms from left to right in a frenzy. Three more strides, and he tripped, face down on the hot sand. His vision suddenly darkened, but he thrashed until his muscles burned and the storm dimmed.

*

Jesse arrived at the hospital just ten minutes after Emily phoned him. The doctor on call had phoned her because she was listed as Ravi's next of kin. Her son had suffered an episode at the beach. As Jesse strode from his car to the front foyer, he saw Bailey sitting on the curb with her head resting on her knees. At first, he thought she was a kid, but she peered from up under her baseball cap and cried out. 'Oh, Jesse!' Her eyes were red-rimmed. 'Ravi lost the plot.'

'Bailey, are you okay?'

'Not really. I can't believe that was Ravi. He went insane. I've never seen anyone act like that before.' She wiped her tear-streaked cheeks. 'I was so scared. I had to run from him until he calmed down. Even Hank was terrified.'

'What do the doctors think?'

'They're transporting him to Whyalla for another MRI and to see a specialist. I'm unsure if they think it's a tumour, drugs, or seizures.' Bailey wrapped her arms around her chest and rocked back and forth. 'Jesse, I think Ravi's going to die!'

'No Bailey. Everything will be fine.' He felt a pang of shame as he said the words he didn't quite believe. 'You need to keep away while the doctors do their thing. Ravi isn't well and could do something – out of control.'

'I filmed him,' she whispered. 'I showed it to the doctor.'

'Really? Can I see it?'

She sniffed, wiped her nose on the end of her sleeve and fumbled her phone from her pocket. The footage was shaky. Bailey had filmed as she ran backwards through the sand. The image slanted to one side when Hank must have pulled against his lead, but it steadied again. At first, the man on the screen didn't look like Ravi; the face didn't look human, more animal. He seemed to erupt from the shallow waves. A force. A murderous-looking force. And the sound he made was awful. It was beast-like and angry. The video continued as he took a few steps and fell to the ground, obviously seething as he blindly thrashed. Then the vision went wobbly again as Bailey stepped closer and threw a towel over his head. In a few more seconds Ravi was quiet and still.

'Jesus,' Jesse muttered. 'That's a long way from normal. It looks like he pitched a fit.'

Bailey's head drooped, and she sobbed soundlessly beside him. Jesse touched her head, about to repeat his lie once more, but stopped. Ravi was not okay, and he would likely never be okay.

This time when Bailey said, 'I think Ravi's going to die.' Jesse agreed.

*

'Are you sure about interviewing the suspect? I mean, is it safe?' Ferdi asked as he watched Molly dress.

'I'll have Ben with me,' she turned to gauge her husband's reaction. 'And besides, Paul De Sousa is recovering from surgery. So he's not likely to be a danger.'

Ferdi slid out from under the sheets and walked towards her. Not bothering to hide his semi-erection. She took a breath as he hugged her. It crossed her mind to undress, but only for a second.

'I have to go.' Molly pointed to his cock. 'Keep that thought. I should be home by eight.'

'Shall I pick you up from the airport?'

Molly smiled, turned back and kissed him briefly on the lips. 'I'll get a cab, but dinner would be good.'

'I'll book us somewhere.'

'No. Let's eat in. Get takeaway.' She smiled. 'We can eat in bed.'

Ben was quiet on the flight to Adelaide, but Molly could feel his needy gaze. It only distracted her the first couple of times. After that, she was too focused on her questions for Paul De Sousa. She had butterflies in her stomach, which was usually a sure sign that she would succeed.

'Jesse would have liked to have been with us today,' Ben said while Molly drained her second cup of coffee.

Her lips twitched with a smile. Ben and Jesse had quite the bromance happening since she dumped him. Only last evening, they shared a beer at the pub. If only there had been such bonhomie from the beginning, they might have achieved so much more, so much sooner.

'Yes. I imagine Jesse would have.' She eyed him sidelong. 'But this is our case, Ben. We are Major Crimes. Besides, he is visiting Ravi Sanders' at the hospital.'

'Do you think Ravi will end up in a looney bin?'

'He is certainly a danger to himself and others.'

'You gotta feel sorry for the poor bastard. He's had shit luck.'

'Yes. But he's made poor choices too. People make their own luck to a degree.' Molly gazed out the window when she felt Ben's hand on her knee.

'Molly…'

'Stop it, Ben. We talk about work or nothing.' She stared down at his fingers as they kneaded her flesh. 'Touch me again, and you'll be unemployed. SAPOL take a dim view of sexual harassment.'

Ben kept his hands to himself. And although he grumbled and pouted occasionally throughout the next hour, Molly enjoyed near-silence for the rest of the flight.

*

Carl sighed loudly when his phone began to ring. He thought he'd switched it to silent, but after the night he'd had, it was any wonder he forgot. The three-car highway accident he attended had resembled a macabre butcher shop. Metal and flesh smeared for dozens of metres along the road. Even a couple of the seasoned cops had thrown up.

He thought about ignoring the call, but he needed to urinate first. As he walked back to his bed, he picked up his mobile. Dorian had been trying to phone him. Carl rubbed his chin; this was a surprise, and the intrigue was too great. Carl called him back.

'Dorian? It's Carl.'

'Oh, thanks for returning my call. I – had something I wanted to speak to you about. It is rather sensitive and perhaps not a discussion we should have on a mobile device.'

'Really?' Carl glanced at his bed, giving up on the possibility of returning to it. 'Oh, okay. What time and where?'

'The Feathers Hotel at eleven?'

'Yeah, sure.' As an afterthought, he asked, 'Is it important?'

'I believe so. And I'm sure you will too.'

'I'll see you there.'

Carl gave one last look at his bed and then headed to the shower. Sleep would be elusive anyway. His mind would be churning with the possible reasons for Dorian's meeting.

When Carl arrived, Dorian was already seated at a corner table in the bistro. Only a few other people were on this side of the room and none were within earshot.

'Sorry about the cloak and dagger, Carl, but I wanted to discuss a sensitive matter.'

'Sure, that's okay.'

'I took the liberty of ordering us brunch. They do a wonderful eggs benedict. I was fairly sure you didn't have any of those trendy eating disorders.'

Carl coughed out a laugh. 'No, I can eat most things.'

The food arrived shortly after Carl had taken his first sip of coffee. Dorian delayed discussing anything until they ate. He dined delicately and slowly. Carl had wolfed his meal in the time it took for Dorian to arrange his eggs and toast. When Dorian finished his food, Carl was on his third coffee and feeling somewhat wired.

Finally, Dorian neatly folded his napkin, which had only been used for dabbing his lips, and said, 'I have been privy to some information regarding the CAS recipients. There have been violent outbursts and attacks nationwide, but you may not have known that two recipients are now deceased.'

'No. I hadn't heard that.'

'Well, people die every day. I suppose the government want people to remain ignorant. One of the two was a woman. She was shot by police in Melbourne after she stabbed a man at a fast-food outlet.'

'I did read about that. However, the article didn't mention that she was an ex-criminal.'

'No, nor her CAS treatment. I think that fact was deliberately supressed. The second deceased was a man who drowned off the Burnie jetty. He had an altercation with a fisherman at the nearby boat ramp. The argument escalated at the end of the pier, and the fisherman pushed him into the water. He drowned.'

'Okay.' Carl wondered where these stories were going.

'Although these events occurred in different states, both deceased underwent post-mortems, and the results were shared with the Health Department and the committee liaising with the Royal Commission.'

'I won't ask how you know that.'

'I'm glad. As you probably realise, I am sticking my neck out by telling you any of this.'

'I won't ask who your source is.'

'No. Of course not.' Dorian took a tiny sip of water and continued. 'On brain examination, both cadavers were found to have white matter lesions in the prefrontal and cingulate areas.'

'Areas associated with emotion-related processes?'

'Yes, Carl. Good to see you still remember your anatomy and physiology studies.'

'Were they related to the CAS drug?'

'With only two cases, this may be a coincidence. But if there is a third, we may be looking at a pattern.'

'We?'

'The Health Department has gathered a group of consultants. Experts in various fields.' Dorian touched his chin with his index finger. 'Similar to the panel group consulted for the CAS drug trials. Now, of course, working to save people from the same drug.' Dorian quickly scanned the room before asking, 'Carl, what was the fate of the man who killed your friend?'

'As far as I know, he was taken to Yatala Prison and received psychiatric care. He didn't die.'

'I see.' Dorian steepled his hands on the table for a moment. 'I was hoping he may have been – accessible.'

'No, I don't think so. But, Dorian, given their propensity for violence, it seems only a matter of time before there are more deaths of CAS recipients, so you'll soon have more cases to prove a pattern.'

'Of course, but delays.' He shrugged. 'We were hoping to find someone a bit sooner.'

Carl thought of Paul de Sousa and said, 'These white matter lesions would show up on MRI scans, on living people, wouldn't they?'

'Well, yes, of course.'

'And wouldn't they be operable, as with some lesions that cause epilepsy?'

'Maybe.'

'So, these people could be helped?'

'In theory, perhaps. Of course, first, we need to prove the pattern.'

'I know one of the CAS recipients who has had a recent MRI scan. He'd suffered memory loss and violent outbursts he couldn't recall. Perhaps you or your colleagues could request his test results? Then you might have your pattern and be able to help other patients.'

Dorian displayed a knowing grin.

'Oh, I see,' Carl said, dropping his gaze. 'How stupid of me. That's why we are having this conversation, isn't it? You already knew about him.'

'Yes, Carl. Your father mentioned the case to me. I didn't like to be underhanded. I wanted you to come to the decision yourself, and to see that this information sharing is for the best. Please text me the patient's details so we can access his files. I would be extremely grateful.'

Carl smiled and shook his head. 'Dad always said you were a smart bloke.'

'And your father always said you were a fine human being.' Dorian smiled. 'And he wasn't wrong.'

Carl would have ordinarily blushed at such a compliment, but he felt too excited to react just then. Instead, for the first time in a long time, he was filled with hope.

*

Ravi remembered the rage overtaking him at the beach, but everything was a blur after that. He knew that something terrible had gone down, or he wouldn't be lying in a hospital bed. Jesse and Bailey sat silently on the other side of the room, waiting for the radiologist to tell Ravi the conclusion of his tests. Ravi was dreading the news and couldn't make eye contact with either Jesse or Bailey.

Just before the tests had been carried out, the head of the diagnostic imaging department told Jesse that the results would be sent to Ravi's GP promptly. The man explained that sharing the results with anyone else was not the imaging department's protocol. Ravi, and everyone else in the radiology waiting room, had witnessed Jesse lose his temper with the man.

'Haven't you heard a word I've said? Ravi is a ticking time bomb. He's had the CAS treatment. The same drug that has caused other recipients to go crazy and kill people. So you can stick to your timely manner where the sun doesn't shine. If you can't tell me the results, you can tell him! He's the patient, and I *will* be in the room. Now get those results right now, or I'm going to charge you with impeding a homicide investigation!'

That had been more than twenty minutes ago, and the tension in Ravi's room was palpable.

Another ten minutes passed before a radiologist, holding a laptop, timidly poked his head through the door. 'Um, Ravi Sanders?' he asked. 'My name is Doctor Spencer

Franks. I am the chief radiologist based here at the hospital.'

'Yes,' Ravi said. 'Please come in.'

The man hadn't reached the end of the bed when Jesse charged across the room. He told the radiologist to hurry up and give them the news.

'Well,' Franks began. 'I have some images to show you.' He paused to open his laptop, glancing at Bailey, who had also moved closer. 'To all of you, I suppose.'

'It's okay,' Ravi said. 'They need to know what's wrong as much as I do.'

'Sure. In the most basic terms, Ravi, we are seeing areas of abnormal myelination in the section of white matter in your brain.'

'As a person with epilepsy might have? Don't they have operable lesions sometimes? I read that somewhere,' Bailey said hopefully.

'Well, yes, but this is different.' Franks paused and took in Ravi's perplexed expression. 'The white matter of the brain communicates with areas of grey matter. Part of the white matter is made up of myelin, so communication can be lost when there is abnormal myelination.

Jesse and Bailey glanced sideways at each other. Ravi drooped his head.

'So,' Franks continued. 'One of the most common diseases where we see this disruption is MS or other inflammatory neurological conditions. However, as

Ravi has recently been a recipient of the CAS treatment, I suspect the aetiology may be of a toxicological nature.'

'Is that good or bad?' Bailey asked.

Franks' lips flapped as he exhaled. He shook his head. 'I really couldn't say. I suggest more tests to first rule out vasculitis, metabolic disease or other possible causes.

'But what can be done if the cause is the CAS drug?'

Franks shrugged. 'I have no idea.'

'How come?' Jesse asked.

The cop's frown transformed his ordinarily placid face. In fact, he looked quite scary. Ravi felt sorry for the doctor, so he butted in. 'Please, Doctor Franks, have you ever seen a case like this before?'

Franks chewed at the inside of his cheek before answering. 'Obviously, with so little information, it's hard to know. I suspect, and this is just a guess, that we could be seeing a toxic encephalopathy, perhaps due to the drug or part of its chemical makeup that was administered to you.'

'Can that be reversed?' Bailey asked the same question that Ravi was about to voice.

'The government has yet to give any details to my department, or indeed any other hospital department, on how to deal with such an issue. To be blunt, no one here has a clue what the drug components are. Until we know that, we are in the dark about how best to treat you.'

'So, how much clout does this hospital have? Does anyone here have to balls to get that information?' Jesse asked.

'We can request it, sure, but it's the Health Department.' Franks shrugged. 'I don't know how they will react.'

'This lack of transparency needs to be reported to the media and the Royal Commission,' Bailey said. 'Because Ravi is unlikely to be the only person to need help.'

'Yes,' said Franks. 'I agree. I can certainly ask for the information…'

'What do I do in the meantime?' Ravi asked.

'You must make yourself available for a whole raft of tests and scans.' Franks shook his head. 'Your – unusual behaviour and any other issues will have to be treated as they occur, symptomatically.' Franks turned to Jesse. 'I take it that Ravi was brought here under Section 57?'

'Oh, um.' Jesse glanced at Ravi. 'Yes, I verbally explained to him Section 57 and the definition of care and control.' Jesse raised an eyebrow and asked gruffly, 'Didn't I?'

Ravi began to shrug but had a feeling he needed to agree. 'Yes, yes, he did.'

'And you agreed?' Franks asked.

'Yes.' Ravi shot a worried look at Bailey. She stared back, slowly shaking her head.

'Very well then. I will send someone from the psychology department, and you can hand over control to them.' Franks cocked his head at Jesse. 'I guess you can get on with your work.'

Jesse nodded. 'Yeah, yeah, that's good.' He turned to Bailey. 'I guess you'll want to stay here?'

'Can I?' Bailey glanced from person to person.

It was Franks who spoke first. 'As long as the handover has been completed.' He picked up his laptop and sighed. 'Good luck Ravi. I'm sure I will see you again. Bye.'

'What did all that mean, Jesse?' Ravi asked.

'Consider yourself sectioned.'

'Like what? A nut case.'

'Ravi, if the shoe fits.'

'That's not fair, Jesse,' Bailey said.

'Okay, I'm sorry. But realistically Ravi. You and everyone else are safer while you remain here.' Jesse had the decency to look apologetic.

'So, they can restrain me?' Ravi asked.

'Only if they need to.' Jesse dropped his gaze to the floor. 'I'm sorry, kid, but you must stay here.'

'He understands,' Bailey said.

And Ravi did, but he was shit scared.

Chapter Twenty-one

When Molly first entered Paul de Sousa's hospital room, he leered at her. She wore her usual work attire, black trousers, a white shirt and a black vest. Not tight fitting nor revealing and, she thought, quite undeserving of such a lecherous glance unless, of course, Ben's opinion counted. Molly kept watching De Sousa. Noting his change of expression when Ben walked in a moment later.

'Cops,' De Sousa spat. He pulled the bedsheet over his head and rolled away from them.

'Hello, are you Paul de Sousa?' Molly asked.

'Piss off,' came Paul's muffled reply.

Molly and Ben exchanged a look before noisily positioning an armchair on either side of his bed.

'I hear you are being discharged tomorrow. I wanted to ask you a few questions.' Molly waited two minutes and then added, 'We can move this interview down to the station if you would rather talk there?'

De Sousa pulled down the sheet and sat up. He glared at Molly. 'I don't talk to pigs.'

'Well, you will today,' Ben said.

'I've got nothing to say.' Paul glanced from one to the other. 'So, fuck off.'

'Okay,' Molly stood and grabbed hold of the sheet. De Sousa squealed as the bedding was pulled away and flung onto a nearby chair, exposing his flimsy gown and naked legs. 'Cuff him, Ben, and we'll take him to the station.'

'No, wait a minute!'

De Sousa's face was livid, but Molly saw him wince as he struggled to pull the cotton gown over his knees.

'Come on, Paul,' she said in a soft voice. 'We don't want to see you suffer. Just have a chat with us.'

'Do I need a lawyer?'

'I don't know, do you?' Ben asked.

'So, ask your questions and then get out of my room.' Paul pointed to the bedding and then to his bed. Once Molly had replaced it, he crossed his arms over his chest and tilted his chin upwards.

His expression reminded Molly of Khalil's, as did the tattooed dashes, indicating a cutting line from the bottom of his ear to the middle of his Adam's apple. She pointed to the inkwork and asked, 'Is that a club tattoo?'

Paul's hand went to his throat, and he grinned. 'Not really, more like a group of buddies getting the same ink. We got them done after a big night out.'

'Amos Khalil has the same tattoo,' Molly said.

'Probably lots of people do.' Paul stared at her breasts instead of her face.

'Did you drive to the town of Henderson and fire a semi-automatic rifle into a house on the fourth of December last year?' Molly asked.

'No.'

'We have your prints on a shell casing that matches the gun used.'

There was no change in de Sousa's smug expression, but Molly noticed him breathing harder.

'Amos Khalil asked you to drive to the house where Ravi Sanders was staying and spray some bullets around. You were supposed to scare him. But something went wrong, didn't it?'

'No comment.'

'You shot and killed an innocent woman. You were told later that you stuffed up, weren't you?'

Paul stared straight ahead. 'No comment.'

'The difference between being charged with unlawful discharge of an illegal weapon, and murder, is about fifteen years,' Molly paused until De Sousa had resumed eye contact. 'Twenty-five years on top of the time the CAS has already taken from you, well, I would say that's a death sentence for someone in your state of health.' She gazed at Ben. 'What do you think, Ben?'

'For sure. But on the other hand, ten years, meh, you could probably do that standing on your head.' Ben smiled.

'I didn't murder anyone.'

'Okay, then, who did? Who fired the shots at Edith Sanders' house.'

'No comment.'

Ben was on his feet, lifting the side of the bed until it tilted dangerously. Two magazines slid to the floor.

'Hey, fuck off!'

Ben dropped the bed with a clang, and De Sousa again winced in pain.

'Come on Paul. Be smart. If this incident went pear-shaped because you were having issues with your head, then tell us. It could make a huge difference to a court, especially with all the media coverage. CAS recipients are big news right now. You would have the public on your side.'

'Who says I have head problems?'

'Are you saying you don't?' Molly asked.

'Was it that ambo? Did he tell you that? I fed that guy a bunch of lies because he wouldn't leave me alone. The guy's a stalker.'

Ben leaned over the bed. His face was only inches from de Sousa's. 'We have your prints on a shell casing. We have the rifle. We also have the car you dumped with your prints all over it, and guess what? There were a bunch more shell casings inside that car. You are gone for this, De Sousa. Finished.'

'Wait,' Molly said. 'It doesn't have to be like that. If you were hired to do a job and things went wrong,' she spread her hands, open-palmed. 'You didn't know you were sick. You weren't to know the dreadful side effects of the CAS treatment, were you?'

'No,' Paul whispered. 'I didn't know.'

'In your own words Paul,' Molly said softly, 'tell us what happened.'

Ben jotted notes while his phone recorded the events that Paul de Sousa described. There was no mention of Amos Khalil's involvement. When Paul spoke of arriving in Henderson, Molly stopped him.

'Wait, back up a second,' she said. 'You said when *we* arrived in Henderson. Who are *we*?'

'The chick. She led the way. I couldn't have found that rifle range to fire a few practice shots – that was in the middle of nowhere. And I never would have found the house by the beach. I couldn't find a road map for the town, and I don't do that phone map shit.'

'So, a woman in another car drove in front of you?'

'Yeah, nah, she was the passenger. Some bloke, her boyfriend, I guess, he was driving.'

'Do you know their names?'

'Her name was Piper. I didn't know his. He was pretty big.' Paul gestured to his biceps. 'Not hard though. I could have squashed him.'

'Piper,' Molly said. 'Piper Summerton.'

'Dunno her last name.'

'She was a friend of Amos Khalil's?' Molly asked.

'Nah. Not a friend. He might have been rooting her, but he wouldn't have a chick as a mate.'

'Not a sensitive new-age guy then?' Ben asked.

'No. He's not. He's a biker.'

'A proper tough guy,' Ben taunted.

'Fuck you mate!'

De Sousa lunged towards Ben, and Ben grasped his hand, bending it at an angle until he screamed. The overbed table was knocked in the scuffle, and a water jug and lunch implements were scattered across the floor. Molly hit the nurse's call bell as both men continued to wrestle. Ben got the upper hand in a few minutes and restrained De Sousa. Molly cuffed him to the bed rail. De Sousa lay in stony silence, and no amount of prompting could make him speak.

'Okay, we do this at the station,' Molly said.

After a doctor certified that De Sousa was fit to travel, an ambulance was called to transport him to the city police station. He was to be held until Molly and Ben were ready. They wanted to give him time to think, or perhaps re-think, his answers.

In the meantime, Molly and Ben rode in the back of a squad car, neither speaking much. The butterflies of excitement had left Molly's stomach. Things were falling into place, but she wondered if, instead of catching a cold-blooded killer, the perpetrator may have just been an unfortunate criminal dealing with unforeseen health problems.

'I could kill for decent coffee,' Molly muttered, 'before we find Sydney Summerton's boyfriend.'

Ben reached over to hold her hand. She was so weary she acquiesced.

The Up-tight gym on Pitt Street was a modern establishment with a vast glass window frontage. Passers-by could have a bird's eye view of the sweaty bodies using treadmills, exercise bikes, ellipticals and cross trainers. Molly and Ben passed the scantily clad patrons as they walked to the weights area. Lines of machines were being utilised by dozens of men and women. A subtle waft of sweat and liniment tainted the air. Molly self-consciously sucked in her stomach as she passed them. Wishing she had bothered with her fitness a little more.

At the far end of the section, they saw a man wearing a hot pink company shirt. Molly waved to him, and after a moment, he walked towards them.

'Can I help you?' he asked.

Molly flashed her badge. 'We are looking for one of your employees. But, unfortunately, we only have his first name, Andreas. Do you know where he is?'

'Andreas quit back in December. I'm not sure why, but I guess he gave the boss a reason.'

'Can we speak to the boss?'

'Sure. I'll go and ask her. Follow me.'

The man walked behind the service counter into an office with a mirrored door. He emerged only a moment later with a dark-haired woman. She was middle-aged and, although not wearing Lycra, obviously had a well-toned body. Molly sighed audibly, feeling like the most out-of-shape person in the building. Ben glanced at her quizzically, but she shook her head.

The woman extended her hand. 'Nelly Adams,' she said. 'Come on in.'

Molly and Ben followed her into the small office, where a noisy printer hummed and spat out reams of paper. The woman opened a filing cabinet beside it.

'We're a bit old-fashioned here,' she explained. 'But I feel happier having a paper trail.' She selected a file labelled "Staff" and placed it on the only desk in the room. 'Here we are,' she said. 'Andreas gave two weeks' notice on the fifth of December, but he didn't return to fulfil that notice. He didn't answer any of our calls.'

'When did you last see him?' Molly asked.

Nelly frowned and tapped her top lip. 'I guess, the Friday before that. But, of course, I'd have to verify that with the payroll staff.'

'Do you have an address for him and contact details?'

'Sure. I'll make a copy for you.' Then, before Nelly moved, she asked, 'Can I ask what this is about?'

'We want to speak to him about a case we are working on. He may be able to assist with our enquiries,' Ben said.

'Oh,' Nelly rolled her eyes with a look of innuendo. 'I'm not surprised he's in trouble. He was easily led.'

'How so?' Molly asked.

'He was a sucker for a pretty face.'

'Piper Summerton?'

'Oh, so you know her. So yeah, it wouldn't surprise me if she got him into trouble.'

'You didn't like her?' Molly asked.

Nelly shook her head. 'There was nothing to like. She thought she was the only person in the world.'

'Did you ever meet her boyfriend, Ravi Sanders?'

'No, wasn't that the bloke who tried to steal Maryjo's car?'

'You heard about that?' Ben asked.

'Yes. This place is a gossip mill. Maryjo was a nice girl. She doesn't come here anymore. I never could understand why she befriended Piper. They were like chalk and cheese.'

'What have you heard about Piper?'

Nelly smiled and gave a conspiratorial wink. 'Running drugs in Asia somewhere.'

'Yeah,' Molly said. 'Could be. Thanks for your help.'

Ben folded the copied details and slid them into his pocket.

'By the way, how much are your fees per month?' Molly asked.

Nelly rudely looked Molly up and down. 'You would benefit from a personal trainer. Seventy dollars a session. Could take a while, though.'

'Thanks,' Molly said between gritted teeth. 'I'll give it some thought.'

As Molly strode for the exit door, Ben had to jog to keep up.

*

Andreas Martinez had moved from the apartment listed on his contact details, but the landlord had a family address for him. It was in a southern Adelaide suburb which took an hour to get to. The head of Adelaide Major Crimes had taken pity on Ben and Molly. She had given them a car to use while they were in the city.

'God, these suburbs go on forever,' Ben complained.

'Yeah. Urban sprawl at its best.'

Molly turned off the expressway. Three turns later, she arrived at Andreas' parent's home. The place was a cream brick bungalow with a car garage almost the same size as the house. The front lawn was bordered by cascading red and gold russelia bushes. A single stone cherub looked forlornly out at the street. Before Molly had opened the car door, a man wearing a wide-brimmed hat emerged from the front of the house. He had a watering can in his hand.

'Hello, Mister Martinez?' Molly asked.

'Yes.' The man gave a guarded stare.

Molly displayed her badge as she walked nearer. 'We would like to speak to your son, Andreas.'

The man's face clouded. 'He's out the back. Room out the back of the house,' Martinez said in a heavily accented voice.

'Thank you,' Molly said.

She and Ben walked quickly in case the father decided to alert the son, but it seemed the dad didn't bother. Andreas was sitting on the stoop of the granny flat, cutting his toenails. He gave a heavy sigh when he eye-balled Molly's badge.

'You don't seem surprised to see us, Andreas,' Ben said.

'Why do you think we're here?' Molly asked.

'Because of Piper.'

'Why? What happened?' Molly sat on the step beside Andreas. Not her favourite position to observe someone, but Ben remained standing and he would be monitoring the young man's reactions for her.

'She had some dumb plan to scare her ex-boyfriend,' Andreas said. 'But the man who was supposed to do the scaring,' Andreas shrugged, 'he flipped out.'

'Flipped out how?' Molly asked.

'He shot up the house. He seemed okay when we first met up with him.'

'Where was that?'

'A pub just outside of the city. I think it was called Lower Light.'

'What happened?'

'Piper explained the plan to this man. He was a biker. A bit mean looking but friendly enough. Piper told him we would lead the way there in my car, but the man didn't like that idea. He said he worked alone.'

'Why did Piper change the plan?'

Andreas exhaled loudly. 'He never would have found the place otherwise.'

'So, where were you when the shooting occurred?'

'We parked about two hundred metres down the road. I think Piper just wanted to hear the gunshots, because she screamed at me to drive away as soon as we heard them. She didn't want us to be caught. We were back on the highway, even before we saw a cop car.'

Molly broke her gaze and rested her head in her hands. Piper's behaviour was certainly odd.

As though reading her thoughts, Andreas said, 'Plus, she also wanted to be there to ensure the man did the job.'

'Why would she doubt him?' Ben asked.

'Because he said he wouldn't do anything more than warning shots. He was sending a message, and that was all.'

'Piper wanted more?' Molly asked.

'Yes. They had argued back in Adelaide.' Andreas chewed his thumbnail. 'Then she said something to him just before we stopped.'

'When you stopped near Edith Sanders' house?' Molly asked.

'Yeah. He pulled up beside us and wound down his window.'

'What did she say?' Ben butted in.

'She told him he should kill Ravi because he was a child rapist.'

'What? Did she have proof of that?' Molly asked.

Andreas screwed up his face and shook his head. 'No. She told me later she said it to rev the guy up. To make sure he was furious enough to shoot Ravi. Apparently, the biker bloke had issues that stemmed back to his childhood. That was how Piper worked. She knew which buttons to push, and she pushed them.'

Molly stared at Ben. 'We want a full psyche history on De Sousa and any past abuse reports. And we might run that story past Khalil too. He may be able to confirm that something happened in De Sousa's childhood. In fact, I'd lay money that Khalil is where she got that information.' Molly turned back to Andreas. 'Piper really is a piece of work.'

'Tell me about it,' Andreas moaned. 'She already had plans to leave the country. The next morning, I saw the note pushed under my door, telling me she was leaving. By the time I reached her place, I was too late. I wasn't included in her escape plans. I got used, just like Ravi did.'

'But you also withheld this information from us, the police. This is a homicide case, so you'll be charged with perverting the cause of justice.' Ben appeared to take pleasure in telling Andreas.

'I know. I told my dad what happened two days after the shooting. I was going to hand myself in. Everything had turned to shit. I couldn't face work. I was a mess.' Andreas gazed at Molly and then shrugged. 'He told me to keep quiet.'

'Your father? Why?' Ben asked.

But Molly was nodding. 'He was worried about deportation?'

'Yes. He was scared of losing everything.'

'Okay. Come down to the station with us.' Molly stood and offered him her hand.

Andreas glanced across the yard, which resembled a small market garden, to his dad's house. He gave a huge sigh and then got to his feet. 'If it's any consolation, I'm sorry.'

'Bad luck mate.' Ben pointed to the roadway. 'Get in the car.'

*

Carl needed to get out of his apartment and clear his mind, only this time, it wasn't Tash filling his thoughts. He was questioning his actions over the past weeks. Wondering if the ends did, in fact, justify the means. Befriending Paul to discover the truth about Edith Sanders's murder was a low act. And while Paul had committed a heinous crime, was he really to blame? And how would the system treat him now? Carl was sure there was no rosy future for Paul, but there may be sympathy for others like him, judging by the growing number of opponents to the CAS. Paul's medical records had been obtained by Dorian's department, and as far as Carl knew, they had proved helpful to his research, so there was a silver lining to all the shit that had gone down.

Carl hit the ignition, and his Ninja roared to life. It was overcast, and rain was likely. The Indian summer was finally at an end. As he climbed higher into the Adelaide Hills, the roads were damp. A heavy fog or a sprinkle of rain left them slick and smelling of ozone. He stopped at a street-side café for tea, watching as dozens of motorbikes passed this popular riding patch. The surrounding small towns were packed with visitors. Carl watched them milling about as he sauntered to the public toilet across the road for a leak. He didn't want to endure the downhill run to the city while needing to pee. More bikes passed in a pack as he threw his leg over the bike and hit the ignition.

The sun had broken through the clouds, causing the damp roads to steam as he flipped left to the right through the tight corners. He grinned. This was precisely what he needed. As he slowed for a tight left-hander, two bikes muscled past him. Carl wasn't afraid of fast riding, but these two clowns overtook him on the wrong side of the road, on a bend. And Carl wasn't a bike snob, but he did sneer at the Harleys as they passed. The riders bedecked in total black, sent an unwanted shiver up his spine. Perhaps, he later thought, that tremor caused him to lay off the throttle, and maybe saved his life.

He laid the bike over for the next right-hander, committed to the corner, but the two Harleys had slowed to a crawl, one in the middle of each lane, only twenty metres in front of him. Carl cursed, fogging his visor as he slammed on the brakes. The bike low-sided, skidding from under him and propelling him towards the guard rail and the cliff beyond. His boot glanced against the railing, and his upper thigh met with a tree, but the momentum spun him back onto the slick road. He held his arms jammed against his sides and hands up to his chin, trying to protect himself. Then, from the corner of his eye, he saw the Harleys disappear around the bend, and on the next spin, a car was almost upon him. He screamed and waited for the impact, but it didn't happen.

The following hours were a blur. A bumpy ride to the hospital, watching the paramedic perform procedures that Carl knew by rote, the IV line and drugs which made the ordeal bearable, the chaos of the emergency department, the x-rays and scans, and blood draws. At some point his father's face hovered over him, asking him questions he didn't know how to answer. Finally, at some time in the afternoon, he slept.

When he awoke, it was as if from a bad dream. But then the pain kicked in, and the dream became a nightmare.

Chapter Twenty-two

R avi's head was covered in a growth of black fuzz. The neurosurgeon had said there was no need to remove all the hair because only a tiny area of Ravi's skull needed to be accessed for the craniotomy. But Ravi told the preoperative nurse to take off the lot. He figured if he lived it would soon grow back. So now his head itched like a bastard. He touched the cotton cap he wore because it made him think twice before scratching. It was a minor inconvenience.

The neurosurgeon from Sydney's Royal North Shore Hospital explained the procedure to Ravi days before the surgery, and it sounded scary. A laminectomy. This operation was usually carried out on severe epileptics whose similar lesions, or in some cases, the irritation to brain tissue surrounding the lesions, triggered their seizures. But the doctor was quick to add that although the EEG and MRI scans placed his lesions – presumably caused by the still unknown contents of the CAS treatment – in areas of his brain specifically responsible for mood and behaviour, this surgery was, at best, guesswork.

This doctor came recommended by Dorian Lindqvist, a family friend of Carl Carruthers. Carl had apparently helped Jesse and the other cops find his grandma's killer. Jesse was full of praise for the man, so Ravi agreed to the recommendation.

The surgeon had little else to say. Ravi wasn't sure if the man was concealing his doubts about success or was terse by nature. Since the operation, Ravi had undergone many psychological examinations and tests to elicit the violent outbursts that had plagued him earlier. Thankfully, they had all failed. It seemed nothing could provoke the temper that had once been so quick to ignite.

Immediately following the procedure, Ravi lost some motor skills and underwent intensive physiotherapy. Now, four weeks postoperatively, he was given a clean bill of health.

The government had paid for his treatment and the costs incurred during his stay in Sydney. But Ravi saw little of the city outside bus rides to the hospital and back to his hotel. He missed the quiet of the country. Most of all, he missed Bailey.

A knock at his hotel door startled Ravi from his reverie. He wasn't expecting anyone. At first, he didn't recognise the woman. He'd never seen the cop smiling so brightly. The expression transformed her. She really was attractive.

'Senior Sergeant Hunter? Come on in.' Ravi gestured to the small table by the window.

'Please, Ravi, it's Molly. You look good. Really good.' She pulled up a chair opposite him, sitting primly with her legs crossed at the ankles.

'Thanks. I feel great. A bit itchy, but all things considered, getting back to normal.'

'You look a little…' She pointed to his eyes.

'Younger?' Ravi nodded. 'No one can explain it, but since the removal of the lesions, the ageing process has reversed a bit.'

'The CAS was a slow-release drug?' Molly speculated.

'Maybe. Even after the damning reports from the Royal Commission, there is still so much secrecy surrounding the CAS. It seems like everyone who was in the know has disappeared.' Ravi scratched his head through his cap. 'Anyway, what are you doing here?'

'Well, after the last few months, I felt like I deserved a break. So Ferdi and I are having a second honeymoon. We're travelling up to the central coast this afternoon. To Port Stephens.'

'Nice,' Ravi said. 'What about Ben?'

'Um, he transferred to Port Augusta station. I guess he wanted a change. Anyway, I've been following your progress,' Molly fidgeted with her wedding ring. 'I thought you might have questions about the case. I think I owe you answers if I can.'

'Carl Carruthers? What happened? Did someone get to him for helping me?'

'Ah, yes. Paul de Sousa has some unsavoury mates. Unfortunately, they were all too happy to dole out some revenge.'

'But Carl wasn't hurt?'

'Nothing that won't heal. Mostly his pride. Since then, he's decided to live like you. Somewhere remote and anonymous.'

'Witness protection?'

'Something like that.'

Ravi grinned. 'You can't tell me?'

'No, I can't. But I do suspect the details in the CAS expose published in the *Australian* last Friday may have come via Carl. The details of the fatal attack on Tash Pawlowski couldn't have come from anyone else.'

'He needed to say his piece.'

'He certainly did that. Feathers have been well and truly ruffled.'

'And what about Piper?' Ravi asked.

'Well, crime has made an astute businesswoman of her, apparently.' Molly tapped her painted nails on the arm of the chair. 'You know, one thing that didn't make sense to me was why Khalil went to such lengths for her. I mean, getting someone to carry out a shooting, that's next-level stuff. Of course, a job like that requires repayment. She owed him a large debt.'

Ravi felt his smile disappear. 'Piper is nothing if not persuasive.'

'Yeah, I get that, but someone as hard as Khalil doesn't get pushed around by a pretty girl. I knew there had to be more. Despite my attempts to set up a dialogue with Thai officials, nothing was ever followed up. I knew the treaty that Australia has with Thailand has its deficiencies, especially regarding drug trafficking. Still, I was not prepared for the stonewalling on our side of the pond.'

'What does that mean?' Ravi said.

'I think Piper is under investigation by someone with more clout.'

'Like who? Like Interpol?'

'I don't know which law enforcement the AFP is working with, and likely, I never will, but it's safe to say she will be brought to justice, eventually.'

'Does that mean someone is hunting her down?' Ravi felt his smile return. The idea of Piper on the run and fearing for her life was pleasing.

'The AFP believe Piper and two other men have been transporting heroin through shipping containers under the guise of home furnishings. Allegedly, there is camera footage of the three at Laem Chabang Port before moving one of the containers. The investigators suspect at least fifty kilos a week were getting through until last month.'

'What happened last month?'

'Something scared her. She took a flight to Beijing.' Molly held out her hands and shrugged. 'Since then, no one can locate her.'

'Khalil hired the right person. You must be slippery to handle that kind of work.'

'Yes. I'm sorry you were caught up in her revenge.' Molly leant across the table and patted his forearm. 'Her deviousness has certainly escalated since then.'

'I'm sorry too. I miss my grandma every day.' Ravi gazed out the window. 'But you know, I'm not angry anymore. I know what happened, which makes me sad, but I understand the futility of dwelling on it.'

'That's great Ravi. That's the attitude that will get you through this. And what about Bailey? How have events affected your relationship?'

'I don't know. She has her studies now. I've heard she spends a lot of time in Adelaide, so I guess her life will move on.' Ravi coughed to clear his throat. 'She knows I'm going home soon. But there's the stuff about her covering for her grandfather, which I understand now, but I treated her badly, and I know I scared her. So I'll have to wait and see if we have a chance. If not...' He gave a dismissive shrug.

'You'll be fine, with or without her, Ravi.'

'Sure. I know.' He lied.

'Have you heard from Jesse Plackis?'

Ravi suspected that Molly was subtly changing the subject, and he was pleased about that. 'Yeah. He and my mum – have this thing.'

'Oh.' Molly dropped her gaze. 'I kind of suspected something like that.'

'Yeah, well, they're talking about marriage.'

'Oh Ravi, that's lovely news!'

Ravi rubbed his nose to hide the grimace. 'I dunno. I guess time will tell. My mum likes working and living in the city, so I don't know how life in a tiny town will suit her.'

'But she was brought up there, wasn't she?'

'Yeah. That's what I mean. Like most other kids, she couldn't wait to get out of there. Now Jesse expects her to move back.'

'They'll find a happy medium. They are smart people.'

'I guess.'

Molly peeked at her watch. 'Well, Ravi, can I do anything for you?'

'No. You did a lot. You found grandma's killer. You unravelled the whole story.'

'I had help.'

Ravi levelled his gaze at her. 'I know you suspected me. I know I scared you. Unfortunately, I scared too many people, and I'm sorry for that.'

Her eyes crinkled with a smile. 'Ravi, you did scare the shit out of me. But it wasn't you, not really; it was the treatment forced upon you.' She wagged a finger in front of his face. 'And, I hope you'll be part of the class action. You get that compensation out of those bastards!'

'Yeah.' Ravi chuckled. 'That's what Jesse says too. So I guess I will.'

'Good. Seriously, you are owed something out of all this.' Molly pointed to his head. 'After all you've been through.'

Ravi shrugged, and as he got to his feet, Molly hugged him. 'Take care, Ravi.'

'You too Molly.'

*

Jesse dragged the third desk into the cell room. He pushed it up against the wall and smiled. It was good to have the station to himself once more. He admired Molly and Ben for their work, but Jesse liked a quiet life. The odd escaped horse or cow, and no more murders would suit him perfectly.

The bell on the reception desk sounded, and a second later, someone said, "Hello."

'Bailey?' Jesse asked from the hallway.

'Yeah, sorry, are you busy?' She was holding two takeaway coffee cups.

'No. Not really. Is anything wrong?'

'I wanted to talk to you.'

'Sure. When did you get home?'

'This morning. My study block doesn't finish until the end of the week, but my mum phoned.' Her face was glum. 'It's not good.'

'Is it Maury?' Jesse asked as he pointed at a seat for her to sit on.

'Yeah. His Parkinson's dementia is now at the moderate stage.'

'I heard your mum was looking for him yesterday.'

'Yeah. Brad, his farmhand, couldn't find him. The house was empty, and the ute was parked by the back door. Brad looked all over the farm and found him at Colin's monument. Grandpa had walked there in the heat. It's over six kilometres, and he had no water.'

'Oh, jeez, that's no good.'

'He's in hospital, under observation and on IV fluids for dehydration.'

Bailey's lips were pressed tightly closed, perhaps to stop them from trembling. Jesse reached over and held her hand.

'Is there something I can help you with?' he asked.

'Yeah, there is. We'll have to move him off the farm. He can't stay out there alone anymore. Mum wants him to live in my flat at the back of the house. I think he should too.' Bailey paused to wipe her eyes. 'He's going to take it badly.'

'Yeah. I get that. Well, I can certainly be present when you move him there.'

'Would you? Oh, that would make such a difference. I mean, Dad's there, but I think he'd rather avoid any....'

'Conflict?'

'Is that what you call it when someone is unreasonable *and* incapable but still wants things his way?'

'I'd call it a shit show.'

Bailey snorted and laughed despite the situation. Then, for the next few moments, she blew her nose and collected her thoughts while Jesse drank his coffee.

'Ravi is home tomorrow,' Jesse said. 'Emily is picking him up from the airport and bringing him here. So you must come to his homecoming party.'

Jesse watched her, gauging her reaction, but her face remained solemn. Then, finally, she gave just the slightest shake of her head.

'So, it's over between you two? Is there someone else that you met on campus?'

Bailey broke into a smile. 'No. It's not anything like that.' When she shook her head, her smile disappeared. 'Ravi didn't want me to visit him in the hospital. He didn't want me there when he had the surgery. I mean, if you are in a partnership, then you are there for each other, aren't you? I thought he'd want me to be there when he opened his eyes to tell him everything was okay after his operation, but he didn't.' Bailey squeezed the bridge of her nose and sniffed. 'I guess we've just run our course.'

'Nonsense! Ravi is crazy about you,' Jesse insisted.

'Sorry Jesse, but his actions say otherwise.'

'Listen, Bailey, Ravi wouldn't let his mum see him either.'

'Really? Why not?'

Jesse had thought about that question himself. 'I guess he was afraid it wouldn't go well. That operation involved a lot of risks, but he went ahead anyway. Maybe if it went wrong, he wanted to spare you and his mum from seeing him that way.'

'I dunno.' Bailey looked unconvinced.

'I think I'm right because he said *I* could come and see him.'

'You?'

'Yeah. And I might not be the *last* person he cares about, but I'd be in the bottom few.'

Bailey chuckled for a moment. Jesse laughed too, but soon they both fell silent once more.

'So, what's it going to be?' Jesse finally asked. 'Do you want to come and see him at the house?'

'No.' Bailey shook her head to punctuate her answer.

'Really? You don't want to be here when he gets home?'

'No.'

Jesse's shoulders slumped. Ravi would take this hard.

'I want to be at the arrivals gate. At the airport.' Bailey's eyes were misting. 'I want to see his reaction, and then I'll know. He can't hide the way he feels. If he doesn't want me, I'll walk away.'

Jesse stood and said, 'Bailey, he won't walk away.'

She merely shrugged.

'So, what would you prefer? Pizza or a chicken platter?' Jesse asked.

'What? What are you talking about?'

'For tomorrow afternoon? For Ravi's homecoming?'

'Jesse, I just said…'

'I know. I'll organise both chicken and pizza.'

Bailey's hands were on her hips. 'You're pretty sure of yourself, aren't you?'

Jesse gave a smug grin. 'I have been known to be right more often than wrong.' He picked up a box of paper files for shredding. 'See you when you get back from the airport tomorrow.'

Bailey had no answer for that, but she smiled.

Milton Keynes UK
Ingram Content Group UK Ltd.
UKHW031209111124
451035UK00006B/573

9 789367 952368